Secrets from the Pink Chair

A Struggle for Life Among the Dead

A novel
Based on a true story

To Janet
Happy Birthday
Love,
Patty Mahoney

Secrets from the Pink Chair

A Struggle for Life Among the Dead

A novel
Based on a true story

Patty Mahoney, M.C.

info@inkwellproductions.com

ISBN: 978-1-939625-65-6
Library of Congress Control Number: 2013916548

Published by Inkwell Productions
10869 N. Scottsdale Road # 103-128
Scottsdale, AZ 85254-5280

Tel. 480-315-3781
E-mail info@inkwellproductions.com
Website www.inkwellproductions.com

Printed in the United States of America

Dedication

To young people who feel lost

Table of Contents

Synopsis

Secrets from the Pink Chair

Jamie is an average child of the1950's, except that her residence is so bizarre. She and her family live in a mortuary. She is such a frequent visitor to the embalming room there that her mother moves a child size pink chair into it. She is never allowed to express her alarm or disgust at anything she observes, nor is she ever shielded from the atrocities of sight, sound or smell that permeate her living environment.

Her father, Francis, devotes himself entirely to business enterprises, not because he enjoys them, but to fulfill his perceived duty to the dead.

Jamie's mother, Gertrude, is so emotionally unstable, she is incapable of attending to the needs of anyone but herself. Her struggle is to get through the day without resorting to explosions of temper and outbursts of rage.

Jamie's sister, Rosarita ,is the apple of Francis' eye. She bears a strong family resemblance to him and gains his affection effortlessly. But, he remains indifferent to Jamie, in spite of her constant attempts to gain his attention.

Carol, her half-sister, is a bright spot in the family constellation for Jamie. A product of Gertrude's first marriage, Francis is not fond of her, either. Jamie finds comfort with her half-sister as they share their feeling of family alienation.

Secrets from the Pink Chair

Chapter One

Pickled Eggs

"Don't touch anything," Mother ordered as the wide door creaked open. My eyes watered from a smell so strong it made my nose burn.

Mother and I stepped in without a word. Daddy nodded toward Mother, but ignored me. He stood between two shiny, white tables which were tilted toward a sink at the end of the room. People lay on their backs atop the tables. They didn't talk to us. I held Mother's hand as I looked up at the white sheets covering them.

Maybe they're so uncomfortable they don't want to talk to anyone. Those tables look cold and they don't have any blankets.

Daddy threw the cigarette dangling from his lip into the deep sink at the end of the tables.

"Are you girls ready for lunch?" he asked. His voice was so loud, it startled me. Again, he ignored the people on the tables.

"Shhh, they're sleeping," I chided him. Then, with exaggerated tiptoeing, I headed for the door.

Daddy let out his loud guffaw and Mother smiled as she caressed my hand.

"It's a good thing you didn't wake them up," Daddy joked.

"I'm so glad we've trained our children not to be afraid of everything. It makes me so mad to stand in line at the store for hours on end while kids Jamie's same age scream and cry when they have to sit on Santa's lap for their Christmas pictures. Those kids are afraid of somebody with a beard, and my little girl can come up with a cute remark when she's looking at a dead body," she said as she gave me a loving gaze.

"There's nothing to be afraid of from dead people. It's the live ones you have to watch out for," Daddy chuckled. "We need to hurry, girls," he urged. "I can't be away too long."

"Do you think you can stomach a bowl of chili from Lola's?" Mother asked. "That's the fastest way I know of to eat and get back here in a hurry."

"Christ, Mother, I'm still eating Tums from my last visit over there. Jamie, I suppose you want to go there so you can watch yourself in the mirror behind the counter. Who the hell wants to see a reflection of themselves guzzling food?"

I hate the greasy food at Lola's Café, but it's fun to gawk at people when they're eating.

"Look out for the traffic," Daddy boomed as I waited for a rusty '43 Ford to lumber past before I stepped onto Fifth Street. I slowed my pace as we approached the deep gutter on the opposite side.

Mother will be furious if I splash mud onto my new Buster Brown socks. She hasn't discovered my new hiding place for the sticker of the little boy and his dog that comes on the shoes and socks. This time, I pressed it to the metal leg of my bed. With

2

the bedspread over it, she can't tell I haven't thrown it away like she said I should.

I smelled the familiar odor of toast burning as Daddy opened the screen door of the café with one hand and swatted at the flies covering it with the other. Mother darted for a red Naugahyde booth at the end of the knotty-pine-paneled diner.

"It's more private here than sitting at the counter," she whispered in my ear as Daddy shook hands and talked to everyone in the place. He told and retold how I thought people were asleep on the hard tables. Everyone turned to look at Mother and me and laugh.

Most of these people spend the whole day at the counter, drinking coffee and smoking cigarettes. They're not used to having kids around. They don't think it's really funny about the sleepers; they just want to be nice to Daddy because he knows them from the American Legion.

We ordered a bowl of chili for each of us, cups of coffee for Mother and Daddy, and a glass of milk for me. Daddy grimaced when he took his first bite, but kept on eating until he took a sip of the coffee.

"You been boiling this since yesterday, Lola?" he shouted as he held up his green mug. He glanced at his wristwatch, shoveled down the chili, gulped the entire mug of coffee and announced our departure in an instant.

"No more, no more," he waved his hand over the empty mug as Lola approached with the coffee pot. "We need to get back before everyone wakes up from their naps." All the customers and waitresses laughed again, even though it was the second time Daddy made fun of me.

Daddy got a good laugh out of everybody at Lola's, but I know a lot more about his secret names than he thinks I do. I watch carefully and figure things out for myself. Just because I don't ask him, he thinks I don't know what's going on around me.

Where the people are on tables is "The Place." Daddy never calls The Place a mortuary like everybody else does.

The biggest of all the black cars parked by my backyard is "The Coach." It has velvet seats and satin ropes that tie back curtains on the windows. "Maguire's" is written on the back window in silver letters. My sisters and I can never ride in it, even though our last name is written on it. Only people in caskets can ride in it.

"The Call Car" is for bringing people back to The Place after they're dead. It's not fancy like The Coach, but we girls still can't ride in it. There's only enough room for three people in the front seat. The back seat is replaced by a cot, and we all know not to touch it. My sisters and I know what a "Stinker" is, too. It's somebody who's been dead too long before they got to The Place. When a car marked "Coroner" brings in Stinkers, our back yard has a smell that makes us want to throw up even though we don't have the flu.

Our favorite of all the cars is the ambulance. It has red lights on top of it, a loud siren, and Maguire's written on it, too. Sometimes after a "Big Phone Call," Daddy hangs up real fast. He runs out the back door, slamming the screen door behind him. We can hear his brother, my Uncle Max, doing the same thing next door. Rosarita and I run to the dining room to watch them race across the back yard. Carol doesn't watch with us anymore. She says she's already seen the race too many times already.

Rosarita and I cheer for Daddy to be the first of the two to reach the ambulance; that means he gets to drive. When he turns on the siren, all the other cars on the street get out of the way. He and Max pull out of the driveway so fast that dust and gravel spray out behind the wheels. Daddy always looks like he's mad when he drives the ambulance. He grips the wheel real tight, looks straight ahead, and doesn't laugh or smile at anyone. It's still exciting to see grown-ups running and then roaring the ambulance out of the carport, though.

Ambulance calls are the only thing fun about The Big Phone. When it rings, no matter what we're doing, we have to be absolutely silent. We have to do this so no one knows kids are around when they're talking about dead people. The Big Phone rings every time somebody needs Daddy to come get somebody who's dead, whether it's in the middle of the night or in the middle of our favorite television shows. "The Little Phone" is for our family, so we can answer it and make noise when it rings.

It's confusing trying to remember the secrets and who knows about which ones. But I'm getting better at it all the time.

"Come on, Jamie. We're going to the grocery store," Mother announced.

This isn't an invitation; it's a command. She's given up on making Carol go with her, and Rosarita makes too much fuss. But, I'm the youngest and Mother doesn't let me out of her sight. She knows I hate shopping. People at the store call her "Gertrude." She could shorten it to something cute like "Trudy," but she won't. My face turns just as red when someone says "Gertrude" as it does when they call Daddy "Francis." It makes him sound like a girl. Why doesn't he say his name is "Frank"? Maybe that's why they call each other "Mother" and "Daddy" instead of their real names.

Carol continued her giggling gossip with her teenage girlfriends, and Rosarita dressed and undressed her doll about a million times so Mother would know she was busy and wouldn't get into trouble while we were gone. Like it or not, Mother and I were off to the tiny grocery store on Mill Avenue, and my sisters got to stay home.

Just as I feared, the butcher yelled out "Hi, Gertrude" the minute the bell over the door chimed. Mother smiled demurely and headed through the produce section to the cold part of the store where the butcher stored the meat. I didn't really like the meat display. Blood drained out of the freshly cut meat onto the silvery trays surrounding it. When the white, napkin-like paper that lined the trays absorbed the blood, it reminded me of the big tub of cold water outside the door at the mortuary. That was where Daddy and Max put sheets from the ambulance. They soak there before the laundry picks them up for cleaning and pressing. The human blood colored the white sheets exactly like the beef blood oozed into the white napkins in the butcher's case.

I never looked away from the human blood gradually dying the water red, and I looked unfazed at the meat case that contained their gory reminders.

Smug as I was about looking in the display case without reaction, I didn't know yet about the new items for sale at the meat case. Just above the glass window that displayed the various cuts of meats sat a transparent glass jar filled with a murky fluid, in which floated pickled eggs. I watched as they remained suspended within the liquid, sometimes slowly spinning in a circle.

Like the bloody meat before it, the sight of the smooth, white eggs immediately reminded me of yet another of the secrets. The pickled egg jar looked just like another jar sitting on a shelf not far from the white tables at The Place. Suspended in it were not eggs, but a human baby. Its tiny arms and legs curled into its body made it no larger than a golf ball. Mother pointed it out to me one day when we were alone at The Place. She told me how a lady in Tempe gave birth at home to a child who was too big to be called a "miscarriage," but too small to be labeled a "stillborn baby."

"Remember when a man handed Daddy a little white diaper with something wrapped in it?" Mother prompted. "The father brought the baby right through the front door of The Place."

Mother retold every grisly detail of the entire incident. Daddy snatched the baby from the arms of the grieving father, she said, and quickly put it out of sight in the embalming room. Meanwhile, Max eased the breathless father into a chair and wrapped him in a blanket. Ducking into the office next door, Max dialed the "0" on the telephone and waited impatiently for the numbered disc to revolve all the way back to the finger-sized metal catch before "The Operator" came through the receiver. She gave this part of the story extra emphasis to underscore the importance of the telephone operator, a job she held before her marriage.

"Marge, it's Maguire's," Max said quietly, so that he wouldn't be overheard in the next room. "Ring any doc that's on call and tell them to come to the mortuary. It's not a death; we just have someone here who needs a doctor."

"Max, are you all right? Did something happen to one of Francis's kids? Don't tell me one of those bodies over there wasn't really dead yet." Mother shook her head at the unprofessional behavior of the operator.

"Stop asking me stupid questions and get a doctor over here. I don't care which one it is. Just find somebody," Max answered.

"All right, all right," Marge huffed. "You never tell me anything."

"You're right. Get a doctor." Mother laughed at Max's dismissal of the nosy woman at the other end of the line.

While Max and Marge tended to the father, Daddy dashed to the ambulance, Mother bragged. He turned on the siren and began a hurried drive to the home where the birth—and death—occurred. He didn't need to look up an address; Tempe was so small that he knew the location of every resident's house without asking.

He drove quickly down Myrtle Avenue, slowing only slightly as he crossed Fifth Street. When he reached the right house on Sixth Street, he backed the ambulance into the driveway for easier loading of the cot later. He ran full speed across the front lawn and vaulted over the porch railing. Without knocking, he threw back the screen door and stepped into the living room. He followed the sound of the mother's cries to reach her in the bedroom.

The linens and mattress of her bed were saturated with red. The mother sat in the middle of the blood pooled around her. She had been screaming so long, her voice was hoarse. Mother lowered her voice dramatically during this retelling so Daddy wouldn't overhear her sharing secrets of The Place.

Max and Daddy usually made ambulance calls together, but with Max tending to the father back at The Place, Daddy made the ambulance call alone. He hoped someone was at the house to help him transfer the mother from bed to ambulance cot. But the woman was alone. He bolted for the front door and yelled, "I need some help in here." Mother boasted how brave Daddy was to take such independent action, but smart enough to ask for help when he needed it.

Joe England, a mechanic at the filling station on Apache Boulevard. appeared on his front porch across the street. He gave his hands a quick swipe down the legs of his grimy overalls and sprinted to Daddy's side. The two men rushed to the bed of the blood-soaked woman, Mother said.

"We have to lift her over to the cot without hurting her."

Daddy leaned in as close as he could get to the mother's screaming face. "Lie down," he shouted.

She stopped screaming, gazed at the two men in confusion, stretched her legs out, and lay back on the bloody pillow.

"You get down by her feet and grab on to the sheet underneath her, England. When I count to three, we'll lift the sheet and use it to shift her over to the cot. Got it? One, two, lift." Mother had seen this procedure so many times that she knew exactly how it had transpired.

The mechanic obediently thrust his grease-stained hands onto the sheet beneath the woman's legs, and he and Daddy gingerly deposited her onto the cot. They steered it through her home and into the waiting ambulance outside.

"Shut that door," Daddy yelled to England, who was now covered in grease and blood. As England gave the back door of the ambulance a hearty slam, Daddy ran the length of the vehicle and scrambled into the driver's seat. He sped away to the hospital with siren blaring, leaving England in the middle of the street, watching.

"Hi, Francis! What's up?" Ethel, the registered nurse who managed the front desk of the emergency room at Mesa Southside Hospital, asked as he hurried up to it, alone.

"This one's bad. She's lost a lot of blood," he told her.

"Bring her in," Ethel said. She looked confused. "You made an ambulance call alone? Where's Max?"

"It's a long story. Just get somebody to help me get her out of the ambulance."

Ethel rang the buzzer that summoned an orderly, Mother continued, and the two men ran outside to the waiting ambulance. As soon as the woman was inside the emergency room door, Daddy rolled the blood-soaked cot back to his ambulance and began the ride home.

Upon his return to the mortuary, he deposited the bloody sheets in the galvanized tub and went back into the office area where it had all begun. Marge had come through and located a doctor to tend to the father, who sedated the shocked man and gave him a ride back to his house by the time Daddy returned from the hospital.

But now the difficult question had to be addressed, she said. What were they going to do with the baby? Daddy couldn't just show up at the hospital and tell them to dispose of it. And embalming in the conventional manner was definitely out of the question for a body so tiny. The apparatus for doing so was not designed to work for something so small, and the veins were too underdeveloped to circulate the fluid the way it needed to.

It would be too insensitive to call the parents to ask, "What do you want me to do with your dead baby?" Without a word spoken, Mother repeated, the family and the mortuary came to an agreement. None of them would ever mention the death again.

On a shelf in the embalming room, the jar of formaldehyde and its infant contents remained, day after day, becoming year after year, moving only when the shelf was jostled by an embalmer accessing another bottle of fluid. No one claimed it, yet no one disposed of it, either. It became another secret of The Place.

But now in the grocery store, surrounded by others, the unexpected similarity of the pickled eggs at the butcher and the pickled baby at the mortuary took me by surprise. The shock on my face was obvious.

Don't cry. Don't gag. Get some color back in your face.

What if someone sees you're upset?

I stared at the checkerboard-tile floor at my feet for several minutes. Then, with hands clenched in two tight fists, I trailed out of the store behind Mother, acting as though nothing had happened.

"Hi! I didn't know you guys were back already," Carol called out as Mother opened the front door. She ran to grab the heavy grocery bags. Rosarita didn't look up from her doll-dressing. I was off the hook now that we were home, but images of the eggs in the jar intruded into my thoughts well into the night.

Carol and Rosarita are so lucky I went along. Mother makes the baby of the family stay by her side no matter what. I bet she treated them the same way she does me, but they got out of it when Mother focused her control on me. But I'm just guessing. We know not to talk about things like that—Mother might overhear us. We have almost as many secrets about the living as we do about the dead.

Chapter Two

500 Pounds of Flesh

"Here you go, Jamie," Mother said cheerily. "I fixed a little place for you to sit while I'm working. Isn't this a lot better than just standing next to me the whole time I'm doing hair? And it's just your size."

Now that Mother knows I understand what she and Daddy do at The Place, she thinks I don't mind being here all the time.

"Thank you, Mother," I said, lowering myself onto the child-sized pink seat. It was a lot better to sit in the chair than to stand, but it was not fun being in the cold room filled with the pungent smell of formaldehyde, watching Mother primping the hair of a corpse.

"How come Rosarita doesn't have to come here?" I ventured. "We could bring a little chair for her, too. We have four of them at home." I knew Carol was too tall to use this baby furniture, but Rosarita wasn't much taller than I was.

"Rosarita doesn't have time to sit around over here; she's in school. When you get to be a big girl like her, you won't have much time to be here, either. That's why we should enjoy our time together now. Just sit quietly and I'll have this hairdo all done."

I bet Carol and Rosarita enjoyed their time alone with Mother as much as I'm enjoying mine. I cannot wait to be in school. I would do anything to get away from the pink chair. But I can't tell Mother I don't like it here, especially after she went to the trouble of making a special place for me.

As the date for my school enrollment neared, I began to have second thoughts about how wonderful it would be. Could I really escape my mortuary home just by being a school kid?

"Do you think the other kids will think I'm a boy because my name is Jamie?" I hounded Mother. "Do the teachers know I'm named after a dead guy?"

"If anyone wants to know about your name, you tell them you're proud to be named after your grandfather, James. He died just before you were born."

"I don't know any other kids who are named after dead people."

"What about your sister, Rosarita? She's named after my dead sister, and no one bothers her about it."

"That's because she's the only white girl in school with a Mexican name. Everybody thinks that's so weird that they don't get to the part about dead people's names."

"Her name is not weird. It's exotic and romantic, the way we like names to be in the South. My sister loved having an unusual name. Nobody thought she was Mexican."

"How come Carol isn't named for somebody who died?"

"You know better than to ask me that," Mother answered sharply. "Her birthday is in December, so we called her our little Christmas Carol."

14

"My birthday is in June. Why didn't you name me for something in the summer?"

Mother's silence indicated the discussion was over.

"I just don't want anything to come up about dead people when I'm at school. I don't want to let any secrets of The Place slip out."

"Trust me, worrying about keeping secrets will be the last thing on your mind when you get there. You aren't like anybody else at Ritter School. The kids who live in those adobe huts along Rural Road have nothing in common with you. They don't even wear shoes. You have a nice house and proper clothing."

"Aren't some kids from church going to be there?"

"No, those kids are going to the new school on the west side of town. You have to go to Ritter because we live in the business district. Things will be fine. Just don't get too close to the Mexicans; they have bugs in their hair."

When summer dragged to a close and I clutched the plastic handle of my blue-and-white lunch box, heading out to my first day away from The Place, my fear gave way to an excitement I'd never known. School was all I'd hoped for and more. From day one, I was thrilled to sit in a chair that wasn't pink, to breathe air that didn't smell like formaldehyde, and to interact with people who were alive. I loved it.

I was always prepared for class with the proper materials and eager to learn. My peers, often undernourished and always unprepared, provided the perfect conditions for me to have the best grades in the class. I was soon so far ahead of the others that my teachers gave me special privileges, like turning the pages of books they read to the class, to reward me for my efforts.

"Class, who do you think can count the highest?" my teacher said while smiling at me.

"Jamie," the others responded in unison.

"Don't be afraid to try it, children. I'll have Jamie help you if you can't remember all of them," my teacher said.

School is great! I'm out of the pink chair and I have all the right answers.

But my moments in the spotlight faded to black when the bell for recess sounded. Standing in line for the swings, it made no difference if I knew all the letters and numbers. What mattered to the other children in the school yard was the ability to capture attention without grown-ups around.

My athletic talents were limited at best, and certainly not enough to impress fellow five-year-olds. I couldn't hang upside down on the monkey bars or even run as fast as most. Intimidating others by picking fights to gain attention was entirely out of the question for me, because the "bad girl" role on the playground might threaten my "star pupil" status back in the classroom.

Pedro, a scrawny Mexican boy who lived in the adobe huts across the street from the school on Rural Road, could draw a crowd that would hang on his every word at recess. I could tell the teachers didn't like his thick accent and his inability to learn quickly. His dirty clothing and trips to the school nurse to check for lice in his hair marked him as a child not likely to entice people of any age to approach him. Yet he clearly had magnetism to the schoolyard gang. Children ran from the classroom door to the shade tree where Pedro began his story-telling. They paid rapt attention to his tales and repeated them throughout the rest of the day.

"There was a lady in Mexico, in my old town," he said in a loud voice so everyone could hear. "She didn't keep no statues of Jesus, or Mary, or even any saints in her house," I made out despite his heavy Mexican accent. "And, when she had a baby. . ." Here he paused for dramatic effect and the group responded by leaning in even closer to catch every word. "It was a devil baby!" he shouted.

The entire group gasped at once. Some of the little girls let out screams of terror. A few of the boys tried to act brave by laughing. To my amazement, no one asked for clarification of this ridiculous tale. Does a devil baby have horns? Does it have a tail? Does it have fire shooting from its eyes? Can you bring it to school so all of us can see it?

I was immensely jealous of Pedro. I knew I could enthrall his followers and steal his limelight in an instant. Yet I was prevented from upstaging him by the vow of silence that came with being one of the Maguire family.

These stupid kids don't even know what dead people look like. I could tell them all about it. Then we'd see if they still think Pedro is so fascinating. I have a million details I could include that would keep them listening for hours. If he doesn't shut up soon, I think my mouth is going to fly open and blurt out everything I know. But what about Mother and Daddy? I can't ruin their lives by telling all our secrets. They've warned me so often. I know how terrible it would be if I let out even one little tidbit about dead people.

"Never repeat anything you hear at home," Daddy warned my sisters and me. "Any kids who are curious about the mortuary business can come to see me. You don't know anything about anybody who dies in this town, understand?"

Mother added, "Daddy is right, girls. If families thought you were saying things about their dead relatives, your father would be out of business. If you want to keep living the nice way you do now, just keep your mouths shut. It's all up to you."

On most occasions, the promise never to tell wasn't bothersome. But when I, too, stood in the shadow of the spotlight cast upon the unattractive Pedro, listening to the source of his newfound fame among peers, the burden of silence became unbearable.

Everyone, even Protestants whom I knew didn't keep any religious statues in their houses, accepted Pedro's ridiculous account as though it were true. I suspected some of them didn't even believe his story; they just wanted to jump around and act scared so they could be part of the crowd. To be the source of this much attention for telling a three-sentence, obviously untrue story that could scarcely be made out through his heavy accent, was an outrage to me. I had true stories with much greater shock value. They consisted of more than three simple sentences, and I could speak English clearly so all could understand. Yet I could not reveal them and ascend to my rightful place as the master of schoolyard horror stories.

I'm in the pink chair mentally even when I'm not there physically. School isn't the refuge I thought it would be.

The greatest disappointment in my imagined rise to fame

came in the spring, when the circus came to town. Prior to its arrival, the town offered little entertainment. With Tempe Beach—the public swimming pool—closed until summer, kids had only two choices for leisure activities; they could go to the College Theater where a new movie arrived once a month, or they could drive to Harmon's Ranch Restaurant out on the highway, where a chain-link cage contained a mountain lion. Someone captured the unfortunate animal years before and displayed it in front of the restaurant which claimed to serve fried chicken that tasted like homemade.

"Every woman in town, including me, can fry chicken that tastes better than the expensive stuff they serve out there," Mother informed Daddy. "The Harmons installed the mountain lion cage in the parking lot near the highway in a desperate attempt to provide another reason for patrons to come to the restaurant," Mother said, defending herself. She went on to say that they hoped bored passersby would stop to stare at the lion. Gazing at a miserable beast trapped in the desert would somehow whet their appetite for expensive chicken, she scoffed.

Directly adjacent to the restaurant and its mountain lion was a vacant lot. It was here, when I rode down Apache Boulevard in the back seat of Mother's tan Studebaker sedan, that I saw the seedy carnies, new to town, begin to erect the tents and stands that would comprise a circus. I could see locals, young and old, stopping by after gawking at the mountain lion next door to watch the thrilling rides being set up, or to count how many tents were needed to display freaks. The anticipation of new entertainment was the talk of the town. As soon as the gates were opened, people would be standing in line to get in.

Even though the kids at my school came from families who often lacked the funds to afford basic food and shelter, they managed to find money for tickets to the circus, Daddy told our family in disgust. Everyone was going to the circus, regardless of their financial status.

People just wanted to do something different for a change and the new circus was it, Mother added.

But the Maguires were not going to the circus, both Mother and Daddy confirmed.

"We're not spending money on dirty food served in a dusty tent on a vacant lot on the highway," Mother said. In fact, she wouldn't even stop the family sedan to let Rosarita and me stare at the mountain lion next door.

Mother's fried chicken was, in fact, delicious, I thought. I watched nearly every Sunday when she heated oil in the frying pan until it was so hot that, upon dropping the flour covered pieces of chicken into it, the grease popped from the pan. It splattered throughout the kitchen, but especially onto Mother's unprotected hands. Sustaining severe burns to her hands and arms, she shrieked in pain as she ran entire sticks of butter over the blisters. Then she let the tears streaming from her eyes drip down onto the elaborate gauze bandages she applied with yards of adhesive tape.

"Don't try to help me. This is just what I have to do to provide for my family," she whimpered every Sunday. Daddy, Carol, Rosarita, and I watched silently as Mother cooked and sobbed and bandaged until the meal was fully prepared.

"This chicken is really good, Mother," Daddy said to break the steely silence at the dining room table.

"I'm glad you can enjoy it. I certainly paid a high price for it," Mother answered as she moved her bandaged hands from lap to tabletop.

Mother is hurt just because we were hungry. I know we should be grateful that she suffers for us, but I still want to go to that circus. In fact, I wouldn't mind looking at the mountain lion and eating at a restaurant, either.

Knowing we wouldn't be able to suggest going to the restaurant and easing our way into the circus next door, we slowly surrendered to Mother's will and began to accept the litany of reasons why we shouldn't go.

At school, the others were recounting which rides were the most fun and which treat tasted the best. I remained silent. I couldn't enter into a conversation about which freaks were real and which were fake. Mother was successful in convincing us that anyone who went to the circus was doomed. If they ate circus food, they would become violently ill. If they didn't die as a result of some malfunction of a carnival ride, they would starve because they spent their last penny to see a sideshow freak created not by nature, but by smoke and mirrors. She even twisted everyone else's attendance into a perceived hazard.

"With all those people there, you don't think some of them will be coughing out their tuberculosis germs? I heard that most of the circus people have big, open sores on their bodies from syphilis. Do you want them rubbing up against you in a crowd?" she pestered us.

In the time it took for the tents to be erected, Mother successfully built her case for aversion to the circus. We could recite how we didn't want our bodies mangled by a poorly assembled ride. The poverty we would bring upon our family by purchasing tickets would bring more shame than we knew we could bear. All three of us hated throwing up. Why would we sentence ourselves to a lifetime of it by eating one bit of filthy cotton candy? Most of all, we didn't want to go insane in the final stages of syphilis we would catch by coming into contact with the carnival workers' open sores. The Maguires were not going to the circus, and that was the end of the story.

With a twist of fate unimaginable to us in our anti-circus brainwashing, nature intervened in the lives of one of the freaks on display at the carnival. I knew there was no half-man/ half-horse without the clever curtain dividing the two halves. I was aware that the bearded lady just removed the fake hair glued to her chin when the show was over. But the fat lady at the circus was a really fat lady who let people pay to look at her. "Lovely Lulu, the 500-pound lady" really did weigh 500 pounds. She managed to turn her obesity to profit for more than thirty years, the *Tempe Daily News* reported. I was soon to see that the strain of carrying that much weight had taken its toll on her by the time she arrived on Apache Boulevard.

"Maguire's," I heard Daddy say into the phone in his most professional voice. "Name of the deceased," he continued. "Location at time of death," he said in his usual tone. "We'll be there immediately," he said in conclusion. After a slight pause to listen, he uttered a surprised, "Oh!" followed by, "Can

I have a number where I can reach you when we have made the appropriate arrangements?"

Instead of dashing out the door to collect the remains as we'd watched him do a million times, he replaced the receiver in its cradle, stunned, saying "Jesus Christ." Turning to Max for support, he said, "She weighs 500 pounds. It's the fat lady at that goddamned circus. We don't have anything that can hold 500 pounds. Now what in the hell do we do?"

Max, too, repeated the "Jesus Christ," but offered no further solutions. "She's not going to fit in the ambulance. She's not going to fit in the hearse," Max fumed.

"Let's call the cop house. They'll know what to do," Daddy interrupted.

Daddy's just saying that. He knows the cops won't come, but he wants to calm Max down.

"The cops aren't going to know what to do, either," Max screeched. His voice was getting higher as his distress increased.

"At least they could help us lift her into something that can hold that much weight. Even if we had a car that could hold her, we couldn't get her into it," Daddy fussed. "I'm not calling in the volunteers from the fire department. They're not going to come down here just because we can't get a dead woman in the car. You call the cops and see if they can spare somebody to help us lift," he insisted.

Max reluctantly dialed the police.

"Max, the whole force could turn out and we couldn't lift a 500 pound dead body," the front desk cop said in answer to Max's plea. "Why don't you get a hydraulic lift or something?"

he suggested.

"We can't be seen at some circus tent swinging a body from a tow truck or crane. People will know it's us out there; we can't be that disrespectful of the dead. We'll be out of business if people think that's how we treat bodies," Max argued.

After much hand wringing, Max came up with a way to get the fat lady back to the mortuary.

"We're in a hell of a jam here," he whined to Sherman Brooks, the owner of a casket company. With a few carefully worded hints from Max about what a good customer the mortuary was, Sherman agreed to let Max borrow the truck he used to deliver caskets. He would still need considerable manpower to roll the body from the hydraulic lift at the fender into the covered cargo portion of the truck, Max explained, but at least he could get Lulu out of the circus tent where she was most certainly beginning to decompose in the heat.

"Gertrude, go to Tempe Hardware and see if there are any Mexicans in the alley who will do day labor. Drive them out to the tents and we'll handle them from there," Max directed.

"Francis, tell your brother that I do not drive down Mill Avenue or Apache Boulevard with a bunch of Mexicans in my car. The whole town will be gossiping about me," Mother demanded.

"All right. But at least, take them as far as the cop house. Nobody will see you going two blocks. Have the Mexicans ride the rest of the way with the cops. People will think they were arrested for something," he instructed. "You'll just have to bring the cops that won't fit in the squad car with all the Mexicans riding in there. People won't gossip if they see you driving the cops around, will they?" he asked desperately.

"It's a lot better than parading through town with a carful of vagrants," she pouted.

I knew this was my only chance to go near the circus, so I jumped into the family sedan immediately. Since Mother was bringing the day laborers, I managed a front row seat at the circus event of the year.

I watched out the car window as a bizarre caravan of police cars and private vehicles, led by a truck with "Brooks Casket Company" printed boldly on both sides, made its way down the highway to the circus tents. I saw a police sergeant playing the role of traffic cop, organizing the group and positioning the casket truck to lift Lulu from her cot and raise her to the level of the cargo bay. I heard Max instruct the group of five cops, two morticians, and three Mexican day laborers to combine their strength and transfer the dead body from the lift platform into the interior of the truck.

I couldn't wait to see the whole operation take place. The lift eased beneath the legs of Lulu's cot, and the truck pulled forward to move her from the confines of the tent. As the driver began to slowly raise the lift to transfer her, bed and all, into the truck, Max screamed, "Wait! Wait!"

The driver halted the hydraulics, leaving the deceased woman and her bed still outside the shelter of the truck. Lulu's cot, unlike the ones designed for ambulances, did not have wheels attached to its legs. She couldn't be rolled into the truck. She would have to be dragged, Max said.

"Four of you come inside the truck, and another four push from outside," Max instructed. "I'll take the inside group, and Francis and the rest of you stay outside pushing as hard as you can. We'll move her as far as we can and then rest. We can move her a little at a time until we get her completely in."

Lulu was much wider than her mattress. To reach the rails of the bed beneath her, the men had to extend their arms full length while bending at the waist. I groaned when I saw that this position placed their faces firmly into the rolls of fat that were Lulu's claim to fame.

"This is going to break my goddamned back. Jesus Christ, isn't there any other way to do this? I can't even breathe with my face in all this blubber!" the complainers yelled.

Their protests did them no good, though. Max was already setting the process in motion.

"One, two, lift," I heard Max order time after time as the cot moved inch by inch into the truck.

"Max, goddamn it, how much more of this do you think we can take?" the cops whined. "Christ on a crutch, can't we just leave her here and let the mountain lion eat her?"

"Shut your goddamned mouth, you. We don't talk about bodies like that," Daddy yelled from his post at the side of the cot.

The group toiled laboriously until, at last, Lulu and her bed were inside the casket truck.

The caravan back to the mortuary moved at an especially slow speed. The driver of the truck told Max he was being careful not to jostle the body around in the back of the truck.

"He was also providing those cops enough time to get over their bellyaching before the final part of their moving job," Max told Daddy.

I watched intently, hoping to catch another look at the fat lady, as the casket truck backed up as close to the door of the embalming room as it could. The crew of cops, undertakers, and laborers climbed in to drag the cot onto the lift to lower it to the ground.

"This is the last time I'm ever helping you, you son of a bitch," one cop whined.

"I feel like I'm going to vomit," another one griped.

"I can't believe I let you talk me into this. I didn't know I'd have to bury my face in some freak's belly while I break my back trying to lift her," yet another yelled at Max.

"We do stuff like this every day. Quit your bitching and lift," Max replied angrily. "It's almost over. Then you can go back to helping little old ladies cross the street. Everybody move slowly and try to lift at the same time. I'll count to three again just like before," Max instructed them.

"I'll try to hold back and not do the whole thing myself," a sarcastic cop threw in. "Do you think we're a bunch of goddamned idiots?"

Suddenly, Lulu's weight shifted atop the cot and she began to roll toward the edge of the lift. In one last desperate attempt to preclude the body's freefalling several feet to the pavement below, Max grabbed a leg of the cot just as Lulu careened over the side of it. His scream was one of pure anguish.

"Mother of god," Daddy cried as he watched Lulu land

face down on the asphalt outside the embalming room door.

I ran from the car when I heard Daddy yell. I arrived at the doorway just in time to observe the group of men drag, push, shove, and roll the fat lady's body from outside to inside the mortuary. It was a scene of massive body parts being contorted into impossible positions straight from the screen of a horror movie. Only later did I hear the siren of the ambulance begin to whine as it rushed Max to the hospital on a backboard, where he remained in traction, under heavy sedation, for days.

I didn't get to see the piano case used as a casket because Lulu couldn't fit into even the largest one made. I didn't see that the fat lady was embalmed on the floor because no one could lift her onto one of the hard white tables. I didn't watch Mother style her hair or observe Daddy apply her makeup while they crawled around on all fours around her. But I knew all these things were happening just a few feet from my back door. When I returned from school the next day, I did see a gigantic dress hanging on the embalming room door and I knew exactly who would be wearing it when Lulu's funeral began.

But none of these observations or eavesdroppings could be shared. Mine were the makings of playground stardom when retold to the other kindergarteners, I knew. I again stood silently watching as Pedro basked in the glory of celebrity earned by stories that were untrue, and certainly not as riveting as the ones I could tell. Instead, I played over and over again in my mind the only part of the circus I had been allowed to be a part of. It didn't really matter if I had seen Lulu, dead or alive, because no one would ever know I had.

I might not be in the pink chair at school, but I haven't really left it behind.

Chapter Three

Negro Baby

"You did a good job on that, Jamie. It's hard to hit the right keys when the typewriter wobbles around so much on this TV tray. Maybe someday we can put it on a real desk and you can see how much easier it is," Carol encouraged as we sat side by side on her lumpy mattress.

"I want to learn to type real fast, like you," I told her. I sat as close as I could get to her on the end of her bed. She wrestled with the flimsy tray as it nearly collapsed every time the little bell rang and she returned the carriage to begin a new line.

I wished I could do this forever. I liked to sit with Carol and just watch whatever she was doing. Sitting quietly here is nothing like sitting quietly in the pink chair. This is even better than school; I don't have to worry about keeping any secrets here. Carol already knows all about The Place. And she knows never to talk about it, too.

Carol, Rosarita, and I shared one bedroom in the small house behind the mortuary. Our lumpy mattresses were squeezed so closely together that we had no room to walk between them. Every night, all three of us crawled on all fours the full length of our beds to reach the ticking-covered pillows mashed up against the wall at the opposite end. If I fell out of bed during the night and became trapped between Carol's bed and mine, Carol never complained. She helped me twist and turn among the metal bedsprings until I could get back on top of my mattress. She knew just how to plump my pillow so the sharp spines of the feathers inside it didn't poke through the pillow case and scratch me.

She was nice to me during the day, too. She let me empty the contents of her purse onto the floor as I searched for a pack of chewing gum. I complained only once that I didn't like clove gum; after that, she bought only Chiclets from then on. She gave me bike rides to the Dairy Queen on Mill Avenue and even paid for my treats. She let me wear her barrettes after she brushed and curled my hair into a new style. She let me play with the keys on her portable typewriter. Even though she had homework to do, she waited patiently while I used up a whole page of her special typing paper just to type my name. JAMIE JAMIE JAMIE.

Then a boy named Henry started taking Carol to the movies every Saturday. He invited her to a dance that was so fancy only kids in high school could go. Mother made Carol a taffeta dress with a gathered net skirt so it looked like she was wearing her crinoline on the outside. Mother sewed tiny little pearls all over the net skirts and Carol had satin shoes dyed to match the pink of the dress. She looked beautiful in it.

Mother waited until the last minute before starting to sew the dress. She said she was stalling, hoping that Carol would get a better date than Henry. Mother slammed the bedroom door real hard and cried for a long time after Henry pinned a carnation corsage on Carol's dress and they drove away in his '55 Chevy.

I liked Henry. He didn't treat Rosarita or me like we bothered him. One time he caught a toad in the irrigation water in the back yard, trapped it in a jelly jar, and gave it to me. I didn't see anything wrong with him taking Carol to movies and dances. But, as he came to the house more often, Mother and Daddy began arguing with Carol almost every day.

"Don't you know he isn't good enough for you?" Mother began.

"He's a nice boy, Mother. I like him," was Carol's weak answer.

"None of those kids you run around with are any damned good," Daddy grumbled.

I didn't know Daddy knew any of Carol's friends. Whenever anyone came to visit Carol, Daddy read the newspaper the whole time they were there. He dipped the paper below his eyes just enough to catch a glimpse of whoever was there as he was turning a page. He never said a word; he just continued smoking his cigarette and reading.

Mother and Daddy and Carol had longer, angrier, and more frequent arguments. Rosarita and I had to leave the room when they started.

"Rosarita, take Jamie and go play somewhere else," Mother yelled in the quivery voice she had right before she started crying. I waited in our bedroom until Carol eventually joined us.

"It's all right," she assured us. "Everything's going to be

just fine," she said as she put her arm around me and squeezed gently.

But everything wasn't all right. In a whirlwind of activity at the end of the summer, Carol and Henry got married. Carol moved to her own house south of Apache Boulevard. Before I knew it, I shared a bedroom with only Rosarita, and the hours of sitting quietly with Carol never returned.

People can vanish from your life in an instant. Just because you love someone doesn't mean they'll be around you forever.

I still had school to keep me away from the pink chair, but summer vacation presented a whole new challenge. Few places in Tempe were fun for kids. The businesses along the major street weren't any fun. "Keep the kids off Mill Avenue," blared the headlines in the *Tempe Daily News*. Daddy read aloud from the editorial page when merchants wrote letters to the editor warning parents about lax supervision when school was not in session. He peered over the top of the newspaper page as though I were a vagrant. Staring directly at me, he raised one eyebrow in a silent incrimination.

Apache Boulevard wasn't a getaway, either; it consisted of four lanes and some gas stations. The few restaurants along the highway weren't interesting for kids. The neighborhoods were rows of houses that all looked exactly alike. Even though some of them housed kids my age, they were too far away from the business district where I lived to be available for fun. Daley Park had playground equipment I liked, but it too was a long way away.

Rosarita was no fun to play with, either. She rode her

bike so fast I couldn't keep up with her. She won every board game we played. Instead of being grateful to me for diverting Mother's attention from her, she was irritable and competitive in all but one activity. Every afternoon, right after "Queen for a Day," the two of us walked across the alley and through the back door of The Spud-Nut doughnut shop. There we ordered the same things each visit—two scoops of chocolate for Rosarita, and two of strawberry for me—atop tall, crunchy cones. But as soon as we lapped down the ice cream, she found something to do that didn't include me.

Everywhere in town, the heat of the Arizona sun was oppressive. I could be outside for only a matter of minutes before I had to retreat to the shelter of the indoors. A few minutes of biking or skating left me running for the shade of the cottonwood trees that grew along the banks of the irrigation canals.

"You can slip off the canal bank into that dirty water, and no one can hear you screaming for help. Is that how you want to look in your casket, all puffed up like drowning victims?" Mother asked. "Even if you don't drown in the filthy water, the crawdads will bite you so many times you'll be all scarred up. Everyone will know for the rest of your life that you were a little girl who didn't listen to her mother and played at the canal," she continued.

If she thought I was still unimpressed with her reasoning, she tacked on another threat. "River bums live along the canal. They do bad things to little girls who go there to play."

I didn't know what "bad things" were, but Mother wouldn't tell me something that wasn't true.

I wanted to be an obedient kid, but I could not resist the lure of the canal banks when the temperature soared above 100 degrees. The wind made a pleasant hum as it traveled through the dense leaves of the cottonwoods bordering the water. Their massive roots made fascinating shapes and textures in the ground surrounding them. Wispy pieces of the cotton for which they were named flowed through the air like fairy dust. I could have spent hours on the muddy bank that bordered the fishy-smelling canal, but I didn't dare linger very long. As I felt the only moist soil for miles around squish through my small hands, I envisioned Mother watching the kitchen clock.

I can't stand to spend any more time in the heat. I need to be here where it's cool. But I'll pay for this later. Mother knows where I am.

The only other cool spot in town was Tempe Beach. Mother had not forbidden it, so I could be cool and unafraid at the same time there. Each year, at dawn on Memorial Day, I began the daily ritual that occupied each day of the blistering summer. "Can we go swimming today?" were the first words out of my mouth. I asked to go to the pool every day just in case somebody died during the night and Mother demanded that I accompany her to the embalming room while she prepared the corpse.

Being at the pool all day means no chance of being in the pink chair all day.

If I could brave, bare-footed, the 100 degree temperature of the cement sidewalks leading up to the ticket window at Tempe Beach, I could save the ten-cent price of renting a locker to hold my shoes while I swam.

"Don't pay for a locker. Just leave your shoes at home. Mother won't know we're going barefoot until after she gives us our money," Rosarita advised me. "That way we can buy taffy at the concession stand."

"I can do it, Rosarita. We can swim and eat sweets. Are you sure Mother isn't going to know, though? She can tell when I go to the canal bank. She'll figure out what we're doing at the pool and we'll get in trouble for that, too," I argued.

"It's fine with me if you're too chicken. But don't ask for even one bite of my candy if you've wasted all your money on a locker," Rosarita threatened.

By midsummer, I could make the trip to the pool in bare feet with only mild discomfort. I considered a few hops and jumps on the blistering cement to be a small price to pay for a sweet treat. I wanted to experience all the pool had to offer.

I came to be identified by my summer-long sunburn. My shoulders were in a ceaseless process of blistering and molting. The pain was over as soon as the blisters broke, so the peeling process was unsightly, but not irritating. Just like running barefooted over the hot cement, I thought the burn was worth it to be able to go to the pool daily. My nose, however, had been burned so severely so many times that the blister became so inflamed it would bleed a little, leaving a scab on top of the bright red skin surrounding it.

"I don't think it's red, Mother," I lied. "Everybody looks like this in the summer. It's not ugly," I replied to Mother's comments.

Some of the lifeguards wore a pasty white nose coat to protect themselves from such a mark, but I thought the white cream looked stupid, so I opted to bear the natural consequences and have an open sore in the middle of my face all summer instead. As though the red, peeling shoulders and the scab on my nose were not enough, I suffered the fate of all the blondes in town.

The Tempe Beach water was so highly chlorinated that the residue of the chemical collected in light-colored hair after many swims. As the chlorine content of my hair soared, I moved from being a blonde at the beginning of the summer to being green-haired a few weeks into it.

For once, I'm like all the other kids. Everybody can tell I go to Tempe Beach just by looking at me.

Most of the people my age were available to play within the sparkling oasis of the pool. Rosarita found her own group, too. Water games and splashing fights filled the sun-baked hours I spent there. I played with kids I knew from school, along with strangers I'd only just met. Everyone was open to playing or racing or dousing everyone else with no formal invitations or introductions required. I no longer had to beg Rosarita to play with me.

I loved laughing and shouting with the others, but I also loved the underwater silence. Just by holding my breath and bending my knees, I could instantly transition from being part of the noisy crowd to being completely uninterrupted in the silence under the water.

I can do whatever I want here. I can have a million

friends if I choose, or I can vanish into the water all alone whenever I please.

But one fun-filled day I made a huge mistake in my underwater escape. I rolled my body into a tight ball and held my breath. I stayed in the refuge under the water as long as my lungs allowed. As I began to paddle to the surface, another kid splashed into the water close to me. Instead of floating peacefully to the water's surface above me, I slammed into the rough plaster of the pool siding. Bouncing off the side instantly reminded me of the baby floating in formaldehyde at the mortuary.

I may be having fun now, but I'll soon be back in the pink chair. I'll have to watch the tiny baby bang against the side of the jar the same way I hit the pool siding.

I didn't abandon my summer refuge, though I didn't spend much time underwater after that happened. And another problem soon tainted my joy at the pool.

Tempe Beach was a public swimming pool where everyone was welcome, even Mexicans. I could still see the rectangle of bright paint where there once was a sign that read "No Mexicans."

Everybody knows the sign was there and what it read. It might as well still be there; you can see right where it was. A lot of old people are mad that they took it down. I don't think Mexicans like to swim, anyway. I never see very many of them here.

Each afternoon at four, Mother parked the family sedan at the curb in front of the pool. Rosarita had accepted a ride from a friend's mom earlier in the day, so Mother had only me to pick up. She leaned over the chain link fence dividing the grassy lawn around the pool from the hot sidewalk. She had to use her hand as a visor to shield her eyes from the harsh reflection of sunlight off the pool water.

"Hey, Jamie," the older boys at the pool taunted, "Tonto is on the lookout for you again."

"She doesn't look like Tonto. She's keeping the sun off her glasses so she can see me," I retorted.

I dogpaddled to the coping around the pool as fast as I could. I didn't wait my turn at the ladder; that would take too long. I threw one leg up out of the water onto the edge of the pool, hoisted my weight to the cement above, and dashed to the fence trying to avoid more references to my mother's pose. However, I could hear the boys continuing with their "Lone Ranger" comments as I ran.

"Get out of there," Mother yelled. "Come over here this instant."

I could tell by the volume of Mother's demands that I needed to comply immediately.

"Do you see those boys over there?" Mother said as she glared at me through the diamond shapes of the chain link fence. She pointed not at the boys making fun of her, but at three other boys on the opposite side of the pool. Their skin was darker than the Mexicans I knew, and their hair glistened with beads of water.

"Yeah," I answered. I felt as though I could cry with dread.

"I have just one rule for you to follow at this place. When Negroes jump into the pool, you are to jump out of it. Do you understand me?"

"I didn't do anything wrong, Mother. I didn't know that was a rule. I didn't even know Negroes were here."

"Just get your towel and get in the car with me. If your grandmother knew this was happening, she would have a fit."

This is really bad. She's even talking about Grandma.

The only time Mother mentioned my grandmother was when she invoked her Southern heritage to condemn the ways of the Southwest. No one could remember what the issue was that separated three generations from one another, but everyone knew not to mention the name of Mother's mother, much less call her or drive the short distance to Mesa where she lived. All I knew was that my only surviving grandparent vanished from my life. Her disappearance made me feel the same way I did when Carol got married.

I ran to get my towel and scampered across the hot cement to reach the car. Mother was already continuing the discussion as my bare legs skidded across the hot car seat.

"I'm sorry, Mother," I said. "I don't want you to be mad at me. I won't ever do it again."

I wasn't exactly sure what I was apologizing for, but I realized it must have been something I should have known.

I figured out so many secrets about the Place, but now I have to know stuff about other places, too.

"Jamie, do you know what a Negro is thinking about when he sees a blonde little girl in her bathing suit?" Mother asked.

I knew from Mother's tone that this was a question I should know how to answer. My mind raced trying to come up with the right response. I paid rapt attention in school; I would have remembered Negroes and blondes if they had been part of my lessons. I began to panic as I came up with—nothing.

"Well, do you?" Mother demanded when I hesitated to answer.

"No, Mother," I finally admitted, my eyes focused on the floorboard.

Mother was so upset that her voice trembled when she spoke. "They are not thinking about swimming. That's for darn sure."

"I knew that. I just didn't know I had to get away so fast before they started thinking it, that's all. I promise to do better next time," I said.

Mother broke the silence with one last comment. "You know, it's situations like these that get little white girls in trouble when Negroes are around."

"I know," I mumbled, even though I had not the slightest notion of my mother's meaning.

The minute we arrived home, I stripped off my wet suit, the very thing that had incited some kind of bad thought in the Negroes' minds, and draped it over the faucet in the bathtub to dry for tomorrow. I knew I had to learn what Mother meant or I could be forbidden from the only cool recreation in town. Not even a trip to the canal bank made Mother as mad as she was today. I was headed on a course that led straight back to the pink chair.

"Come here," I said in a stage whisper when I spotted Rosarita just outside the bathroom door. I shut and locked the door behind us once she was in the room. Carol had taught me long ago that any of the secrets we shared were discussed in the bathroom only. Even Mother respected the sanctity of the only locked door in the house.

"Do you know about Negroes in swimming pools?" I blurted. When Rosarita didn't respond immediately, I added, "It has something to do with bathing suits on blonde girls."

Even with the additional hints, Rosarita couldn't figure it out. She responded with a shrug of her shoulders. I knew I had come across a serious offense if it was so bad Rosarita didn't even know about it

I waited until nightfall, when everyone was in bed, before I consulted Rosarita again. I had to keep the discussion short, because Mother and Daddy were just down the hall in their bedroom. The sound of the cooler was the only mask for our nightly talks and, fortunately, it was gushing air at a furious pace tonight.

I whispered into the darkness, "Do you think Carol knows about Negroes in swimming pools when they see blonde girls in bathing suits? It makes white girls get into trouble."

"Call Carol. I'm tired," Rosarita mumbled. "You're always scared about something. It's probably no big deal."

I knew I could trust Carol to tell the truth about little girls and Negroes. But now that she lived across town with Henry, I would have to risk a phone call outside Mother's hearing.

"What are you talking about?" Carol grumbled sleepily. I called so early she hadn't even taken down the pin curls she put in her hair every night. I heard the bobby pins scratching against the receiver as she talked. "Does Mother know you're calling me? You'd better be careful or she'll find out," she warned.

"Mother thinks she told me about it yesterday, but I don't know what she means and she's too mad for me to ask her. Just tell me so she'll keep letting me go to Tempe Beach. I know you know, Carol. Come on, just tell me," I pleaded. "I couldn't even sleep last night."

"When Mother says girls get into trouble, she means they are going to have babies and they're not married yet," Carol finally answered.

"That doesn't make any sense. I don't want to have a baby," I replied. "Even if I did have a baby, I wouldn't want it to be a Negro baby. I'd want it to be brunette, like Rosarita."

"Just be quiet about it," Carol said. "No matter what Mother says about the swimming pool, you are not going to have a Negro baby. That's all you need to know for now."

"Do you think I can go back to the pool?"

"Not if you don't hush and hang up."

I lay awake again the next night. I didn't want to have a Negro baby, but I did want to play at Tempe Beach, no matter who else was in the Olympic-size pool at the same time.

After what seemed like hours of tossing and turning, I took a long, deep breath. I knew I could trust Carol to have told the truth.

In the wee hours of the morning, I finally developed a plan. I would keep a watchful eye for Negroes at the pool from now on, and leap from the water the moment I spotted them. I just had to hope I had escaped the contaminated water two days ago in enough time to avoid having a Negro baby. It was all I knew to do. Even though I still had red skin and green hair, I didn't have the same joy going to the pool any more. In the back of my mind was always the knowledge that even the best places in the world held hidden dangers that I was unaware of. I had a funny, tight feeling in my stomach every time I put on my bathing suit now.

Chapter Four

Lost Arm

The only other place in town I truly loved, besides Tempe Beach and the forbidden canal bank, was Billie's Flower Shop next door to the mortuary. It filled the void left by the seasonal closing of Tempe Beach from Labor Day to Memorial Day.

The flower shop was a feast for all my senses. From the moment I pushed open the glass door, I was aware that the shop was different from every other place in my world.

A little bell above the doorway announced my entry with a jingle, accompanied by a waft of cool, fragrant air. No pungent odors of chemicals or choking puffs of dust could be found in the little shop—just an array of delights. The walls were layered with shelves reaching to the ceiling, each containing plants so well tended they billowed from their ceramic containers and cascaded down the wall.

Beyond the potted plants stood the cooler, containing every flower of every variety, or so I thought. Standing in buckets of water, the blooms beckoned through the dewy glass doors, inviting me to reach for the handle and pull. When I did, the refrigeration misted out to coat my face. The combined fragrances of carnations and roses and flowers I didn't even know the names of created a perfume to accompany the sensation of the mist as I held the door open. In those few seconds, even the tight feeling in my stomach went away.

Every time I went to the flower shop, the kind couple who owned it welcomed me.

"Hi, Jamie," Billie called out from behind the counter. "Let's pick out a flower for you to take home."

I chose a carnation every time, but I debated laboriously before coming to my conclusion. In the cloud of fragrant, cool mist, I reached for the container that held the red carnations. I lingered as long as possible before I found the tallest of them all. Letting the water from the bucket drip down my dress from the newly plucked flower, I buried my nose into the very middle of the jagged petals and inhaled as deeply as I could.

I want this beautiful scent to go to every part of my body, inside and out.

Then Billie motioned for me to come behind the counter with her. There, thin dowels of wood held spool upon spool of ribbon of every color of the rainbow, and each of the different colors draped over the edge of the spool. With the carnation in one hand, I extended my other arm and walked slowly past the ribbons. I let each color drape fleetingly across my flesh only to be picked up by the following color until every shade had thrilled my sense of touch as well as sight.

Billie let me choose not one, but two colors of ribbon to go with my carnation. With great care and intense pleasure, I pointed to two different shades of pink, one just slightly paler than the other. With the red of the carnation, they blended into a symphony of my favorite colors. I watched, captivated, as she took my flower and ribbons from me and, with a short flurry of movement, created a bow of both ribbons tied deftly around the stem of the flower. Then Billie pulled on the spools containing my chosen colors and created streamers that were even longer than the stem of the flower. As I walked away, they drifted around my body.

I love it here so much. What if something happens to take this away from me?

By the time I arrived back at Mother's door, the tight feeling in my stomach was already strong. On a spring afternoon, a telephone call turned my vague fears about losing the joy of the flower shop into a panic.

"Oh, Jesus." Daddy grimaced as he said it. "We're on our way," he spoke into the receiver, and the conversation ended.

"Max, did you hear that?" Daddy called out. Extensions of the Big Phone in our house and Max's allowed Daddy and Max to communicate with each other once the caller hung up. "It could be Duane. We have to get out to the groves," Daddy urged.

Duane was Billie's husband. He owned several acres of citrus orchards along Baseline Road, just west of the Japanese flower gardens. I thought that place too was somewhat magical, like the flower shop, because the blossoms on the trees created a beautiful scent that spread for miles around. In the groves, the heavy foliage of the trees provided a blanket of shade. The combination of the perfumed air and the cool temperature created an oasis in the hot desert. And, just like at the flower shop, I always left with a gift. At the orchard it was an orange I was allowed to pick from a tree myself. Duane pointed out the ones that were ripe and sweet, and held me by the waist as I reached among the branches to pull one from the twig. He then produced a pen knife from his pocket to cut away the peel. All the way home I put sections of juicy orange into my mouth whole, biting down to release the squirt of juice and spitting out the seeds as we drove along. Trips to the orchard were a rare treat for me, which made them and Duane all the more dear.

Often when I visited the flower shop, Duane and Billie would be together, working among the flowers. They seemed genuinely pleased to welcome a little girl into their beautiful surroundings. I knew and loved Duane, so hearing his name associated with the trouble that accompanied calls for the ambulance sent a chill through me. I knew, though, that now was not the time to ask questions. Max and Daddy ran from their houses, slamming their screen doors and the ambulance doors as well. All I saw was Daddy driving the ambulance with Max in the passenger seat. They were driving fast and the siren was going full blast. Something was terribly wrong, I knew.

The call was from one of the few English-speaking employees at Duane's orchard. Most of the people who worked there were Mexicans. I had seen the campsites among the orange trees where they lived during picking season. They worked from dawn to dusk every day to harvest the citrus crop. Their only assistance in doing this came from an apparatus similar to a dump truck. As the workers threw the oranges from the burlap sacks they wore to collect the fruit while they were picking into its bed, a hydraulic lift scooped the oranges up and moved them to the front, making more room for the next burlap bagful to be tossed in.

I overheard Daddy telling Mother what happened at the orchard which had sent him out the door so quickly. Somehow, when Duane was in the field with the Mexicans, his burlap sack became twisted around the hydraulic mechanism, causing the machine to scoop up his bag along with the oranges. As he reached in to retrieve it, the machine clamped down on his arm. The force was so great that as it began to lift the oranges to move them back, it began to lift Duane by the arm.

"My arm! My arm!" he screamed to those around him. "Stop the truck," he pleaded.

The Mexicans couldn't understand his English words, but they saw what was happening as the machine stayed in motion and Duane dangled in the air by his arm. They raced to halt the mechanism, but none of them really knew how it operated. They panicked. It took several minutes of yelling in Spanish and men from the entire grove crowding around before the truck stopped, Daddy said.

"All the pulling and grinding and lifting of the heavy machinery just ripped Duane's arm from his body," Daddy stated in a matter of fact tone. When the truck finally stopped, Duane dropped with a thud into the blood-soaked ground beneath him. The Mexicans were hysterical, screaming at each other to help him, though none knew what to do, Daddy continued.

Max picked up the story where Daddy left off. Max was always more excitable than my father, I knew, so I listened even more intently when he told what he saw.

"'Mano! Mano!'" they screamed to the English-speaking foreman as he drove up," Max told everyone.

"There's nothing wrong with your hands," the foreman shouted back in confusion. Only when he saw the trail of blood leading to Duane's limp body did he realize they were speaking of their boss's hand, not their own.

"Oh, God," he mumbled as he rolled Duane's body over to reveal his missing limb.

The wives of the Mexican fruit pickers emerged from their tents and fell to their knees, praying the rosary in Spanish as fast as their fingers could move through the beads. With the approach of the foreman, the Mexicans who had originally struggled to help Duane now stood back helplessly, Max said. They thought their boss was dead.

"Call an ambulance," someone shouted. "Get Maguire's out here," another yelled.

The foreman ran to his truck and raced off in a cloud of dust. When he finally reached a phone and had Maguire's on the line, he added, at the end of his frantic call to Daddy, "Tell Billie. She doesn't know."

"Got it. She's next door at the flower shop," Daddy answered.

"Mother, go get Billie. She won't be able to drive to the orchard after she hears this," Daddy told Mother.

I knew I wasn't allowed to stay in the house alone. Just like the day when Lulu, the circus fat lady, died, I rode along to the scene of this call in the backseat of Mother's sedan.

"Duane, buddy, Duane, old man, we're coming. It's Francis and Max. We'll take care of you," Daddy yelled as he and Uncle Max ran through the trees with the ambulance cot.

They made their way through the grove to the site of the accident and lifted their injured friend onto the rolling cot. Billie, Mother, and I stood watching at the edge of the grove. Daddy kept up his encouragement all the way down the path that led back.

"Duane, oh my god, Duane," Billie screamed when the blood-soaked trio came into view. She ran toward the cot.

"Billie, no," Daddy yelled. He jumped to the front of the cot to shield her view of her mangled husband. "Don't do this to yourself now. Wait until we get him cleaned up before you see him. Everything's going to be fine. Just wait over there by Gertrude," he told her.

She continued to scream for Duane, but Daddy and Max ignored her as they scrambled toward the ambulance as quickly as they could. Mother put her arm around Billie's shoulder, but she shrugged it off and kept screaming.

"Christ, can't you hurry up?" Daddy yelled at Max.

"What more do you want from me? Jesus, I'm pushing the cot with one hand and using the other one as a tourniquet. Every time the cot hits a clod of dirt, I lose my grip on this vein. He's going to bleed out if I let go too many times," Max said.

I hoped Billie was still screaming so loud she didn't hear him say that. She looked like her knees were going to buckle beneath her any second.

By the time they approached the ambulance, Max and Daddy were as soaked with blood as Duane.

"God damn it," Max moaned when his bloody right hand

slipped off the ambulance door handle. He was successful with his left, though, and the back of the ambulance opened to receive its cargo. I watched silently as Daddy and Max hoisted a blood-covered body, which looked nothing like the Duane I knew, into the ambulance.

Once the cot was secure in the back, Daddy sprinted to the driver's seat to begin the trip to the emergency room. Max rode in back with Duane, fumbling to find something that would help him put enough pressure on Duane's arm to stem the tide of blood coming from it.

"Francis was driving like a bat out of hell," I heard Max tell the admitting nurse at the hospital. Once they had bounced and jostled their way through the grove, they lost no time when they reached paved road, he said. Through red lights, school zones, and the heavily trafficked business district of Mesa, they flew well beyond the speed limit in their quest to save their friend. Mother, Billie, and I followed behind them at a more reasonable speed.

It seemed like hours before the familiar neon "Emergency" sign came into view at Mesa Southside Hospital, Max said.

"We need help out here," Daddy began screaming before he and Max got the cot out of the ambulance. "Get a doc. We've got a bad one here," Max added as they pushed the cot toward the emergency room door.

By the time the doctor, who had been running down the hallway to meet them, arrived at Duane's side, Mother, Billie, and I found seats in the waiting room. We could hear everyone's conversation in the treatment area next door.

"This arm is gone," Daddy said.

"Where is it?" the doctor asked.

"What do you mean, where is it?" Daddy said, irritated. "I just told you. It tore off."

"I can see that," the doctor countered. "Do you have it?"

"Are you listening to me?" Daddy asked. "His arm is in a conveyor out in the middle of an orange grove. The man would be dead if we hadn't been able to get him out of there."

"So you don't have the arm?" the doctor asked again.

"The machine has the arm. What in the hell are you talking about?" Daddy yelled.

"If you had the arm," the doctor said with sarcastic slowness, "we could assess the damage to the musculature and circulatory systems without performing surgery after he's lost so much blood."

"Are you telling me that you need the torn-off arm to best treat what's still attached?" Daddy asked, incredulous.

"That would be standard diagnostic procedure," the doctor replied. I recognized his tone of voice; it was the one most people reserved for speaking to children.

"Oh, Christ," Daddy said to Max, whose mud-and-blood soaked clothing had dried to a crust, covering his body.

I saw Daddy and Max both run out of the hospital without a word to each other. "Stay here," Daddy shouted to us as he trotted past the waiting room.

"By the time we got back to the grove, the oranges in the truck didn't even look like fruit. They were so saturated with blood, they had congealed into something that looked like one giant mass," Daddy told us when he returned. He recounted the gory retrieval in a voice hoarse with fatigue.

Crouching over the mess like dogs preparing to bury a bone, he and Max used their bare hands to shovel orange after orange between their feet, praying that their hands would eventually land on the flesh of a human, not an orange. As they dug deeper, the little cuts and scrapes on their own hands became soaked in orange juice that stung bitterly. And they were beginning to sweat so much that their dripping perspiration was rehydrating the dried blood into a sticky liquid again, making it even more difficult to grasp the oranges. From time to time, they pulled themselves up from their crouching positions to peer into the fruit pile, hoping to spot the arm. Each time they tried this, it became more difficult because the sun was going down. In an hour, they would be standing in complete darkness with no chance of finding their quarry.

"Then my hand hit something that felt like metal," Daddy said. "It felt harder than oranges. With both hands, I grabbed onto it and pulled it from the fruit. It was a man's wristwatch," he said.

"Seconds later, we had Duane's arm," Max interrupted.

They ran for the ambulance. With the arm between them on the front seat, they traveled the same path they'd used earlier that same day. As they careened through the streets to reach the hospital again, their clothing stuck to their skin and hardened there.

"Where is your injury?" the admitting nurse asked them on their second arrival at the emergency room.

"It's Francis and Max," I heard Daddy say. I could see the nurse was still struggling to recognize them through the mud and blood covering them.

Then she saw it. Daddy held Duane's arm out to the nurse.

"We found it," was all Daddy had the energy to say.

"What is that?" she asked as she took a step backward.

"The arm," Daddy said. "The doc said he needed it so he could figure out how bad the veins and stuff were so he wouldn't have to do surgery, and he didn't want to do surgery because Duane's already lost too much blood," I heard Daddy spit out in one sentence. I could see he was too exhausted to manage further explanation.

"Oh," the nurse replied.

I watched the two bloody, citrusy, sweaty men stand mute as the nurse slowly put on rubber gloves and strolled into the treatment room to deliver the arm. When she returned to the waiting room several minutes later, she found them standing silently exactly where she left them.

They stared straight ahead in a stupor as she announced in a flat voice, "We can't use it."

"It's not a donation, for Christ's sake," Daddy answered. He became more animated the longer he talked. "It's Duane's arm. The doc needs it to treat him." As an afterthought, he added quietly, "He did make it, didn't he?"

"He didn't expire," the nurse said flatly. "You know, it's been three hours since you brought him in here," she added as though she were scolding boys who had missed their curfew.

The men looked at each other, turned around simultaneously, and shuffled past the waiting room where we sat. I saw them get into the waiting ambulance. Daddy paused before he started the engine. He sat silently with his head resting on the steering wheel. Neither brother spoke. Slowly, Daddy let his hand drop onto the gear shift. Then he lifted his head, and I saw the ambulance ease out of the emergency entrance.

Mother and I waited while the nurse ushered Billie through double swinging doors marked "Emergency." No one uttered a word when she came back. Mother and I got up and Billie followed us, zombie-like, across the hot asphalt and into the stifling heat of Mother's parked car. I sat silently in the back seat as we rode past the beautiful flower gardens and into the acres of citrus groves. Billie cried quietly as we returned her to her home among the fragrant orange trees.

Many weeks later, Duane was strong enough to come to the flower shop again, but I didn't really like going there anymore. The sight of Duane's empty shirt sleeve secured with a safety pin soured the thrill of the pretty flowers and the colored ribbons. Every time I looked at the now one-armed man, I was reminded how quickly things I loved could be taken away.

My affection for Duane and Billie had not diminished, but my fear of losing the beautiful parts of my life was too strong to let me enjoy the flower shop and its owners the way I used to. Just like the pool and Carol and my grandmother, Duane's arm was a reminder that everything I loved was at risk of being whisked away in an instant. The tight feeling in my stomach was so strong I could hardly breathe.

I have to find a place where I feel safe. But where? I was dumb to think there was happiness at the flower shop. It's next door to The Place and the pink chair. I should have known better.

Chapter Five

Vanished Playhouse

Daddy and Mother never missed an opportunity to remind us of the threat we posed to the dignity of Daddy's business and, therefore, the financial stability of our entire family.

"Rosarita, get off those swings this instant," Mother yelled out to the back yard. "You saw the hearse pull out of the garage just like I did. You know very good and well that means there's a funeral at the mortuary. What would we do if your father came out with a grieving family and found you playing merrily right in front of them?"

"Jamie, do I have to wait for you to hush every time The Big Phone rings? You can hear it just as well as I can. You know I can't have a family call and hear kids yammering in the background," Daddy lectured.

"I don't care if you are married," Mother scolded Carol. "You are not to come to the mortuary wearing shorts. People in your father's business expect girls to wear dresses. None of you girls will be happy until you run us out of business," she raved.

When Rosarita and I decided we wanted a playhouse in the yard that separated the mortuary from our family home, we knew Daddy would object. If he spent time making us a playhouse, he'd have less time for embalming or funerals or bookkeeping or anything else related to the mortuary. We'd never get it.

"Jamie, quit being such a whiner and help me think of how we can convince Daddy to get us a playhouse. It'll be so cute with little curtains in the windows. We can have tea parties for our dolls out there. Come on," Rosarita plagued me.

"If we say we'll play in it, he definitely won't say yes," I said. "The more we're outside, the more chance there is that a dead person's family will see us. You know Daddy won't like that. Neither will Max," I continued.

"All right, you big baby, I'll get it myself. You wait and see. I'll talk him in to it."

Rosarita can have anything she wants. All she has to do is smile and her dimples will convince anyone.

"You're right. Go ahead and ask him yourself. He'll tell me no," I retorted.

"We're not putting anything else out where you girls can be seen or heard by families," Daddy said that night at the dinner table. "I wish you would learn to enjoy what you already have instead of wanting even more. Have you even played with those new jewelry boxes I brought you last week?"

"Those aren't jewelry boxes," Rosarita countered. "They're sample caskets from that salesman."

"Well, I had to ask him for two. Each mortuary usually gets only one, but I said I had two kids, so I needed two samples. Don't you think that was humiliating, begging for toys for you two?"

"But, they're not toys, they're little caskets. They say so

on the stickers inside them. I can show you right where the name and number of the casket company is."

"They're lined in cedar, you know. Have you even bothered to smell them?"

"We like the casket samples, but we want a playhouse, too. We'll be nice and quiet, Daddy. Some kids by our school have a playhouse that looks just like a little tiny version of their real house. We want one like that, too," Rosarita pressed.

"We'll see," Daddy conceded after the first argument.

Two weeks and fourteen dinner-table arguments later, Rosarita landed on my bed with a jump. "We're getting a playhouse! Daddy said so!"

"Are we getting the playhouse tomorrow?" were the first words out of Rosarita's mouth every night at dinner for weeks. I didn't comment except for an occasional "me, too" to support Rosarita's campaign. Nothing was so important that I would risk Daddy calling me "Chatterbox" in front of everyone again. My stomach got so tight after he squelched my conversation that I couldn't eat dinner the last time I spoke up. Then I was in trouble with Mother for not eating.

If she doesn't stop begging for it to be here tomorrow, we're not going to get it at all. Daddy's getting sick of hearing about it.

Rosarita and I had expectations of a miniature replica of our own home. After all, if our parents could make dead people look alive again, they could surely make a toy house that seemed real. We had good reasons for our faith in our parents' ability to create something from nothing; both Mother and Daddy were highly respected for their skill in what's known as the "restorative arts".

Some families brought photos to the mortuary so Mother could copy the hairstyle their loved one had in life. Many of the pictures showed the deceased when she was half the age she was at death, though, so they weren't much help. Mother used her own creativity to construct hairdos appropriate for burial. She was so accomplished that she could even comb wigs to look natural on the bald ones who'd died after chemotherapy or brain surgery.

"Always come back and check bodies after they are in the caskets," she instructed me. "Daddy and Max mess up their hair while they're dressing them. And putting them in the casket can make the sides look mashed down if the pillow comes up too far," she continued, as though she were teaching me my future job.

When Daddy worked on bodies, he allowed no one in the room. It was illegal for anyone to be present during embalming except the immediate family of the deceased, but he had artistic, not ethical, reasons for keeping everyone out. Daddy allowed no distractions as he applied makeup. No corpse ever left his preparation room without structural defects to the face entirely masked from view. He could mix various tints of makeup to match precisely the skin tone the person had before death. He blended the creams and powders deftly into the collar or the hairline. There were no lines of demarcation on a neck or an ear where makeup ended when families viewed a loved one prepared by Maguire's.

Almost every time we were around other morticians in the area, one of them would comment on Daddy's expertise. His ability with lips was unmatched by any mortician in the region, they said. He used the precise amount of wax needed to seal the mouth shut without making the face look like it was smiling at its viewers from the casket. Daddy understood the need to underplay the color of lip tint, especially on men. No family was traumatized by seeing its patriarch sporting women's lipstick to his own funeral, he bragged to us.

And now all that attention to detail is going to be spent on our playhouse. This thing is going to be the mansion of all playhouses.

Rosarita and I ran straight for the yard when we got home from school the next day. "Let's go see it," Rosarita yelled as she skipped out the back door.

"Go on out," Mother encouraged. "Daddy is just finishing it up. He made it for you girls himself."

We both came to a screeching halt when we saw the new playhouse. It was definitely not a miniature version of our house.

Where we expected to see little windows with curtains on them, we saw the crudely stenciled words "Fragile" and "This End Up" on unpainted plywood. Where we thought there would be a little front door on hinges inviting us in, there was a rectangle sawed into the plywood so roughly that it was fringed in giant splinters. When we wanted to bend down to avoid hitting our heads on the low ceiling of our new playhouse, we looked up more than six feet in the air before we caught sight of the ceiling, more plywood.

"Is this the playhouse?" Rosarita finally asked.

"Yes it is. And if you don't like, I'll tear the damned thing down," Daddy growled back. "You girls know I don't have time to be messing with this. I've got a funeral to run this afternoon, a visitation tonight, and two bodies waiting for makeup in the preparation room. I don't know why I wasted my time on this in the first place," he said, walking back to the mortuary before we could answer.

"He didn't get a playhouse at all. He just turned a casket shipping crate on end and sawed a hole in it for a door."

"Nobody has a playhouse that's only half as wide as it is tall. You'd have to be a skinny giant to be able to play in here," Rosarita observed.

We angled though the splintered doorway and stepped inside, standing nose-to-nose to fit, yet having more than a yard of space over our heads.

"I could have told you it would be this way," Mother gloated when we showed her the playhouse. "Your father doesn't care about anything but that mortuary. If you doubt me, just go take a look at our kitchen ceiling. You certainly don't see mashed potatoes all over the ceiling in the chapel, do you? That's because he gives a rip about the business. But our home, ohhhhh, nooooo," she dramatically drew out the last words.

I had to admit that the ceiling in our kitchen was unlike any I had ever seen. The manner in which it came to be so unusual was equally bizarre. Mother, in her haste to begrudgingly prepare dinner one evening, failed to completely seal the lid on the pressure cooker filled with potatoes.

Bam! Pow! Deafening explosion came from the range as the lid flew to the ceiling at warp speed, where it left a perfectly lid-shaped dent in the plaster, then blasted down to crash to the floor.

Mother assumed the position of hands protecting head, just like I learned at school during air raid drills, and ran headlong into the living room where Rosarita and I were watching television.

"What happened?" Rosarita shrieked.

Mashed potatoes covered the entire kitchen. They stuck to the curtains over the window and all over the refrigerator. Potato stalactites covered the ceiling surrounding the dented circle. Big, white, starchy blobs blotched the back of Mother's housedress, where they had landed in the midst of her escape.

Rosarita looked at me, knowing I would laugh, but we had to gauge Mother's reaction before we allowed ourselves to smile.

"Help me clean this up before your father gets home," Mother said from the safety of the living room. When the three of us dared enter the potato-blasted kitchen, even Mother had to laugh. Rosarita and I thought we'd avoided the dreaded emotional outburst from Mother.

We cleaned everything we could reach before Daddy got home.

"No potatoes?" Daddy asked as we passed the meat and vegetables.

Rosarita and I burst into laughter.

"What's so funny about that?" he challenged.

Rosarita pointed to the ceiling textured with potatoes.

"What the hell is that?" Daddy asked, then exploded into laughter along with us. Mother laughed too as she told Daddy how we couldn't reach the point of impact on the ceiling, but cleaned the rest of the damage before his arrival.

"I need you to scrape it off before it hardens. You may need to spackle that pot-sized ring while you're at it."

"All right, all right. I'll do it when this visitation is over. I need to get back to The Place now. Try not to have the rest of the house in smithereens before I get back," he laughed

Mother fell into a steely silence about the kitchen ceiling when it still had potato stalactites hanging from it months afterward.

"This is how much your father cares about our home," Mother pointed out. We weren't really sympathetic, though, because we could still remember how funny it was when the explosion happened.

We came to appreciate Mother's warnings, however, when Daddy finally decided it was time to repaint the whole house. He ignored the potato ceiling as he began rolling the smelly enamel onto the kitchen surfaces. He painted the entire kitchen sunshine yellow, including the dent and the remaining potatoes.

"Nobody else will even notice," he said when Mother saw the mess. "You wanted it painted, so now it's painted." That statement precluded all further discussion of the texture of the kitchen ceiling.

"We won't ask Daddy to improve it," Rosarita said when she saw Daddy's excuse for a playhouse. "I'll get one of Mother's old dresses and we'll drape it over the hole like a door," she said. "Then it will seem more like a real house."

"I'll get a rock from the alley and we can hold the dress

back with it when the door is supposed to be open," I piped up. I started to think we could make the casket crate feel like a playhouse after all. Each of us took off in a different direction to begin our fix-up work. By dinner time, we were feeling good about making the best of the casket crate.

"We put a door on the playhouse, Daddy," Rosarita announced as she passed a bowl of summer squash to him. "We put a rock on one of the boards that sticks out a little above the hole. It holds a dress up to cover the hole. If we want to leave the door open, we just tuck the dress up underneath the rock," Rosarita reported proudly.

"You're using rocks to hold a dress up? And just what is going to keep that rock from falling down on one of your heads and killing you?" Daddy asked.

"It's just a little rock, Daddy. We'll be careful with it, though," Rosarita threw in quickly.

"Jesus Christ, can't you leave anything alone? You wanted a playhouse, I gave you a playhouse. But, oh no, what I gave you is not good enough. You two have to drag in rocks that could kill somebody. I knew better than to waste time on this in the first place. Who do you think is taking care of The Place while I spend all day making toys in the yard for you?" he ranted.

Neither of us responded. Not even Mother dared comment further.

"What do you think is going to happen to the playhouse?" Rosarita whispered to me when we were in bed later that night.

"We shouldn't talk about it anymore. Daddy's right. What if he wasted too much time on it and now people are mad because their funerals weren't good?" I asked.

"You're no help. Just go to sleep. I'll take care of it myself," Rosarita snapped.

Again the following day, Rosarita and I ran home from school to see the playhouse. We stopped short when we reached the yard. All that remained of our playhouse was a square indentation in the grass where it had stood. The dress and the rock to hold it had vanished, too.

We turned around slowly and walked silently back into our home.

"It might have ruined somebody's funeral," I said.

Rosarita didn't answer me. No one ever mentioned the playhouse or its disappearance again. Just like the potato ceiling before it, we pretended the playhouse never existed.

While we were looking for rocks, though, I discovered something that interested me more than the playhouse anyway. At first, I thought it was just an old plank of weathered wood. When I came closer to it, I saw it was a ladder stretched out along the grass of the yard for such a long time that it had faded from a tan wood color to a soft shade of gray. Each rung was so worn that the edges were no longer sharp angles, but gentle curves. The ravages of the Arizona sun had furrowed deep grooves in its long sides.

I leaned down and ran my hand along one side of it. Unlike the splintery playhouse casket crate, the ladder looked smooth and comfortable, almost inviting. It was lying near the side of the house, so no one really knew it was there. The tall grass that escaped the mower grew up through the rungs to make an orderly pattern like a garden path. I found it irresistible.

I stepped from rung to rung for hours upon hours until the grass between them was flush with the ladder. The dark green of the blades still shimmered between the light gray steps to make a beautiful landscape that was just steps away from the harshness of the mortuary and my home. I invented a hopscotch game in which I not only stepped on top of the rungs, but also between them and into the grass. It wasn't long before I could jump over every rung on the whole ladder in one try. I became so good at it that I began counting the alternating rectangles of wood and grass as I hopped along. Between the exertion of jumping over the rungs and the mental distraction of counting them, I was happily exhausted by the end of each day. In fact, I found myself spending almost all my time playing on the ladder. I stopped begging Rosarita to play with me; the ladder and its number sequences were far more satisfying.

I often lost my balance and fell across the evenly spaced steps, which left me with bruises in perfect intervals from my ankles to my knees. I didn't mind falling or bruising my legs; it was such fun being in a private, pretty place that the discomfort didn't matter.

When I was counting the number of hops I could make, the tight feeling in my stomach was replaced with a sense of relaxation and pleasure. The constant counting also relieved me from the need to chew my fingernails so much. In fact, some of the fingers didn't even have little scabs on them anymore.

One, two, three. I missed. I'll start over. One, two, three, four. Start over. You missed one. One, two three, four, five.

Start over.

I developed patterns of jumps that I followed each time. Jumping eight consecutively without a miss, followed by six more were my special favorites.

Eight, six. Eight, six. Eight, six. Eight, six. You missed. Eight, six. Eight, six.

Soon, I was so proficient at eight and six that I added another set of six, and then five, to my pattern. It was even more challenging now, but I knew I could master it.

Eight, six, six, five. Eight, six, six, five. Eight, six, six, five.

The ladder and its numbers occupied my body and mind any time I could escape there. Even when I wasn't on the ladder, I could calm myself just by repeating the numbers in my head.

I was so accomplished as a ladder jumper and counter that now I added a third set of numbers to my routine. I jumped until I completed—without a fall—first eight, then six, then six more, then five, plus seven more, followed by three. I always began at the same end of the ladder, never taking the steps in reverse or beginning the series on a middle step. The series of jumps had to be executed and counted exactly the same way each time or they didn't count.

Jumping, counting, jumping, counting, jumping, counting.

I felt so much more relaxed after counting on the ladder that I began incorporating counting into almost every task I tackled. I wasn't anxious because I wasn't deciding anything; the numbers determined my every movement and thought.

"Hurry up and get dressed. We're going to be late for school," Rosarita ordered on most school day mornings.

I looked into the drawer filled with different-colored socks and silently started counting them again. My sequence ended on a pair of red socks. I would have to sneak past Mother to make it out of the house in them. Mother had chosen a pink dress for me to wear; she would never allow red socks with a pink dress. I grabbed the red socks, put them on and dashed past Mother before she could inspect my outfit. Numbers were so much more important than colors that I didn't care how much my dress clashed with my socks.

On the sidewalk leading into school, I began to see a pattern similar to the one made by the grass and the ladder rungs. I knew immediately that I had to use the number sequence or I couldn't get into the school. I took eight steps in one square of cement, then six in the next, six again on the following one, until I completed the whole sequence I used on the ladder. I had to take eight tiny steps on one square, lengthen my stride to only six for the next one. The most difficult one came at the end when I took seven steps on the next-to-last square, but only three on the last one. If I lost my balance and took the wrong number of steps on each square, I had to go back to the beginning of the sidewalk and start all over again. The rules for the sidewalk were the same as those for the ladder.

"You look like an idiot. Walk like everybody else," Rosarita scolded as I hobbled and stretched to maintain the sequence. "Why are you going back where we just came from?" she complained.

I couldn't answer her. She interrupted the numbers.

Eight, six, six, five, seven, three. Eight, six, six, five, seven, three.

I set increasingly more difficult challenges for myself as I continued the ladder game.

I could read a whole book now while only allowing myself to inhale after I read the number of words in the sequence. With all the reading and counting and breathing, my mind was so full that my thoughts never drifted to things that made me bite my nails or get the tight stomach feeling anymore.

"Oh my God, what happened to your legs?" Mother shrieked one day when she finally noticed the evenly spaced bruises.

"Nothing, Mother," I answered. The tight feeling was in my stomach again.

"Your legs are all bruised. Did you fall down?"

"No, I don't know how those got there. I didn't even know they were there."

"You don't know how you got all those bruises? Don't they hurt?"

"No, they don't hurt. I don't know how they got there."

"I knew it. It was only a matter of time. It's in the blood. How much more of this can I be asked to endure?" Mother asked, with her eyes watery and her lower lip beginning to quiver.

"Mother, don't be upset. I didn't bleed. I don't know what you're talking about," I pleaded.

Mother was on her way to the bedroom. In a second, she slammed the door shut and began wailing loud enough that everyone could hear it.

"Now what did you do?" Rosarita accused as she opened

our bedroom door. "When Mother goes in her room like that, the crying can go on for days. Daddy's going to be mad that you made her do that again. This is going to be just like when Carol said she was getting married. Do you want her locked up in there like that again?"

"I didn't do anything. She saw bruises on my legs and ran into her room. She said it was something about blood."

"We have to call Carol to come over here and get her to come out before Daddy finds out. Go beg her to come out and stop crying."

Outside the door, I called, "Mother, I didn't mean to upset you. Please come out."

"Mother, will you come out for me? I know you're mad at Jamie, so just come out for me," Rosarita begged.

"I don't want to talk to anyone. Just leave me alone," Mother whimpered back.

"Can we call Carol, Mother? I bet she can make you feel better," Rosarita offered.

"I said to leave me alone," she screamed.

"I'll come over," Carol said when we called. "Maybe I can get her to open the door before Daddy finds out."

"She's dying! She's dying!" Rosarita and I eavesdropped through the door once Carol had gained entry into Mother's room.

In a few minutes, Carol and Mother emerged from the room, Mother still sniffling.

"Don't tell Daddy or we'll all be in trouble," Carol warned us. "Mother thinks Jamie has leukemia because her legs are so bruised. She says her sister who died from it bruised very easily, so Mother thinks Jamie inherited leukemia and her leg bruises prove it."

"I just don't know how much more I can take. I lost my sister; now I'm going to lose my child. What have I ever done to deserve this?" she whimpered to Daddy when he came home for dinner.

"Maybe the bruises aren't as bad as you think, Mother," Daddy tried. "Let me have a look at them. You know we studied a lot about disease when I was in embalming college. I'll be able to tell if something is wrong. Come here, Jamie, let's see what has your mother so worried."

I walked silently toward my father. As I lifted my skirt to reveal the full extent of the evenly spaced bruises, Daddy yelled, "Jesus Christ! What the hell have you been doing?" Then, to Mother, he ordered, "Call Feldstein tomorrow morning to get an appointment. We're going to need him to treat this one. Jews are the only docs smart enough to handle these serious situations. This kid is all bruised up. Something is really wrong with her."

Mother told anyone who would listen about her dying child in the week it took to get an appointment with Dr. Feldstein. She told her story in the hushed tones that made people hang on her every word. I watched in horror as my mother systematically became the object of pity everywhere she went.

Just as I feared, Feldstein really was as smart as Daddy said he was. He took one look at my legs and said, "What did you fall on?"

"I've been playing on an old ladder. Sometimes I fall,"

was all I uttered.

"She's fine," Dr. Feldstein said as he turned and left the examining room.

Several weeks passed before anyone dared mention Dr. Feldstein again. Nobody stopped us in the grocery store anymore to put their arm around Mother. Phone calls to inquire if Mother was able to come out of her bedroom today stopped. Carol didn't come over any more to coax our mother into normal functioning. After a while, Mother put away the photos of her dead sister that had appeared around the house during the wait to see Feldstein.

Just like the playhouse before it, the ladder in the yard disappeared after my confession about playing on it.

When I took my bath that night, I felt a stinging sensation on the tips of my fingers. As I lifted them above the soapy water, I saw the little scabs were back where I had chewed my nails past the quick.

Chapter Six

Happy Holidays

"I love holidays," Rosarita said, as we made plans for the Fourth of July. "We can go shopping at night when they have Midnight Madness. With the stores open past seven, you don't have to get all sweaty while you're shopping. And after it turns dark, the fireworks show caps off the whole day."

"If you like it so much, why are you always complaining when we have to stand in the heat to watch the parade?" I asked.

"That's the worst part. Once all those boring guys march past in their uniforms, we can start the fun," she replied.

"It is neat to see all the shops open at night, but I like celebrations better when they don't include those long speeches in front of city hall. The only time those are interesting at all is when somebody passes out from the heat."

"I thought I was going to die laughing when that kid in the high school band keeled over," Rosarita laughed. "He squished his trombone so bad when he landed that the whole instrument was as flat as a pancake. He looked like a total jerk, all sprawled out on the cement with his mangled instrument underneath him."

"That didn't turn out to be so funny, Rosarita. Daddy had to take that kid to the hospital. When he came to, he threw up all over the back of the ambulance," I reminded her.

"Yuck, I'm glad we didn't have to see that part. But the smashed horn was hilarious. How do you always know about the sickening stuff? I just enjoy the comical parts when people are acting dumb."

"He wasn't dumb. He was sick. Can you imagine how hot it is to wear one of those band uniforms in July?"

"That's what you get for doing stupid stuff. If he didn't play in that goofy band, he could have been wearing shorts like the rest of us and been just fine."

"You're not very nice to people when they're sick, Rosarita. I couldn't believe you laughed at that girl who passed out in church during Easter Mass, either."

"Oh, that was hysterical. I knew she was going to crash when she started weaving back and forth while she was kneeling."

"She was white as a sheet when she finally tried to get out of there."

"That was the best part. She was so dizzy, she was staggering down the aisle like she was drunk. She'd hit the pews on one side and then wander back over to crash into the pews on the opposite side. "

"She could have been hurt when she tried to make it down those steep stairs outside."

"Well, she wasn't. She made a good show out of the most boring part of the day. Then we got to come home and eat the candy in our Easter baskets. Last Easter, though, was the best of them all," Rosarita started.

Mother insisted upon making each of us a dress every

Easter. She said the dresses in stores were too expensive.

"Why don't you just buy them dresses?" Daddy asked. "It isn't worth it to have you all nervous and upset every year. We can afford it."

"Well, it's not just the money. Those store dresses are constructed so shabbily, they fall apart after one washing. Do you want your kids going to Easter services in clothes that are falling apart?"

"Not all of them can be made poorly. Maybe you need to shop in Phoenix, where they have nicer merchandise. I'll give you the money right now."

"Oh, so you're ashamed to have your kids wear homemade clothes? You don't think I'm a good enough seamstress to make them look nice?"

On and on the argument raged, year after year, until Mother eventually finished the dresses and everyone commented on how beautiful and well-made they were. She waited until no more than a week before Easter before she began sewing. Last year, she chose a pattern of rows upon rows of ruffles that covered the gathered skirts. Making the ruffles took days, and affixing them to the skirts required even more time. Mother stayed up after everyone else was in bed, her portable sewing machine humming into the night. By morning, she was so exhausted that she could explode at the slightest irritation.

Everyone in the household was on pins and needles as Easter approached and the dresses were still not complete. When, at last, Easter morning arrived and we appeared in our pink gingham ruffled finery fresh from Mother's needle, everyone heaved a collective sigh of relief.

"Everyone looks real pretty, Mother," Daddy began.

"Do you think they look all right? I only finished them early this morning," Mother simpered.

"They'll be the prettiest girls in church, Mother. You wait and see," Daddy cajoled as he donned the suit coat that would be soaked in sweat not five minutes into the service.

"Everybody looks so nice. I stand out like a sore thumb. I don't think I'm going to church, Daddy. You take the girls. I don't have anything new to wear and my old dresses are worn out," Mother said. "You can go without me this year."

"No, no, no," Daddy consoled, putting his arm around Mother. "You look just fine. Why didn't you buy yourself something new?"

"We can't afford it. I want the girls to look nice, so I make theirs first. There's not enough money for me to get anything for myself by then," she continued, tears streaking her makeup. "You go on now. I'll just wait here at home and make the ham for dinner," she pushed.

"You're just as pretty as a picture, no matter what you're wearing," Daddy groveled. "Come on and go to church with us. You want to take credit for making those beautiful things for the girls, don't you?"

"We want you to go, too, Mother," Rosarita chimed in. "Everybody will want to know how you made these dresses. You'll need to be there so you can show them you did it yourself."

"Oh, all right," Mother said, wiping the back of her hand across her wet cheek.

Shortly, our family, dressed in our Easter finest, began the short walk to the church. We travelled down College Avenue, Rosarita and I covered in ruffles from head to toe, on the side where the most passers-by could admire our dresses.

"It's getting hot," Rosarita said. "I hope I don't make a sweat mark on my new dress."

"Let's speed up a little," I offered. "We're almost to that orchid tree that makes so much shade. It'll be cooler there."

Rosarita and I rushed ahead of our parents and walked hurriedly to the shady part of the sidewalk ahead.

"Those dresses look mighty good from the rear, too," Daddy called after us, still trying to calm Mother.

"Yuck," I screeched. The tree that provided the cool place for us to walk also provided a cool place for pigeons to perch. Rosarita turned at my exclamation to see a streak of bird droppings splashed down the front of the dress Mother had just finished sewing.

"You're looking real good now, Jamie. Your dress has more decoration on it than anyone else's in the whole church, I'm sure," Rosarita scoffed.

"Look at Jamie's dress," she shouted back to our parents, laughing. "The birds like it, too," she said between gasps.

Daddy took a step back from Mother and began shaking his head no at Rosarita to get her to stop laughing. She sobered up instantly, but it was already too late.

"Oh my God," Mother yelled when I turned toward her. "How did you manage that, Jamie? Everybody in church walks under this tree and you don't see them covered in bird poop."

Daddy smirked as he tried to control his own laughter.

"Nobody's going to notice," he began.

"Not notice? Are you blind? It's down the whole front of the skirt. Every ruffle is covered in it," Mother wailed. "We're going home," she continued, grabbing my arm and beginning to walk toward home.

"We don't have to go home, Mother," Daddy pleaded. "Don't you have a Kleenex? We can just wipe it off and go on."

"Oh, so now I'm not only the family seamstress, but the public laundress, too? You want me to stand out here in front of all these people and wipe bird poop off my own kid?"

Daddy stopped smiling. "Here," he said sourly, "I'll do it myself with my bare hand."

"Now you're going to be the big hero. You haven't been up until all hours sewing these dresses. I have. Now you come to the rescue at the last minute and take credit for saving the day." Her voice quaked in the way I knew was the omen of open sobbing.

"Oh, Christ, are we really going to do this now?" Daddy snapped.

"We're going home," Mother sobbed. "Rosarita, if you want to go on to church, go ahead. You're the only one who looks decent now. You can tell them that your little sister couldn't manage to stay clean for even a few minutes."

"I'm sorry, Mother," I said. I wanted to cry, too, but I knew Daddy would be even angrier if I did.

"That's okay, Mother," Rosarita said. "If everyone else has to go home because of Jamie, I'll come with you, too. It's not fair that I'm the only one who gets to go."

All of us walked home in silence, with me holding my ruffled skirt away from my body so the bird droppings didn't soak through to my legs.

"Good job," Rosarita laughed when we were in our bedroom alone. "You and your bird poop dress got us out of a boring church service. Let's go hide Easter eggs," she said as she headed out the door.

* * *

Unlike Easter, when I fended for myself, Max and Grace eased the tension of the Christmas holidays. They insisted that we call them as soon as we got out of bed every Christmas morning. With flashlight in hand, Max led the way across the backyard. He held Grace by the hand as the two of them stumbled through the pre-dawn darkness until they reached our house. The lights of our home, as well as those on the Christmas tree, were blazing by the time they reached their destination. Without knocking, they threw open the back door and Max yelled, "Merry Christmas!" That was the signal that the annual fun could begin.

Daddy typically looked exhausted before the festivities even began. His reluctance to begin the day was a stark contrast to Max's eagerness.

"Oh, Christ, are you girls up already?" Daddy griped when we woke him around 5:30 a.m.

"Come on, Daddy. Santa came. We want to open our presents," Rosarita begged.

As he laboriously rolled out of bed and reached for his pack of Camels on the bedside table, he grumbled, "Does anybody care that I've been up all night embalming bodies?"

No one listened to his complaints as we raced for the tree. I knew about the Christmas "rush" at The Place. Drunk drivers and old people waiting to see one last Christmas meant that Daddy and Max worked extra long hours every December and January. But I didn't let the many deaths interfere with my anticipation of Santa. As soon as Max and Grace arrived from next door, everyone pulled up a chair around the tree to get as close to the action as possible.

Mother decorated it with exacting symmetry. Every ornament on one side of the tree mirrored another one of the exact size, shape, and color on the opposite side. They were also arranged in descending order of size. The largest were on the bottom branches; the rest gradually decreased in size until the uppermost branches were adorned with glass balls so small we could barely see them.

By Christmas morning, the Scotch pine had been standing in its little bucket of water for almost two weeks. The dry desert air reduced it to something that looked more like a tumbleweed blowing down the street than to the fresh conifer dragged down from the mountains weeks before. Brown needles formed a perfect circle on the carpet around its base. Every time someone opened a door, they scattered through the whole house.

"Ow," I cried out when one of the sharp tips of the dead needles pierced my bare foot.

"Shut up," Rosarita warned me. "Mother is already saying the tree is a fire hazard. If you keep screeching every time your foot gets stuck, she'll take it down early."

"Sorry, I forgot," I apologized.

"Do you want to get her started on how stab wounds look after people are dead? Remember how she told us the skin on burn victims looks exactly like the skin on barbecued chicken? She ruined everyone's appetite with that story at Carol's cookout last summer. I couldn't touch my drumstick after she talked about the black crispy parts curled up around the edges and the blisters where the heat hadn't been as intense."

"You're right," I admitted. "No one ate a bite of chicken and Carol worked hard to make a nice dinner for us. I felt really bad for her."

"I felt really bad for me. I was hungry," Rosarita retorted. "Just keep quiet if you step on those needles, or we'll lose the Christmas tree just like we lost that good dinner."

"The tree looks beautiful, Gertrude," Grace said every year, ignoring its obvious state of decay.

"Thank you. I hate decorating it myself, but no one else takes the time to do it right. I can't stand to have some out-of-balance tree in my living room for two weeks," she answered.

"Oh, we couldn't have that," Max laughed, and everyone joined in.

"Gertrude, hurry up with that coffee, will you?" Max called out to the kitchen. "Francis and I are fading fast."

Grace sat quietly, smoking a cigarette she drew from a heavily bejeweled case. She was well groomed and pleasant. Mother, on the other hand, was disheveled in both appearance and mood every holiday I remember.

Once Max had a mug of coffee in his hand, and Grace a lighted cigarette in hers, Rosarita and I attacked the tree.

"Dig in," Max shouted with a laugh.

We grabbed packages and ripped the paper from them as quickly as we could.

"This is just what I wanted," Rosarita screamed over her new doll dress. "I bet you got one just like it. Jamie, hurry up and open your presents. You're getting behind," Rosarita urged.

"It's a Madame Alexander!" I cried out as a piece of red paper gave way to reveal the signature blue floral box of my favorite brand of doll.

Everyone in the room smiled, child and adult alike.

Brrringggg! Brrrringgg! Brrringgg!

At the sound of the third consecutive ring of The Big Phone in the hall, our joyous group fell instantly silent.

"Everyone be quiet," warned Daddy, even though all noise had ceased before he opened his mouth. He plodded through the crumpled wrapping paper covering the floor and reached the phone before it began another set of rings.

"Maguire's," he answered in his low, professional voice.

"We're so sorry for your loss," he said into the receiver after a pause.

Mother threw a wad of wrapping paper to the floor as hard as she could. She looked at Grace and both of them began shaking their heads in disgust.

"Every year," Mother whispered to Grace.

Rosarita and I exchanged a look of disappointment, but

neither of us made a sound.

Max was on his feet, heading for the back door that led to the garage where the hearses were stored.

"Old Man Fernwood didn't make it," Daddy said as he hung up the receiver. "I knew he'd be one to hold out until Christmas."

"So you're going to get him?" Mother asked sullenly.

"It's the Christmas rush, Mother. What do you expect me to do? Leave him at home until it's convenient?"

"We have to go," Max said, interrupting the exchange I knew would result in the same argument we listened to every year.

Grace, Mother, Rosarita, and I sat silently in front of the tree with only half the presents unwrapped. As we heard Max start the engine of The Call Car, we remained motionless. No one spoke until the hum of the engine faded completely as the men drove away.

"This is why I hate this business," Mother said to Grace.

"At least you girls got some things opened this year. Let's play with what you already have," Grace suggested. She lowered herself and her cigarette from the chair to the floor where we sat among our newest toys and the torn wrapping paper.

"Do you know anyone else that doesn't even have Christmas Day to spend with their families?" Mother asked.

"I do get tired of it," Grace conceded. "But Max always says I should be glad to give up a little time with him so we can have the money to enjoy life."

"Yeah, this is real enjoyable. Sitting here alone on

Christmas morning while our husbands are out collecting dead people," Mother grumbled.

"You're not alone, Mother. We're here with you. Right, Grace?" I tried.

"I know that," Mother whimpered. "I just work so hard to make everything perfect for Christmas, and something ruins it every year."

"We did better with the icicles this year, Mother," Rosarita consoled. "We put them on one by one, just like you said. I think it's a lot easier to just throw a whole bunch of them at one time. You get through a lot faster."

"Your mother always has a perfectly decorated tree," Grace said. "It's a shame we don't get to enjoy it with everyone, but those two will be back soon and we can finish opening presents. Nothing's ruined; it's just postponed."

"Where did you pick up that phrase? From my wedding day?" Mother snarled.

Grace pretended she didn't hear, and began talking and playing with us and our toys. Mother proceeded on with the story anyway.

"Here we are," she began. "We're all at the church, ready to begin the ceremony, and the fire alarm starts up. I could understand the volunteer firemen dropping everything to go get the fire trucks, but when your father left me to make that ambulance call, I was mortified," she reported. "You remember that, Grace, don't you?" she pressed. "Here's Francis, the groom, running for the ambulance with Max, the best man, right behind him."

Grace nodded that she remembered and continued to play with us.

"Then your father, girls, had the unmitigated gall to tell me how funny it was to see my wedding ring stuck onto Max's little finger while they lifted a body into the back of the ambulance."

This time, it was Rosarita and I who pretended we didn't hear. We kept on playing with Grace.

"I should have known right then and there what I was getting into. Even though I'm married, I basically live alone. Any time I need anything, there's always somebody else who's hurt or sick or dead who needs my husband more. I'm tired of it. This business is ruining our lives."

"Do you think that little package has a doll dress in it since Santa brought dolls in the presents we already opened?" Rosarita dared.

"Don't start that, Rosarita. You know that we wait until everyone can be around the tree before we open presents. You girls will just have to wait until Daddy and Max get back before you open anything else."

"I bet they wouldn't even notice that we opened just one more without them," Rosarita wagered.

"I'm sure it'll be just a short time before everyone can be here. Mr. Fernwood should be pretty easy to embalm. They won't be gone for more than a couple of hours," Grace tried.

"Thank God it was him and not some accident victim all smashed to hell. They take forever to embalm," Mother retaliated.

Grace showed us how to make our new dolls sit down and

even walk a few steps.

When an hour passed and Daddy and Max had still not returned, Mother said, "I guess I better start roasting the turkey."

"Let's wait until the men get back, Gertrude. You don't want to have a meal ready with no one to eat it," Grace offered.

"When you have children, Grace, you have to keep to a schedule," Mother said condescendingly. "I'm sure you and Max are totally spontaneous in your planning, but I have two little girls over here who need to eat on time."

Grace quietly said "Merry Christmas" to each of us and hoisted herself up from the floor. "Thanks for letting us be here," she told Mother. The sun had risen by now, so she didn't need the assistance of Max or his flashlight to make her way back to her own house alone.

Mother headed for the kitchen.

"Start cleaning up that mess you made with the wrapping paper, girls," she ordered. "I don't want the place looking like a cyclone hit it when your father finally gets back."

"Come on, Jamie," Rosarita whispered. "We can pretend like we're picking up paper, but we can rattle some of these unopened presents to see if we can tell what else Santa brought us."

"You better not, Rosarita," I warned. "Mother could peek her head around the corner from the kitchen and see us doing it. We might never get anything for Christmas again."

"You're such a chicken," Rosarita baited.

"At least I'm not a barbecued chicken," I answered. Both of us laughed loudly.

"Cleaning up shouldn't be enough fun to make you girls laugh," Mother called to us from the kitchen. "I'd better not find paper on the floor when you two are having such a good time."

"We're cleaning, Mother," Rosarita answered. "We're not having a good time at all."

Just then, we heard Mother groan loudly. Next, we heard a metallic thud.

"Mother, what's wrong? Are you all right?" we called as we ran to the kitchen. Mother was slamming the oven door closed on the turkey-filled roaster she just dropped onto the rack within.

"No, no, there's nothing wrong. It's just business as usual around here. I have to put this great big turkey in the oven. Do I have a man here to help me with something so heavy? Hell, no. But then, what should I expect? It's only Christmas morning. Isn't everybody's husband at work today?"

Rosarita and I exchanged a glance. I recognized that Rosarita felt the same dread I did. Mother was escalating into a full-blown tantrum. Carol was at her own home making Christmas dinner for her family and couldn't help us. Daddy was embalming a body, so he couldn't be disturbed. Grace had already escaped back to her own home and certainly wouldn't return under these conditions. My sister and I were left alone in what would soon be the eye of the storm.

"We'll help you, Mother. What do you want us to do?" Rosarita began.

"A lot of help you two are. You'll just make a bigger mess for me to deal with all alone. Don't even try. It's not worth it,"

Mother said. Her voice had taken on that shaky quality again.

I decided to try another tactic.

"I'm sorry you're not having fun, Mother. You should come play with our new toys. Christmas should be fun for everybody, right, Rosarita?" I asked.

"Yeah, Mother, come in here and see our new dolls," Rosarita chimed in.

"You're right, girls," Mother began, as tears began to spill down her cheeks. "It's fun for everyone except me. I don't know what I did in this life to deserve to be treated this way. I work my fingers to the bone. I take care of you kids. I fix the women's hair at the mortuary. And what thanks do I get for it? I'm left high and dry on Christmas and every other day," she moaned.

She threw herself across the scratchy wool sofa in the living room, as far away from the tree as she could get in the small room, and stared straight ahead while we tried to interest her in our new toys. From time to time, she emitted a long, mournful sigh. She rose several times to check the progress of the turkey in the oven. When the phone rang, she ran to answer it.

"You've got to be kidding me," she spat into the receiver after listening for a few seconds.

"It must be Daddy," Rosarita whispered to me.

"We've been waiting here all this time, and now you're still not coming home," she said.

"The Fernwoods want to come right now to make arrangements. They're all upset. I can't tell them to wait until my kids have opened their Christmas presents. Imagine how they feel. You know how hard it is on families who lose someone on Christmas Day," Daddy cajoled.

"I know how hard it is on the families of the morticians who take care of them," Mother began tearfully. "Your little girls have waited patiently the entire afternoon for you to finish your embalming or whatever you're doing at that mortuary. Now their hearts are going to be broken all over again when you still refuse to come home."

"We're okay, Mother," I interrupted. "Don't be upset because of us. We can open the rest of our presents later."

"The turkey is going to be ready in an hour. If you want anything decent to eat, you'd better be home by then, no matter whose funeral is being planned," Mother said.

Rosarita and I watched nervously as the minutes ticked past on the clock atop Daddy's desk. They seemed to race by as the back door remained closed and our father remained at work.

"This is how it always is," Mother started in again. "The meal is going to be ruined because of your father."

Even though Daddy was not home yet, Mother took the turkey from the oven, removed the stuffing and put all the side dishes into serving pieces on the table.

"He's going to be here any minute," I reassured her.

Mother didn't answer, but dramatically wiped away a tear as she put the finishing touches on the Christmas feast.

"I guess I'll carve the turkey myself, too," Mother whined. "I have to do everything else a man should be doing in this house."

Just as she began slicing into the breast of the huge bird,

the back door squeaked open.

"It's Daddy," Rosarita squealed with relief.

"Dinner's ready, Daddy. Come sit down quick," I urged.

"I thought you girls were so anxious to open the rest of your presents that you were heartbroken," Daddy remarked sarcastically.

"No, we can wait for that," I said.

"I'm sorry, Mother," Daddy said after Mother sniffled loud enough for him to notice that she was still crying. "Let's eat now, if that's what you want to do."

"I haven't put the rolls in the oven to warm," Mother protested, still pouting. "Do you think you can wait that long, or will you have to go back to the mortuary before they're done?"

"I'm home for the night. I promise," Daddy said.

"Yeah, until the phone rings again," Mother retorted.

She took the dinner rolls from their cardboard box, placed them on a cookie sheet, and popped them in the oven.

"Jamie, pour the milk," she ordered. "Rosarita, put a paper napkin next to everyone's plate. I forgot to do that—I was so upset."

Before long, everyone was busy with their assigned duties to get dinner on the table, and Mother was placated.

"This is delicious, Mother," I said as soon as one forkful hit my mouth.

"Yes, Mother. This is really good," Rosarita agreed.

Neither of us mentioned the presents that beckoned to us from the living room beyond.

"See, we're having a real nice Christmas after all,"

Daddy asserted.

Mother cracked a half-smile and began to eat her dinner.

"Oh my God," she suddenly shrieked. Everyone at the table jumped in surprise. Then we saw what was wrong. Black smoke was puffing out the oven door. When Mother removed the rolls, I saw they looked like charcoal briquettes. The one closest to the back of the oven had burst into flame.

"This is why I hate Christmas," Mother shouted. She picked up a serving spoon she'd used to take the stuffing out of the turkey and hurled it across the kitchen. It crashed it to the floor in a hail of bread crumbs, onions and celery.

"Now, Mother," Daddy began as he cautiously approached her. There was no telling what would be thrown next.

"Don't try to make me feel better," she asserted. "The whole dinner is ruined because I forgot about the rolls. If we could have eaten on time, I wouldn't have been so frazzled that I couldn't remember anything."

"I don't think things are as bad as all that," Daddy replied.

Mother whirled in a half-circle and, with the back of her hand, swept every dish on the drainboard onto the kitchen floor. Glass and china fragments flew everywhere. Rosarita began picking them up immediately. I stared at my parents in fright. The tight feeling in my stomach was unbearable. I started biting my fingernails furiously. Mother, bawling loudly, was heading for her bedroom, where she would lock herself in.

"Well, will you look at this?" Daddy marveled, as though he'd made a great discovery. "The rolls weren't ruined after all. This one is really good," he said as he chomped into a piece of charcoal in the shape of a dinner roll. "Try one, girls. They're really good," he encouraged.

Taking his cue, I reached for one that was still on fire and hastily blew out the flame. "You're right, Daddy. I don't like it when the rolls are all mushy. These are nice and crispy on the outside," I lied.

"Do you want me to fix one for you, Mother?" Rosarita asked as she piled a small pyramid of butter onto the blackened bread she held in her hand.

"Are they really okay?" Mother whimpered.

"Yes, Mother, they taste fine," Daddy said, and continued, "Now, let's eat this good dinner your Mother made for us." He stepped over the shards of glass and fragments of dishes and food on the floor to get back to the dinner table.

At last, we ate Christmas dinner. By the time we washed the dishes and the floor, it was time for Rosarita and me to go to bed.

"Can we stay up late to open the rest of our presents?" Rosarita asked.

"I'm exhausted," Mother answered. "I'm going to bed."

"So we have to wait until tomorrow?" Rosarita pressed.

I dragged her toward our bedroom.

"You girls go get your pajamas on," Daddy ordered.

Once he had Mother settled in bed, he crept quietly across the hall to our room.

"Open them real quietly. Your mother is in bed," he said, pointing toward the living room.

"It's really nice of Daddy to let us open our presents,"

Rosarita whispered as we sat in the dark, carefully unfolding the wrapping paper from our gifts.

"I don't think he was being nice," I whispered back. "I think that was his way of saying 'Thank you for eating charcoal and saying it tastes good.'"

We put our hands over our mouths to contain our laughter, then tiptoed back to our room so we didn't wake our mother.

"You're not going to have much use for your present from Grace," Rosarita laughed. My eyes shifted from my new pink manicure set to my hands. All I had left were nails bitten below the quick, and scabs where the cuticle should be.

"I guess not," I said as I climbed into bed. "But it was nice of Grace to get it for me, anyway."

Chapter Seven

Desk Blotter

"Everybody up," Mother yelled, walking through the house. "The desk is going to be here any time now. I don't want a brand new desk coming into a dirty house."

"Can't we sleep just a little longer? It's Saturday," Rosarita begged.

"I don't care what day it is; you have to help me clean. The floors have to be mopped and waxed. It will take all three of us to drag the shag rug out to the clothesline. You girls can beat it with the broom to get the dust out of it. You always enjoy doing that," Mother said.

"I love beating rugs at the crack of dawn," Rosarita mumbled just loud enough for me to hear.

She threw back her chenille bedspread and shuffled to the bathroom. I kicked the blanket back from my cozy cocoon and stumbled to the closet in search of my bathrobe. We staggered to the breakfast table to begin the day's activities while still half asleep. No one spoke as we ate eggs and bacon.

"The American Legion is giving the desk to your father for being a war hero and the commander of the local post. He's volunteered hours and hours to help veterans. Everyone in Tempe is very proud to have a Purple Heart recipient as the head of their American Legion. Not many other towns can claim that around here." Mother recounted Daddy's merit for the Legion's gift.

"I didn't know about all that boring stuff. I thought they were giving it to him because he sold the most poppies on Veteran's Day," Rosarita said grumpily.

"Those poppies are sold by the Ladies' Auxiliary, not the Legionnaires," Mother said. "To be elected commander of the legion post is a big deal. You girls should be proud."

"Does this mean we have to stand for those speeches and hear the old men talk about wars and stuff again?" Rosarita asked.

"No, there aren't speeches this time. That's only on holidays."

"That's some holiday—watching a bunch of old guys march down the street. Then we get to stand for hours on end at the cemetery while they prance around the graves shooting off rifles. They don't even have a target. They just shoot those guns off into thin air. Seems like a waste of bullets to me," she went on.

"This has nothing to do with that. The Legion is giving your father a new desk to thank him for being such a good commander."

"What do you have to do to be a commander?" Rosarita pressed. "You don't need a desk to march around or make speeches. They don't even let him shoot the rifles into the air at the cemetery." Rosarita looked at me gleefully, and I giggled silently.

"We need to clean thoroughly and then move the record

player into the hall to make room for the desk," Mother said, ignoring us.

"That's going to put the record player right next to The Big Phone. If somebody calls when we're listening to music, they're going to hear it on the other end of the line," I ventured.

"I hope we aren't playing an Elvis song when somebody across town dies," Rosarita laughed.

"That isn't funny, girls," Mother said sternly. "When The Big Phone rings, you girls know you are to be quiet. Now you need to turn the record player off, too. We can't have people thinking we're over here having a good time when they're mourning their loved ones."

"Why don't we put the desk in the hall and leave the record player where it is?" Rosarita suggested. "A desk isn't going to make any noise. We can keep it as close to the phone as we want and nobody will ever know the difference."

"We want everyone who comes here to see the new desk. The Legion paid a lot of money for it, and they won't want it hidden in the hallway by the phone."

"How will they know? They don't live here or answer the phone, do they?" Rosarita persisted.

"I should think you girls would be thankful to have a father who carries out his civic duty so unselfishly. All you have to do is make room for his desk," Mother scolded.

When the red cement floors had been waxed to a glistening shine, the shag rug had been dragged to the clothesline, beaten unmercifully, and dragged back in, and all six of the ashtrays had been emptied and cleaned, Mother announced that the room was properly prepared for the delivery of the Legionnaire's desk.

She put on a clean housedress and adjusted the two bobby pins on the side of her head to keep her hair out of her eyes. She dabbed the tube of bright red lipstick on her lips just before the doorbell rang.

"Oh, hello, please come right in," she greeted the deliverymen.

Two burly Mexican men maneuvered the huge, blonde desk through the front door and into the tiny living room.

"Where do you want us to put it?" one of them asked.

"Right here," Mother pointed to the empty spot. "We want everyone to be able to see it as soon as they come in," she said.

The deliverymen didn't respond, but put the desk up against the wall as she directed.

"You know, this desk is a gift to my husband from the American Legion."

The deliverymen remained silent as they pushed the furniture into place.

"He's the commander of the legion post, you know."

"Do you want us to move a chair up to it for you?" one of them asked.

Mother looked flustered. "We don't have a chair for it. They didn't send one with you?" she inquired.

"The desk is all we have on the truck," one answered.

"Well, that's all right," she said, despite the fact that her face was turning red.

When the men left, we stood looking at the desk that occupied most of the square footage of our living room.

"We could pull up a chair from the kitchen table," I suggested. I hurried into the kitchen and returned with a yellow vinyl chair which had chrome legs bent into an *S* shape.

"That's going to be stupid," Rosarita warned. "If he leans too far forward, the whole chair will slip out from under him, just like it does at the table."

"It'll serve him right for taking up all the space in the living room," she mumbled under her breath. Mother sat down in the hazardous chair to see if it would be suitable for the prestigious desk. The seat of the chair was so low that her chin nearly rested on the writing surface.

"That'll be real good, Mother," Rosarita laughed.

"This isn't going to work," Mother declared, ignoring her. "Let's just put the chair back at the table and we'll figure out something else."

"The desk isn't going to be of much use if you can't sit down at it, though," I observed.

"He doesn't even use a desk at home. His desk is at The Place," Rosarita said. "Let's tell those guys to take it over to the mortuary, and we can have our record player back where we want it."

"There will be no more of that kind of talk," Mother chided. "We just won't have a chair at this desk."

"Maybe he can just do this," Rosarita laughed as she bent her knees and balanced herself on an imaginary chair beneath her.

I giggled quietly, but my stomach was really hurting now. Rosarita jumped up and became instantly straight-faced as

Daddy and Max walked in to admire the new arrival.

"That's one hell of a desk, Francis," Max told his brother as he slapped him proudly on the back. "Those Legion boys really know how to take care of their own."

Daddy stood looking at the giant desk, beaming.

"For all your years of hard work," Mother chimed in.

Again, Daddy didn't answer, but gazed lovingly at the new furniture monopolizing our living room.

"It's ... incomplete, don't you think?" Max asked. "You need one of those fancy blotters and a fountain pen with your initials on it for a desk like that. Gertrude, what's the matter with you? I thought you would have been to the stationery store and had that all set up by now," Max kidded.

"Who do you think got this house tidied up to receive this beautiful desk?" Mother joked back. "I was a little busy."

Just then, The Big Phone rang. Everyone in the room became silent as Daddy squeezed past the record player in its new home in the hallway and picked up the receiver. "Maguires," he said soberly into the black phone as Max tiptoed out the door to get back to business. Rosarita retreated to our bedroom, leaving Mother and me alone.

Mother lingered in the living room long after the delivery man left. She stared at the desk for a long time before she reached out and rubbed her hand along the shiny finish.

"Isn't this beautiful?" she asked. "It's such an honor to have it in our house."

"It's real pretty, Mother," I answered.

"I know you girls are a little disappointed about moving

the record player out of here," she said. "I'll make it up to you by taking you with me on a special trip tomorrow, okay?"

"Where are we going?" I asked.

"You'll see. It'll just be you and me. You'll like it," Mother replied.

As I walked around the awkwardly placed record player in the hall to get to the bathroom, I remembered my mother's promise for the next day.

Maybe I'll get a new record or something. Mother can tell I'm mad about the desk.

* * *

"All set?" Mother asked the next morning as soon as the breakfast dishes were washed and put away.

"Yeah, I want to see what we're going to do."

The two of us walked out the back door, past the garage where the hearses were parked, and onto the street that led to Mill Avenue.

"We're not going to try on clothes, are we?" I asked. "I hate trying on clothes just so we can copy them later. I'd rather just go to the dime store now and get the material and pattern and not wait to make the salesgirl think we are going to buy a dress. I'm always scared we're going to get caught looking to see how it's made in the dressing room instead of really trying it on.," I admitted.

"No, we're not going to try on clothes. But we're not going to the fabric counter at the dime store, either," Mother said. "We're going to that business supply shop next to the *Tempe Daily News.* Can you guess what we're going to buy?"

"Are we getting more of those Maguire Mortuary stickers to put on little bottles of smelling salts?" I asked. "It was kind of fun when we first got them, but after sticking labels on about a million dinky bottles, I didn't really like it anymore."

"Daddy said you did a good job on them."

"I know, but one time I opened one of those little bottles and smelled it. Boy, if that's what you have to smell to keep from fainting, I'd rather just drop to the ground myself. That stuff stinks. Why do we have to put those next to all the chairs in the chapel, anyway? I never see anybody faint. I just hear them crying. Sometimes the Mexicans shout stuff in Spanish, but I can't understand what they're saying."

"Some people do faint, but your father keeps them from prying eyes. That's why you get to have that cute little bubbler drinking fountain right outside the chapel door, too. If people don't need smelling salts, they can keep from fainting with a nice cool drink. You enjoy getting a drink out of that fountain, don't you?"

"Yeah. It's fun, except when it's so hot the water burns your mouth. That metal handle burns when it's hot, too."

"Well, you could seem a little more grateful for all the nice things you get to have that other girls don't. If Daddy were in a different business, you wouldn't have a drinking fountain at all, hot or cold."

"I know, Mother. I like all the stuff I have."

"Here we are," Mother said as the little bell above the stationery shop door chimed when we opened it.

"How are you, Gertrude?" the lady behind the counter asked.

"We're fine, thanks."

"Do you need funeral programs printed or are you just dropping off an obituary?"

"Neither. We're here to pick out something real special."

"Are you going to change the color of those pens that say □Maguire's' on them? I see people using the green ones all around town. You don't realize how many people attend funerals until you see them carrying those pens around. Those are really good advertising for you."

"We're in the market for your very best desk blotter," Mother announced.

"What's that?" I asked.

"You know. It's thick paper that keeps ink from running through stationery onto the finish on the desktop."

"For the new desk?" I inquired.

"Of course. We don't want it getting ruined," Mother replied as she turned away from me, giving her full attention to the saleslady.

"The American Legion gave Francis an extravagant gift for his years of service to the post," Mother bragged.

She paused, waiting for the shopkeeper to ask for more details.

"Well, I suppose you guessed it was a desk," she added sourly as the clerk attended to business.

"Well, we have some real nice blotters over here on this display," the shopkeeper replied. "What color were you thinking of? Green would match your business cards and pens," she suggested.

"Oh, isn't that pretty, Jamie?" Mother asked as she eyed a forest-green leatherette model.

"Mm hm," I replied through clenched teeth.

"Good, that's decided," Mother said.

"Will there be anything else?" the shopkeeper asked. "These letter openers have a marble handle on them that would look very distinguished sitting on that blotter."

"Oh, you're right," Mother enthused as the clerk placed the opener on the blotter. "I think you're starting to understand what a lovely piece of furniture this desk really is."

"What do you think, Jamie? Should we splurge on a letter opener, too?"

"Sure," I grumbled.

Mother nearly ran back to the house to arrange her purchases on the desk before Daddy got home.

"Aren't you excited? That's going to make up for losing the record player in here. See? I told you I would make it up to you. After all, how many little girls get to choose their father's desk accessories?" she asked. "Of course, most little girls don't have a desk like this in their living rooms because their fathers didn't get a gift from the American Legion."

"I know how he got the desk, Mother," I said.

"Then act a little proud about it, at least."

As Mother predicted, Daddy was pleased by the new blotter and letter opener.

"We don't even get mail here at the house," Rosarita said. "What's he going to open with that letter opener over here?"

"It's just important that he have a usable desk now that the

Legion has honored him with their gift," Mother explained.

After dinner, we gathered in the cramped living room to watch television. As Daddy smoked cigarette after cigarette, the black and white image on the little Zenith in the corner became scarcely visible through the haze. The minute the nightly news was over, the bedtime ritual began.

"Nighty night, girls," Daddy said as each of us approached his green wool over-stuffed chair to place an obligatory kiss on his cheek.

"Nighty night, Daddy," we each answered.

Why does Mother make us give Daddy a kiss every single night? He never gives us a kiss back. Our pajamas smell like smoke from getting so close to his cigarette. Some nights, I rub against the ash tray when I'm getting off his lap. I can smell it all night long, no matter how many times I wash my hands.

Long after the entire household was silent except for the sound of Daddy's snoring, I got up to use the bathroom.

I turned sideways to make it past the record player blocking the bathroom door. When I did, I stood for a moment looking at the side of the desk I could see from the hallway. Then, I walked into the dark living room and picked up the marble letter opener. As my fingers wrapped around the handle, I experienced an urge I had never allowed myself to act upon before.

Gripping the opener as hard as I could, I aimed its sharp tip and, with all the strength I could muster, I stabbed the opener into the green leatherette on the corner of the blotter. Having done it once, I repeatedly jabbed the opener through the fake leather, the padding underneath it, the thick cardboard below, and onto the hard surface of the desk itself. When I stopped, I saw more than ten stab wounds to the little diagonal of leatherette on the corner of the blotter. The gray colored padding was oozing out of it like stuffing from a rag doll.

I'm going to be in so much trouble for this. I'm not even supposed to be touching this, much less poking holes in it. Everyone's going to know I'm the one who did it, too.

I dropped the letter opener like it was hot, ran into my room, and pulled the sheets up under my chin. I lay there rigidly for hours before the alarm clock in my parents' bedroom went off.

"Jamie, come eat. Your breakfast is getting cold," Mother yelled from the kitchen some time later.

I started for the kitchen as though I were climbing steps to the gallows. I had to walk right past the desk to get to the kitchen. I was sure by now someone had seen the wounds I had inflicted on it the night before. I walked as slowly as possible as I passed the desk. I dared only one quick glance at the scene of my crime from the night before.

Did I imagine that? How can this be? There are no holes in it. The letter opener is right where it should be. It looks like nobody touched the desk.

With a second longer look, I saw that the blotter had been turned around. The holes from the letter opener were at the back of the desk now, not the front. With the shadows cast by the wall behind it, damage was scarcely noticeable.

I'm saved. Somebody saved me. They saw the blotter and moved it before I got in trouble. But who? Somebody else in this

110

house knows I poked holes in something that belongs to Daddy. Are they letting me get away with it, or are they just waiting for the right moment to tell everyone?

While we girls ate our bacon and eggs and Daddy drank coffee and smoked cigarettes, no one spoke. The only sound at the table was the rustling of the newspaper pages as Daddy turned them.

The desk, complete with all its green accessories, remained in the living room. The fear that someone would mention the wounded blotter—and expose me as the culprit—flashed through my thoughts every time I passed the desk. No one came forth as the hero who covered my crime, but I never knew when the finger of blame would be pointed at me, either. The threat only made the knot in my stomach bigger.

I will never act on my true feelings, no matter how strong they are. Whatever I feel when I'm upset, I'll simply act the opposite. Then there can be no incriminating evidence against me. Laughing when I feel like crying is much easier than wondering when someone will discover my crime.

Chapter Eight

Deadly Ride

"How would you girls like to take a ride?" Daddy asked on an afternoon that was dragging by at its typical, boring pace.

"Sure, Daddy, we're always ready to go," Mother answered, wrapping her arm around my shoulders.

She's going to pinch my arm if I say I don't want to. I'd better act eager.

"We're going to the Children's Colony in Coolidge," he said.

He's not asking any more. He's telling me I'm going, like it or not.

"Why is there a whole colony just for some kids?" I asked.

"Most of the kids there don't have parents who can take care of them," he replied. "We'll take one of the limousines," he added, sweetening the deal.

It might not be so bad. Who am I to look down on kids who don't have any parents and have to live at the Children's Colony?

"Okay, I'll go," I said, as though I had a choice.

"Oh, good," Mother enthused. "It'll be so nice to take a long drive and really get away from this place."

"Is Rosarita going too?" I asked.

"Why don't you go ask her?" Daddy inquired, in an upbeat mood.

"Rosarita, do you want to go on a ride with Mother and Daddy?" I shouted as I ran for our closed bedroom door.

As I opened it, I saw Rosarita perched on the edge of her bed, putting fingernail polish on her toes. As she slowly drew the tiny brush of bright red paint across a nail, she looked up at me, annoyed.

"You idiot, they're not going on a joy ride. What did they tell you? Are they getting a death certificate signed or picking up a body?"

"They're not picking up a body. We're going to take one of the limousines. You and I could ride on those fold-out bumper seats. Come on, it'll be fun," I encouraged.

"I'm staying right here and painting my toenails. That's going to be much more fun than whatever you're going to do in that car. You wait and see. You'll be sorry you went," she warned.

"Okay, if you want to stay here all day, go ahead. I'm going. Daddy's excited about it and so is Mother. You're the one who's going to miss out. Maybe they'll stop somewhere and we can have milkshakes."

"There isn't any milkshake in the world worth what you are going to endure driving around with them," Rosarita said.

"Okay, this is your last chance. They're ready to go. Come on, Rosarita, I don't want to go alone. It'll be much more fun with another kid along," I begged.

"You'll have plenty of kids along. Didn't you say you were going to the Children's Colony?" Rosarita asked.

"Fine," I said angrily and slammed the door on Rosarita and her toenails.

"Rosarita doesn't want to go," I reported to our parents.

"Well, she'll be sorry," Daddy said.

We're riding in a limousine to a place built just for kids. Rosarita's toenails couldn't be more interesting than getting out of town.

"Let's go," I said, as I began my way to the carport where the fleet of limousines awaited.

Most people have to have somebody in their family die before they get to ride in one of these limos. I get to ride in one just for the fun of it. I'm going to pull down the bumper seat and have it all to myself.

Daddy positioned himself behind the steering wheel with the big Cadillac emblem at its center. Mother slid into the passenger seat. The whole interior of the car was upholstered in plush velvet. I hopped in back and immediately pulled down one of the folding bumper seats. Soon we were gliding down the streets of Tempe, enjoying the cushioned ride available only in a Cadillac. I loved the cool breeze from the refrigeration Daddy controlled just by pushing a button near the radio.

Nobody has air conditioning in their car. We don't even have it in our house. This is great!

As the houses of Tempe gave way to barren desert, I ran my fingers over the upholstery. I moved from one seat to the other, trying out every vantage point in the huge vehicle. When I looked up to the dashboard, I saw the clock had moved to an hour since we left Tempe.

"Where is the Children's Colony?" I asked. "Coolidge is a long way from Tempe, isn't it?"

"What's wrong with you? I thought you liked riding in this car?" Daddy said, irritated.

"I do. I was just wondering where we are," I countered quickly. I knew I was in danger of angering Daddy and having to get another lecture about being a Chatterbox. "I just don't see anything around here that looks like a village for little kids, that's all," I added hurriedly. "It's mostly just sand and cactus out here."

"Leave the navigating to me," Daddy growled as the Cadillac glided through the heat. Soon he said, "Here we are," as he eased the long car onto an access road away from the main highway.

I don't see anything that looks like a village, but I'll just wait. I'm sure I'll see it soon.

Eventually, the paved road gave way to a dirt pathway. Even with the smooth ride of the Cadillac to cushion the blow, the limousine was jarred into moving at a snail's pace as we drove over giant ruts in the road. Finally, we ended our journey at what looked to me like Army barracks, not a village for kids.

"Is this it?" I asked.

"What in the hell else do you think it would be, out here in the middle of the desert?" Daddy grumbled.

I deliberately waited in the car for several seconds before opening the door. I knew I would choke on the dust the car had created as we drove in.

"I'll go see what's up," Daddy said to Mother and me.

"You girls stay here."

I squinted to look at the intense light reflecting off the metal roofs of the buildings near us. One rusty swing set was the only evidence of any children ever having been here. The whole area had the ambience of a ghost town, complete with tumbleweeds rolling around in the wind.

"This is the Colony?" I asked Mother this time.

"I guess so. I've never been here, either. We won't have to stay very long, though. Your father is just picking up a kid," Mother told me.

"Really? We're picking up a kid here?" I inquired excitedly. "Is it a boy or a girl? How old is this kid? Can I ride in the back seat with them?" I asked.

"If that's what you want to do, go ahead," Mother conceded.

Then, I saw the first movement since our arrival in the ghost town. A child—I couldn't tell if it was male or female—limped out the door of the nearest building. Through the dust and the reflecting light I thought I saw the child's legs twisted into a shape that would have prevented most from standing, much less walking. With great effort, the child slowly dragged one twisted leg around another with the help of a single crutch padded with a filthy blanket.

"That's not the kid who's going with us, is it?" I gasped.

"Huh-uh," Mother said so softly I could hardly hear her.

Then I spotted another child. This one could move quickly, and its legs were normal. This one ran as fast as it could, slamming its head into the side of the building at full speed. Instead of crying or falling, it turned around, ran back to the path where it started, and ran headlong into the building again. It continued to do this until a trickle of blood began to show down the side of its face.

"What is that kid doing?" I exclaimed, alarmed. "He's running into the wall on purpose. He's doing it over and over. He's hurting himself."

This time Mother didn't even answer. She just shrugged.

"Mother, there's something wrong with these kids," I stated. "They're all crippled and crazy."

"Why do you think they live here? That's why we have the Children's Colony. It's for kids who are messed up, either physically or mentally."

"And we're taking one of these messed up kids in the car with us? I don't want to ride with one of these kids."

"You said you wanted to go. Why don't you just concentrate on the good things, like getting away from the house for a while? Don't you like riding around in this swanky Cadillac?" Mother asked.

I was speechless. A parade of the most handicapped children I could ever imagine began to shuffle from one building to another. With horror, I saw the ones in the rusty wheelchairs being pushed by others who were my age, but still drooled as they walked. As they came nearer, the smell of urine and feces wafted from their dirty clothes. Several of them made sounds that I didn't know humans could make. I wanted to look away, but I couldn't take my eyes off them.

"Here they come. Don't stare at them," Mother admonished.

Daddy was in the doorway of one of the buildings. I

strained to see what kind of monstrosity was going to be sharing the back seat with me all the way home. But as he stepped into the sunlight, I saw there was no child walking beside him.

Maybe I'm going to get out of this after all. There's no kid with him. I think he's carrying boards or something, though. That's all right. I can stand anything as long as it's not one of these awful kids.

As my father came closer to the car, I saw that his parcel was covered in a blanket. Daddy used both arms to hold it, but he wasn't struggling under any kind of weight. He walked easily to the side of the car.

Mother and I watched silently as Daddy opened the back door of the Cadillac and crouched to place the parcel on the back seat. When a gust of hot wind blustered up briefly, the blanket covering the package blew back at one corner, revealing a brown foot.

It's one of those kids. One of these kids has died and we're bringing his body home with us. He doesn't even have a casket. He's just wrapped in an old blanket. I'm going to share the back seat with a dead kid all the way back to Tempe. I might even have to touch it.

"Is this the kid we're taking back with us?" I asked Daddy, trying to lower my voice to hide my fear.

"Yeah, it's some Indian kid. The family can't afford to get down here from the reservation, so we're bringing it up to the mortuary where it's more convenient for them," Daddy replied.

"It's a shame to lose a child," Mother said. "I just can't imagine what those parents are going through."

"I don't know if it's a boy or a girl, but whoever it is wasn't even living with its parents. How will they notice it's gone?" I inquired.

"Don't talk like that. First of all, he's a little boy. Second, his parents couldn't take care of him because he was too sick," Daddy told me.

"What was he sick from? All of these kids look pretty sick to me."

"The death certificate isn't signed yet, so we don't know why he died."

He probably had something contagious, like polio. Daddy's always picking up bodies at the hospitals or the tuberculosis sanitarium, but I don't have to ride in the back of the car with them when he does. What if this kid had polio and I'm sitting right next to him? That air conditioning is probably blowing his polio germs right up my nose at this very minute.

"You're all right back there, aren't you?" Daddy asked as I squirmed as far from the body as I could.

"Yes, Daddy," I answered on cue. With the turn of the key in the ignition, the Cadillac hummed to life.

The boy's rigid body was motionless most of the time. But when the dirt road became exceptionally rutted, even the Cadillac couldn't prevent him from rocking from one side to the other, then snapping back into position instantly. I was torn between closely watching the stiffened body bump along, feeling nauseated, or staring out the window trying to forget he was there. If he bounced too much, he might rub up against me when I wasn't looking. So I decided it was easier to watch him and make sure not even the blanket covering him touched me.

"Boy, there's sure not much out here, is there?" Daddy commented as we drove for mile after mile through nothing but desert. "That's why I took this car instead of the old hearse. Wanted to make sure we didn't break down out here in the middle of nowhere," he continued.

If we broke down out here, somebody would have to come help us. They would see that I'm cruising down the highway with a stiff little Indian boy bouncing along beside me.

"This air conditioning will keep him nice and cool until we get home and I can embalm him. These new-fangled gadgets for cars come in real handy in our business, don't they?" Daddy asked.

"Oh yes, Daddy," I answered immediately. Mother gave an approving little chuckle from the front seat.

Sure, she thinks air conditioning is a convenience to keep bodies from rotting on the way back to the mortuary. I'm the one getting polio germs blown up her nose.

"Can people get polio from touching people who have it?" I asked, trying mightily to sound conversational and not hysterical. The brown foot was inching closer and closer every time we hit a bump.

"Have you been listening to those old ladies at the lunch counter again? I swear, every time somebody limps, they scatter in all directions. Hell, I've been to that polio ward a million times and you don't see me getting it, do you?" Daddy challenged.

"If you start to limp, it's nothing more than a leg cramp, Jamie, "Mother chuckled.

"You're not sitting back there thinking that Indian kid had polio, are you?" Daddy questioned.

Now what am I going to say? He'll make fun of me for being afraid if I just say yes, and yell at me for talking too much if I try to explain.

"I'm not afraid," I lied. "It's not the dead ones we have to be afraid of. Right, Daddy?" I mimicked.

"Absolutely," he confirmed.

"Hey, there's a root beer stand up here. It doesn't look too dirty. Let's stop and get a float," Daddy said.

We drove up to the barrel-shaped trailer in the sand on the side of the road. Daddy ceremoniously pushed the button to make the automatic window on his side of the Cadillac roll down. A Mexican girl came out to the car and attached a tray to the side of it.

"What'll it be, girls?" Daddy asked, then stated, "We'll have three root beer floats" before either of us had enough time to answer him.

This is just getting worse and worse. If I suck hard enough on the straw to get the ice cream into my mouth, for sure I'll get some polio germs in there with it. If I try to drink it straight out of the mug, I'll spill it if the ice cream sloshes to the top. If I get root beer on this kid's dead body, I'll be in so much trouble with Mother and Daddy. But if I say I don't want anything to drink, they'll know how bothered I am to be back here with the dead kid.

The Mexican girl returned with three mugs, brown at the bottom, white frothy ice cream floating up to the top. She placed them carefully on the tray.

As Daddy gingerly handed one back to me, both he and Mother warned simultaneously, "Don't spill it."

Alternately staring between the mug and the body, I decided it was best to just get it over with quickly. Putting the straw in my mouth, I inhaled deeply and pulled on it as hard as I could. Instead of the float coming up through the straw, it remained in the mug. The paper straw had collapsed under the pressure of my mighty sucking power.

I licked a few of the bubbles off the top of the mug, but knew not to tip it to get any more.

"Can I have a spoon to get the ice cream with?" I asked.

"No. If you put a spoon in the mug, it'll make it overflow. For God's sake, we can't have you spilling root beer on that kid. Just be patient a few minutes and the ice cream will melt. Then you won't have to use a spoon—you can just slurp it up through the straw."

I can't ask for another straw. They'll be mad that I ruined the first one.

Okay," I replied, staring alternately at the mug and the body.

"I guess I wasn't as thirsty as I thought," I said as my parents finished their floats. "Do either of you want mine?"

"You're not going to drink it yourself? You are the pickiest kid I have ever seen," Mother scolded.

"Hell, I don't care. That just leaves more for me. Come on, Mother, let's have another one," Daddy said as he moved straws from their mugs to mine. "This is like being at the malt shop again, with one glass and two straws," he laughed.

My parents polished off my treat as well as their own and began the last leg of our journey home.

At least we're going to be home soon. This will be over. Finally.

Just as we were about to cross the last bridge over a desert wash to enter Tempe again, I spotted the three town police cars blocking the roadway. Several highway patrol cars jutted into the road as well. A pair of officers stopped every car to question the passengers.

How are we going to explain having two kids in the back seat, one dead and one alive? They're going to think we killed this kid. He hasn't even been embalmed yet. They can't say he's sleeping; he's as stiff as a board. We're going to prison. You can't drive around with a dead body on your backseat!

"Afternoon, officer," Daddy said as he pushed the button to roll down the window.

"We had an AWOL at the county jail this morning, so we're stopping everyone who passes through to ask if they've seen anyone unusual while they were driving," the patrolman told us.

Unusual? Wait until you get a load of what I'm riding next to here in the backseat. He's going to search our car to see if we have the escapee with us. Boy, is he in for a shock.

"We were just coming home from a visit to the Children's Colony," Daddy said.

"Oh, I'm so sorry," the cop said. "Well, I won't hold you up any longer." He motioned for the other officers to let the Cadillac through the roadblock.

I slumped back against the velvet upholstery, weak with

relief that I wasn't headed for a life behind bars.

"I hope they catch that jailbird soon. It makes me so nervous when scary people are running around loose," Mother said.

No one else spoke for the rest of the trip. When we pulled into the carport where he stored the fleet of Cadillacs, Daddy opened the door to the back seat, pulled the small, stiff body into his arms, and carried it into the embalming room. He shut the door firmly behind him, the signal for anyone else to go away because he would be embalming before any more decomposition could occur.

He didn't even say good-bye to us. He's carrying that dead kid so carefully that you would think he was delivering precious cargo.

Mother and I walked through our back yard and into the kitchen.

"Well, that was a nice little trip. It's so good to get out of here once in a while," Mother commented.

I had been dying for a drink ever since we left the root beer stand. I went to the refrigerator and pulled out the old pickle jar filled with cold water. I struggled to get the lid off. The many minerals in the Arizona tap water left green deposits around the top of the jar. The lid finally gave way with a grainy sound and I poured the contents into a glass. I didn't even wait for the particles floating in it to sink to the bottom before I guzzled it down in one huge gulp.

Chapter Nine

Piano Lessons

I peered in at the storefront window of Barrett's Piano Store every day on my walk home from school. Music flowed out through the dusty glass onto the sidewalk where I stood. I stared at the beautiful pianos. Some had plain black finishes, others a warm maple. I dreamed what it would be like to play one.

"Do you think we could get a piano? If I knew how to play, I could spend more time inside practicing instead of being out in the yard where mortuary families could see me," I suggested to my parents.

Rosarita always tells them how something she wants would benefit them, too. I hope it will work for me, even though I don't have her dimples to charm them with.

"We'll see," was the answer each time I asked.

"The piano wouldn't be for just me, Daddy," I bargained. "Rosarita could learn to play it, too."

"If I got the thing, would you practice?" Daddy asked Rosarita.

I shot her a pleading look across the table.

"I guess I could try it," she conceded.

Even with Rosarita as my reluctant ally, months went by

with no progress toward buying a piano. I asked about it enough times that Daddy exploded into his dinner table lecture about listening to the Chatterbox while he was trying to eat. I gave up hope that learning music was in my future. I reverted to my old habit of keeping quiet at the table and showing no emotion at all.

So, at dinner, Daddy droned on with his boring accounts of business at The Place while I daydreamed. But during one dinner, my reverie screeched to a halt in midstream. Daddy mentioned Mr. Barrett in the midst of his one-sided conversation. I was all ears after that.

"Barrett showed up at The Place today with the damnedest idea," he told us. As he repeated Mr. Barrett's words, I couldn't believe what I was hearing.

"Francis, I feel terrible I don't have the cash for this bill," Daddy drawled in imitation of Mr. Barrett's speech. "It seems so disrespectful to my dear Edna to leave her burial charges unpaid. She was my bookkeeper, you know. She would never let an account like this go on at the store," he said. "Do you think you would ever have use for a piano to play at funerals? If I gave you one from the store, I think its value would satisfy Edna's account and my conscience."

"I told him no, no, there's no need for that, Barrett, we can wait for payment." Families are under enough stress when they lose somebody. We don't make it worse for them by demanding money when they can't afford a funeral." Daddy repeated his business philosophy for the billionth time.

Why didn't you say, "You bet I want a piano. Then Jamie can learn to play and spend less time in the pink chair."

Before Daddy continued with his opinions about business, I dared to ask again. "Do you think we could take a piano from Mr. Barrett's store, though? I think it would make him feel better about losing his wife, not worse."

"Oh, sure. All of a sudden you're so concerned about Barrett's emotions," Daddy laughed. "I've seen you standing outside his store drooling at those pianos while he plays."

"So, can we get one, really?"

"This is actually up to Rosarita, you know. I'm not letting Barrett off the hook unless both of you girls want a piano."

"Yeah, Jamie, we couldn't get something as big as a piano for just one of you. We have to consider everybody in such a big decision," Mother added.

Does no one remember the desk in the living room? I think that was only for one person in the family.

"You said you wanted it, too, huh, Rosarita," I cajoled.

If I had more time, I could bargain with her. I could tell her she didn't have to give me a quarter for doing her homework anymore. I'd do it free of charge to get the piano.

"If Rosarita decides she doesn't like it, she could always quit later on," Mother finally helped me.

"It's all right with me as long as I don't have to play if I don't like it," Rosarita mumbled in a monotone.

"Well, if both of you girls want it, I'll tell Barrett we'll take one and write off his account," Daddy decided.

I concealed my delight with a quiet "Thank you, Daddy." Now was not the time to risk a Chatterbox incident when I was so close to winning the piano campaign.

Weeks later, the whole Maguire family walked the blocks to the piano store to choose our new instrument. I maintained the same bored expression as Rosarita as we walked through the aisles of pianos, even though I could have danced at the thought of actually having one of them for my own.

"We have a nice line of spinets," Mr. Barrett told Mother and Daddy. "They're the most popular ones now. They don't take up as much floor space in your living room as the old uprights. The acoustics in them aren't as good as uprights, but most people buy pianos now for how they look, not how they sound," he added.

"Which ones do you girls like?" Mr. Barrett said to Rosarita and me.

I became out of breath with excitement when Mr. Barrett offered, "Don't you want to try one? Sit right down here," as he motioned for me to join him on a bench in front of a stunning black and white keyboard.

"No, thank you," I said in little more than a whisper. "I don't care which one we get."

I would give my eyeteeth to really put my hands on those keys. I want the loudest, prettiest piano in the whole world. But I'm not dumb enough to give in to temptation. "Children are not to be seen or heard in public," my parents say. I'm not going to mess up my chances of getting a piano.

"Here's a pretty little number," Mr. Barrett pressed. "Why not try this one?" he offered a second time as he pointed to another instrument.

I shook my head back and forth. I didn't risk using my

voice at all this second time. When I looked at Rosarita, I could see her expression change from boredom to irritation.

We have to speed this thing up or it still might all fall apart. Rosarita doesn't give a darn and Mother and Daddy are doing this mostly for her.

"Well, Mother, I guess it's up to you to make the decision," Daddy said.

"I don't know which one is best, Daddy. We'll get whatever you say," Mother answered, even though she'd told me that she wanted a spinet before we ever left the house.

"I don't want to take advantage here, Barrett. Which one do you think you can't get rid of any other way?" Daddy asked.

"Oh, this one's going to be here a long time," Mr. Barrett chuckled as he pointed to an enormous upright that had been refinished in a gaudy reddish brown shade. "But she does have a beautiful sound," he added as he sat down and pounded a lively march tune on its keys.

"Okay, we'll take that one," Daddy told him.

"You don't need to take the worst one, Francis. Please, look around and find one you and the family can really be proud of," Mr. Barrett replied.

"No, no, this will be fine. It's just for the kids, anyway. We don't care what it looks like. They don't even know how to play it yet," Daddy answered.

"It's up to you," Mr. Barrett said, shrugging.

"This one is just fine, right, girls?" Daddy asked us. "We don't care what it looks like. It's just for you. Mr. Barrett can save these pretty ones for his real customers."

Rosarita nodded with as little movement as possible to indicate she agreed. Mother smiled, but I could tell she was trying not to show how angry she was. Her lips were pinched so tightly together that no red lipstick was visible.

I said "Sure." I didn't risk making a longer statement; I was afraid my voice would reveal my disappointment with the piano's appearance.

After firm handshakes between the men, Rosarita and I were the proud owners of the ugliest piano in the store in exchange for a woman's burial.

"Don't start that again," Rosarita interrupted my thoughts on the walk back home. "You look like some kind of freak dancing along the sidewalk that way. Can't you just be normal for once?"

"What? I'm not doing anything freaky," I denied. I was so consumed with the numbers in my head that I'd forgotten to conceal my actions from the disapproving eyes of my sister.

"You got what you wanted. Now I have to play a stupid piano I didn't even want. The least you could do is walk like a normal person," Rosarita complained.

"You said you wanted the piano, too, Rosarita. Don't blame me if you don't want to play it now," I countered.

"Now all of a sudden you want us to start telling Mother and Daddy the truth? You know how that will work out as well as I do. We don't have Carol around all the time to get us out of trouble like we used to," Rosarita said.

"Okay, I know you had to say what they wanted, but you just go along with it and leave me alone. I can walk however I want, just like you," I retorted.

"Thanks, I've had a really fun day. First I get to say I want to buy a piano when everybody knows I don't want it. Then I get to watch you dancing like a freak all the way home. And then I can get in trouble for not playing the piano the way Mother and Daddy want me to," Rosarita griped. "You owe me. You got us into this piano thing in the first place."

"It's not my fault Mrs. Barrett died. I didn't know Mr. Barrett needed to give us a piano. How was I to know he couldn't pay his wife's funeral bill?"

"You're always either dancing around, lost in a fog, or staring into storefront windows dreaming about stuff we can't have. I'm sick of you."

"Sorry." I was so distracted by counting the steps in the sidewalk that I could hardly hear what Rosarita was complaining about. On the way to the piano store, I forgot the numbers and counting for the few blocks it took to walk there. Now, though, knowing that the instrument I had dreamed about for so long was to be a monstrosity I would be ashamed for the others girls at school to see, the numbers came flooding into my thoughts relentlessly. Nothing could drown out the counting and recounting of the precise patterns I had in my mind. My feet had to cooperate with the rhythm going on in my head or I couldn't take another step.

"Where are we going to put such a big piece of furniture?" Mother ventured when we arrived home.

"Good question, Mother," Daddy replied. "I didn't think about that when we said we could take the upright. We don't have to keep it in the living room. There's plenty of room in the dining room," he said.

"The cool air from the evap doesn't go into the dining room. Aren't you afraid the heat will buckle the finish?" Mother persisted.

"Who cares? It would probably look better without the finish it has now," Daddy laughed.

When the piano arrived the next day, Mother directed the movers to put it into the only room in the entire house that had no form of air conditioning. The room was icy cold in the winter, and so hot in the Arizona summer no one could stand to be in it for more than a few minutes.

"Can I take piano lessons now that we have one for me to practice on?" I asked Mother.

"I'm sure Daddy will let you if you take Rosarita, too," Mother advised.

"Rosarita, please act like you want to take piano lessons. It'll be so much fun. The guy who teaches them is a student at the college. He's cute and funny and really nice. You'll like him. And we can talk to the other girls taking lessons from him," I pleaded.

"Cute college boys don't give piano lessons to you and your freaky friends from school. I'm only doing it if Mother and Daddy make me," she stated flatly.

"Daddy, are we going to take piano lessons now?" I asked again, risking the Chatterbox lecture once again.

"I meant to tell you that I've taken care of that. I'm not paying some smart aleck college boy to teach you music. The lady from the Baptist church—you know, the one who plays the organ for funerals—she's going to teach you for half the price that college kid wants. She's giving me a deal because she wants me to throw the organ jobs her way when families are making funeral arrangements. It pays to know people," he said proudly.

"Thank you, Daddy," Rosarita and I said in unison.

Within a week, Daddy announced the date and time of the first lesson.

"Beulah lives in those houses in the older part of town, but you can ride your bikes there. She said you can start at four o'clock this Thursday," Daddy told everyone at dinner. "If you want to hear her ahead of that, you can open the back door during the ten o'clock service for that guy who was in the head-on out on the highway. The family didn't know any hymns, so I suggested 'Rock of Ages.' Beulah knows that one like the back of her hand. She adds some extra chords and stuff near the end to jazz it up a little. You'll really like it. Some day you girls will be able to play like her."

"Do you think she can teach us how to play duets like 'Heart and Soul,' or some melodies from songs on the radio? Some other girls at school can play those things. The teacher from the college taught them how to play them," I said.

"She doesn't play any of that trash you listen to on the radio. She plays hymns that people enjoy at funerals. I want you to know something useful, not tunes to entertain college boys," Daddy countered.

"That's all right. I was just wondering what our lessons would be like," I replied. "I can't wait for them to start."

"If you keep blabbering about how much you want to take those stupid piano lessons, I'm never going to get out of it," Rosarita complained when we were alone. "We're not going to be able to play anything fun; Daddy already told us that. Can you seriously tell me you want to spend your time playing funeral hymns?" she continued.

"I'm sure they won't all be hymns. I bet we get to play some other kinds of songs, just not rock and roll from the radio. I'll bet you'll like it too, once we get started."

"I'll just bet I will. I can't wait to ride bikes to some old house to learn to play an ugly piano I don't even want. I bet the teacher is some old lady, too," Rosarita griped.

"I'm sure she's a good teacher, even if she is old, Rosarita. Just be nice about it, okay?"I begged.

The next Thursday, we began peddling toward Maple Avenue at 3:30 p.m.; I didn't want to be late for our first lesson. When I spotted the number for Beulah Carlson's address, I felt my heartbeat quicken with anticipation.

"Here it is. I bet Beulah has a real pretty piano, not one like ours. Aren't you excited to play an instrument that's pretty?" I asked.

"I'd rather be home listening to music I like on the radio. Do you know how many records we could buy with what Daddy is spending on these lessons?" Rosarita countered.

Beulah's yard was so carefully manicured that we knew better than to drop our bikes on the grass. We walked them up to the red cement porch in front and parked them as far out of the way as possible.

This doesn't seem like a house where anything has ever been out of place. We'd better not mess it up.

"Where's the doorbell?" I asked as I tried to smooth the wrinkles out of my gingham dress. "I don't see a button anywhere. Do you think we should just knock?"

"No, don't knock. Everybody has a door bell. Just look for it. What's that little black knob? That's where the doorbell should be. Maybe that's it. Try it."

"What if that isn't it? We'll get in trouble for touching it."

"Just push it, you big baby." I tried to push it, but it wouldn't budge.

"It doesn't work," I said.

"You're not doing it right. You can't push it. You have to twist it like this," Rosarita said, as she reached around me and my wrinkled dress to grab the knob and give it a turn.

Bbrrrrrrring. It sounded like a bicycle bell. Both of us jumped back when the sound hit us, and neither of us could keep from laughing.

"Great teacher this one is going to be. She doesn't know the difference between a bike bell and a doorbell," Rosarita giggled.

"Don't make me laugh. I don't want to look stupid the first time my new piano teacher sees me," I said.

"It's going to take a lot more than being serious to keep you from looking stupid," Rosarita finished just as the heavy black door began to open slowly.

As our eyes adjusted from the bright sunlight of the outdoors to the dark interior of the room beyond, we first saw the outline of a large woman. Though we couldn't make out her facial features yet, her silence and slow movements to usher us in gave me the distinct impression that she was not happy to see us.

"Mrs. Carlson, I'm Jamie and this is my sister, Rosarita."

There was no response from Beulah.

"You know, from the mortuary."

No response.

"Francis Maguire is our father."

When Beulah finally said, "Sit over here" and pointed to the chairs beside the piano, I was startled to see she'd painted her lipstick well beyond the natural outline of her mouth. At a closer glance, I also saw that two bright red lines of rouge marked Beulah's cheeks. The bizarre makeup application, combined with her thinning hair which was standing straight on end, gave Beulah the appearance of a clown. But Beulah had chosen an outfit composed entirely of black to accompany the garish cosmetics. When she turned to reach for the books she would use to teach us, Rosarita shot me a look that would have made me laugh if I weren't so amazed.

"To begin, I need to see your hands." Beulah interrupted our silent communication.

Oh, no. She's going to see the scabs on my fingers where the nails should be, and the cuticles all frayed from where I've bitten them. Mine are going to look worse compared to Rosarita's. Her nails are almost as beautiful as her dimples. She lets hers grow as long as they can. They're always polished in a color to match her dress. Beulah's going to say something to Daddy about how ugly my hands are and then I'll be in more trouble.

Slowly, I pointed my ravaged fingers toward Beulah. Rosarita did the same with her manicured ones.

I stared at the old carpet beneath me rather than bear the shame of hearing another comment about my hands. Beulah's gaudy makeup and unruly hair still mesmerized Rosarita. She stared straight at the face of our new teacher.

To my amazement, the teacher scarcely glanced at my hands. Instead, she turned her attention to Rosarita.

"These will have to be cut. You can't play the piano with nails that long. Do you want me to get the clippers for you?"

Rosarita jerked her hands back behind her as though she had been burned by the words.

"No, I'll do it myself. Later," she replied quickly.

"Well, all right. Just make sure they are gone by your next lesson," Beulah ordered.

Even though we played Beulah's pretty spinet and listened to her demonstrate how to read a couple of notes on the scale, neither of us remembered much beyond the hand incident.

As we mounted our bikes for the ride home an hour later, Rosarita announced her plan. "I am not cutting my nails for that crazy-looking old lady."

"You better do it, Rosarita. She'll tell Mother and Daddy if you don't."

"Let her. I'm not cutting my nails for anyone. I can't believe she let you go with yours all chewed to pieces, and makes me cut mine off. You're the one with problems with your nails, not me. At least I can keep mine out of my mouth."

"You liked Beulah, didn't you?" Daddy asked that night.

"Yes, Daddy," we replied.

"Let's hear what you learned," he continued. "Play your mother and me a song."

"We only had our first lesson. We only know two notes yet," I answered. "We know middle C, though, and everything starts from there."

"It took you an hour to learn two notes? We've got a couple of musical geniuses on our hands here, Mother," Daddy chuckled.

"Someday we'll be able to play the songs from this book she gave us," I threw in quickly.

"What is it?" Daddy asked. I handed him the green book Beulah had given us.

"Great!" Daddy bellowed. "You'll be the only Catholics in town who know all the Baptist hymns. This is a Protestant hymnal, Mother," he laughed.

"Is that what that is?" Rosarita threw in. "We're going to play church songs from the Baptists?"

"It's just music, you guys," I defended. "She's just using these songs to teach us music. It's all the same."

"Pipe down, Chatterbox. You think you're Liberace after you've had one piano lesson," he said.

Everyone, except me, laughed.

Day after blistering hot day I went to the un-air-conditioned dining room and practiced the scales and finger exercises and simple songs from my theory books. I learned to peck out the melodies from the hymnal as well. My solitude at the piano

140

became relaxing. The notes in my head replaced the constant numbers rumbling through my mind. Best of all, the amount of time I spent at the keyboard reduced the time I spent in the pink chair. Mother could hear me practicing so she didn't demand that I be within her sight.

I spent entire afternoons practicing, and so I began to play better than Rosarita, who never touched the keys unless our parents demanded it.

"Daddy, I can't keep up with Jamie. She plays that stupid piano constantly, so Beulah thinks she's all great and I can't do anything," Rosarita eventually told Daddy. "Can I just quit taking lessons? I never wanted to play the piano, anyway. I have plenty of music on my radio."

They'll never let me continue without her. She's ruining my chance to stay out of the pink chair.

"Oh, she's not that bad at it, Daddy. I can help her catch up," I added frantically.

"I don't want you girls being jealous of each other. If Jamie is hurting Rosarita's feelings by getting ahead of her in piano, then we'll just have both of you quit the damned thing. I don't need another expense just so you girls can fight," Daddy said.

"Do we have to sell the piano, too?" I asked, timidly.

"We can't do that. Barrett paid his funeral bills with it. We can't make it look like we didn't want it."

"Beulah doesn't like me, anyway, Daddy. She says Jamie is a better player than I am and she wants me to cut my fingernails," Rosarita whined.

"So that's what this is really about," Daddy said. "You

don't want to do anything you think might make you less beautiful. Don't you know you could never do anything to make yourself look ugly? No piano lessons could replace those dimples," he smiled.

"What do you think we should do, Mother?" Daddy asked.

"Jamie's already ruined the appearance of her hands. Those chewed up nails should be used for something," Mother replied.

"Do you want to continue with the lessons, Chatterbox, or should we just cancel both of you?" Daddy asked.

"I want to keep going," I said as softly and quickly as I could.

"You spend the time Jamie is at piano lessons painting your long, pretty nails, then, Rosarita. But don't you ever think that your hands are more important than your face. You couldn't be ugly if you tried. Now, Jamie, on the other hand..." Daddy trailed off. As he cracked a sarcastic smile, the other two caught on and everyone laughed uproariously.

But the next time Mother asked me, "Do you want to go with me to do a woman's hair at the mortuary or do you want to stay here to practice?" I knew who the true victor was in the battle over the piano.

Having long nails is nothing compared to staying out of the pink chair.

Chapter Ten

Flowers

"Be nice and quiet now. Daddy and Max are upset that the next funeral is going to start before they can get the lighting right. Daddy told the new kid to replace all the bulbs and he got the wrong color."

As Mother and I walked into the chapel, we saw the new employee—a college kid—frantically unscrewing white light bulbs and replacing them with pink ones in the torchieres by the casket.

"Why is Daddy so mad about those light bulbs?" I asked Mother

"If you shine white light on a casket, it makes the people in it look dead," Mother answered.

"If you're in a casket, don't you think most people know you're dead anyway?"

"Of course people know you're dead, but they don't want you to look it. The pink lights are there to protect the feelings of the family," she explained.

I wandered away from the pink light bulbs a bit and stepped behind the sheer green drapery that separated the family chapel from the rest of the chapel. I could see Mother on the other side.

"People look different through these curtains, Mother," I said. "The guy in the casket looks a lot worse from here than he does on the other side of the curtains."

"Your father paid a fortune for those drapes. Don't say anything bad about them or he'll make me try to sew new ones. All I need is one more thing to do over here when I have a house to run, too," Mother griped. "We have to have drapes so people won't be able to see families crying. Lots of people try to sneak a peek over at the family when they walk past the casket. They're curious about how the family is holding up. They should just leave them alone at a time like that."

"People can still see them through these flimsy curtains," I argued with Mother. I could see her with just a little distortion when I viewed her through the fabric.

"Just don't tell Daddy. Or anyone else, either."

If he knows the family can see out through those drapes, don't you think he knows that people can look through them to watch the family? Everybody can still see them, even though he has them in a separate room. Some secrets of The Place make no sense.

When the funeral service ended, Daddy and Max whisked the family away before anyone could see them. They ushered them through a secret back door, down a breezeway between the chapel and the Spud-Nut doughnut shop next to it, and into the waiting limousine. Both Daddy and Max calmed down once the family was safely spirited away in The Getaway Car.

Every person in the chapel has had a sideways glance, if not an outright stare, at the family through the drapes. I don't know why it's so important that no one sees them get into the car. If anybody needs protecting, it's the doughnut customers next door. They're wolfing down a chocolate glazed while someone else is sobbing for their relative a few feet away.

My mind wandered to questions of the funeral industry when I was in the preparation room, too. I liked it better when all I had to do was keep my mouth shut about The Place. But I found myself having questions about everything.

"Can't they just lie down flat?" I dared to utter as I watched Daddy painstakingly touching up makeup on a dead face. "That red rubbery headrest looks uncomfortable," I ventured from my post on the pink chair.

"They wouldn't fit on the pillow later," Daddy replied. Mother glared at me to be quiet while Daddy was working. I knew she would answer my questions later when we were alone.

"If you wait until rigor mortis has set in, you'd have to break their necks to put their head on a pillow," she recounted in complete detail. "Some other mortuaries let the bodies go too long before they take care of them. Your father will stay up all night if he has to, to make a body look as good as possible for the family. You'll never see a body from Maguire's with bruised hands because they weren't embalmed fast enough, or a head at a weird angle because they weren't positioned for their caskets soon after death. Those things have to be done quickly, but I hate it that Daddy is out all night doing them. Then when the family comes in the next morning to make the arrangements for the funeral, he has to look all bright and rested or they'll know he's been up all night."

I could tell how much care Daddy put into his work. He was so meticulous with the hands of the dead. The fingers stayed together in a relaxed fold over the waist; he used exactly the right amount of wax to make them look natural. He made sure the makeup extended into the crease of every finger, so no onlooker could see where it ended. His weaving of a rosary through the fingers of Catholics was scientific in its precision, Mother bragged.

"Most people think families only look at the faces, but they don't. They can tell if you hurried with the hands or left the makeup off the top of a bald man's head. Your father protects people from seeing awful things like that on their dead family members," she continued.

I bet he doesn't know the effect those green drapes are having on all his hard work. The minty haze they cast on the pink light bulbs and the perfect makeup cancels their effect. He's struggling to protect the family, and instead, his efforts are making the person in the casket look worse.

Daddy was careful about not just the body and the service, but the burial as well. He and Max demanded funerals be dignified from start to finish. By the time they drove the hearse to the cemetery, they wanted all the flowers that had surrounded the casket at the chapel to surround the artificial grass covering the mound of dirt next to the grave.

The moment the funeral ended at the chapel, everyone had to pitch in to gather all the flowers, load them into the truck borrowed from Billie and Duane, race to the cemetery, unload them there, and arrange them around the gravesite before the family and guests arrived. Rosarita made me laugh by naming this chore "Beat the Clock." Florists, morticians, and their helpers trotted swiftly back and forth numerous times from chapel to flower truck as Rosarita and I watched from our backyard.

"Those carnations look like they've grown feet," Rosarita laughed as Max jogged by with an arrangement that covered his face. "Is that guy smelling those daisies or is he peeking through them so he doesn't fall down?"

"We better help or Mother's going to be mad," I warned. "There are three funerals today—one here and two others at churches. She's going to be overwhelmed."

"I have homework to do," she answered. "You can go by yourself."

"You get out of everything," I yelled over my shoulder as I made my way across our back yard and up to the parked cars.

With three funerals today, every vehicle we owned was serving as flower delivery. Billie's trucks were at the church funerals several blocks away.

"It's all right. We'll put the flowers in the back of the ambulance and just hope to hell nobody needs to go to the hospital until this funeral is over. I have to drive the hearse in the funeral procession," Daddy assured Mother. "I'll make sure we go nice and slow so you'll have plenty of time to arrange the flowers by the grave before we get there."

This is going to be fun. The flowers smell so good and Daddy is really counting on me to help out. Mother and I will have this all done before the family gets to the cemetery. If the grave is a long way from the pavement, Mother will have to run to get everything done before the family arrives. She hates running, especially at the cemetery where she's so afraid she'll step on somebody's grave marker.

The minute everyone was out of the chapel, Mother and I gathered and loaded gladiolas, carnations, and mums into the ambulance backed up to the rear entrance. There were so many flowers that I was winded from dashing back and forth so many times.

"Are you sure that's all of them, Jamie?" Mother asked. "Every single flower has to be at the cemetery. We can't leave any behind. Hurry, make one last trip in to see that we have them all."

I hope there aren't any more. That ambulance is bulging at the seams now, we have so many flowers in it. I have scratches all over my arms from those skinny green wires holding the buds in place.

"All the flowers are in the ambulance already, Mother, and the hearse hasn't even left the parking lot for the funeral procession," I reported. "We'll beat them to the cemetery by a mile."

"I guess we're all set then. I hope I know how to drive this thing. I've never done it before," Mother admitted.

"You're a good driver, Mother. You can do it. Come on, let's go."

"Okay, I have the clutch pressed down and the emergency brake off. I guess I just need to press this starter button and we'll be on our way," she said.

Instead of hearing the engine turn over and begin to hum

its way to the cemetery, the ear-splitting blast of a siren threw Mother and I back against the seat of the ambulance. Arrrrrrrrrr! it wound up as it reached its crescendo, then Errrrrrr! as it wound down. Everyone in the funeral procession turned to look at Mother and me as the siren began another round. The deafening noise dashed any hope of quietly darting ahead of the hearse to arrive at the cemetery quickly. Mother's face was so red, it looked like it might bleed.

Daddy bolted from the hearse and ran back to the ambulance.

"What in the hell do you think you're doing?" he screamed. "The whole damn family can see we're taking the flowers to the cemetery in an ambulance!"

"I didn't know that button was for the siren. I thought it was the starter. I don't know how much more you can expect from me. I cook, clean, fix hair, and now deliver flowers. Do you ever stop to think that I could use a little help, too?" Mother whimpered, tears rolling down her cheeks. "I have to do everything by myself and then I get yelled at if it isn't just perfect."

"You have help. Who do you think is sitting in that seat next to you? I saw her running with flowers, too," Daddy noted as he nodded toward me.

"You call her help?" Mother blurted out. "If you think she's so much help, why don't you have her with you, not me? Then we'll see how much help you think she is."

"Just get the flowers to the cemetery, will you? I have a funeral to run," he said as he stormed away.

"I'm sorry I rushed you, Mother. You wouldn't have

pushed the wrong button if I wasn't making you go too fast," I said quietly.

"That's the way men are, Jamie. Women do all the work and men are still never satisfied. The worst thing that can ever happen to a person is to be born female."

The worst thing that can ever happen to a person is to be born Jamie. Being a good worker is not going to be my way out of the pink chair, either.

By the time we arrived at the cemetery, I wasn't much help. My fingers hurt when I touched the bloody tips of them against the flowers. Sweat running into the million scratches on my arms began to sting the longer I worked. My stomach had such a tight feeling in it, I could hardly stand up straight. What really slowed me down, though, was counting the number of steps I could take from the ambulance to the grave. If I didn't take the right number of them, I had to start all over again.

Chapter Eleven

Summer Camp

My eyes couldn't read the words fast enough. I gripped the bright yellow border of the *National Geographic* cover as though I thought the print would jump from the page if I let go. If I gasped or screamed for joy like I wanted, I'd get kicked out of the periodicals room of the library, so I gulped and read in silence. It wasn't until my third time through the article about Brazil that I looked up to savor the ecstasy of my discovery. I released my grip somewhat on the journal and let my tired eyes drift around the stacks of magazines surrounding me. With deep self-satisfaction, I recounted in my head the events leading to my serendipitous stumbling across the holy grail of my daydreams.

"Interracial marriage over the centuries has created a coffee-with-cream-colored population in which country of origin or genealogical heritage are indistinguishable. They are Brazilians, their own biological mixture of those from every continent in the world," the article read.

I'd dreamed of this place forever. It removes an entire section related to race from my enormous list of rules and secrets. At last I'd found some relief from the constant threat of unknowingly breaking Mother's rules. I could like people with black, brown or white skin. No one could make up rules about which facilities one race could use or claim rights to. I could make friends with anyone who was nice, regardless of their skin color. I could marry whomever I loved and nobody would be mean to my kids because they didn't look like everybody else. The thousands of rules and secrets I have to learn in Arizona would be of no consequence in Brazil. Life there would be completely carefree. I love Brazil! I'm going to live in Brazil! I want to be Brazilian!

My geography report on my country of choice had unearthed the land of no prejudice for me. I immediately launched my own program of Brazilian immersion. I read about Brazilian food, Brazilian weather, Brazilian exports, and Brazilian language.

I wondered how I ccoud learn Portuguese if the high school doesn't offer it as a foreign language. Americans probably don't want a lot of people to learn it. The language barrier is the only negative about wonderful Brazil. If it weren't for the foreign tongue, the entire United States, land of a million impossible rules, could become a ghost town as the population abandoned it for the utopia of Brazil, land of one race.

My daydreaming became solely devoted to plans for moving to Brazil. I envisioned myself, as a member of the new Brazilian race, strolling through the sand of Ipanema. In my reverie, I wore nothing but a scandalously small bikini, but I didn't look scrawny or pale or even sunburned. In Brazil, I too would be transformed.

My reinvention of myself in this new country, with these

new people, fueled my passion to escape from the threat of the pink chair and the difficult culture surrounding it. I began my plan to distance myself, step by step, until I eased over the South American border some day. Until I made it to Brazil, I seized every opportunity to leave home by myself.

"Aren't you getting a little old to be a Brownie?" Rosarita jeered.

"I'm not a Brownie, I'm a Girl Scout now. Remember the Flying Up ceremony?" I retorted.

"I didn't see anybody but those creepy girls prancing around with their sashes covered in dumb-looking patches for all the badges they earned. I didn't pay attention to what they were doing."

"But, you saw what I was doing."

"Don't tell me you want to be like those girls in high school who show up for class in their Scout uniforms. Everybody laughs at them. You'd better wise up before the same thing happens to you."

"Oh, I'm wise, all right. I'm not going to stay in it after next year. I'll quit once I go to camp in Prescott for two whole weeks during the summer. You've never been past the city limits without Mother or Daddy."

I'm going all the way to Yavapai County by myself now. Next, I'll find a way of leaving Arizona, then the United States— through Mexico—further and further south until I arrive in Brazil. This is the first step in my quest to be a Brazilian.

A year of being a Girl Scout can be a long time, I discovered, as I waited for my camping trip to arrive. I didn't feel the delight the other creepy scouts took in earning badges. They did all kinds of things like picking leaves from trees to identify them, rubbing sticks together to build campfires, and plodding over miles of arid desert hoping to photograph a robin's nest or hear a blue jay's call.

Obviously, those who made up the requirements for the badges were not from Arizona. There are no robins in the dry riverbeds near Tempe. Nor could anyone build a scrapbook of autumn leaves when the only plants for miles are cactus and tumbleweed.

"Are you really going to one of those dumb meetings again?" Rosarita asked every Wednesday when I hid my official Girls Scout pin in my purse. "You don't even like it. If you did, you wouldn't be ashamed for everybody else to know. You'd show up at school in your full regalia, like all the other super-creeps who belong to Scouts."

"Just because my uniform doesn't fit is no reason to think I'm hiding that I belong. I'm real interested in camping and fishing and becoming a goodwill ambassador for my country."

"You're an ambassador all right. You don't even talk to anybody else at school."

"So maybe that's why I need to be in Girl Scouts. So I can learn to talk to others."

"And do a good deed every day," Rosarita scoffed.

She can mock me forever, but I'll have the last laugh as the bus to Prescott takes me away for two whole weeks and she's stuck here. My Girl Scout Camp of today is my Brazil of tomorrow.

The meetings were pretty awful, though. The leader wore her hair in a braid so long it wrapped around her entire head. At first glance, she looked like she was wearing a crown. "Queen of Creeps," I silently named her. She gave endless lectures on the virtues of sensible shoes. (She wore oxfords laced up so tightly her ankles bulged over them.) Her daughter was a charter member of our troop. She stayed in the same troop every year because she stayed in the same grade every year. So far, she'd been in fourth grade three times. By now, she was the only fourth grader old enough to have floppy boobs bouncing around when she played jump rope. She was a lot worse than just creepy, like the rest of us. Something was really wrong with her. I wanted to go to camp so much that I acted as though I thought she was normal. I didn't even react when she raised her arms to block someone in Red Rover. Her sleeveless shirt revealed her armpits covered in the blackest hair I'd ever seen on a woman. But I attended and participated in every weekly meeting, a small price to pay for the first leg of my journey to Brazil.

My careful planning proceeded calmly until the Girl Scout office sent home a packing list for all the prospective campers. Mother flew into a tizzy.

"We don't have these things," she whined as she ticked off items like tin utensils for camp cooking, or a sleeping bag to put on the tent cots at night. "And you have to bring a flashlight, too. I wonder what the rest of us are supposed to do when the summer thunderstorms hit, the power goes out, and you have the only flashlight in the house in your cozy tent in Prescott? Stumble around in the dark until you get back?" she demanded.

"We can get her another flashlight, Mother," Daddy mumbled from behind his newspaper.

"So now we're going to have two flashlights for me to keep track of. The junk drawer in the kitchen hardly has enough room for one, much less two," she griped. "I don't know why you want to go someplace that has no electricity anyway, Jamie. This camp makes everything difficult for parents while their kids are off having a good time."

Mother's mood didn't improve as she bought me a second pair of sneakers (in case the first ones got wet) and a raincoat with a hood.

"Five pairs of shorts?" she yelled. "Have these people ever heard of washing? Surely there's a laundry where you can do two or three pairs of shorts and rewear them. No little girl needs five pairs of shorts."

"If they don't have electricity, they don't have a laundry. You better get the five pairs of shorts, Mother," Rosarita chuckled.

"That's always your solution, isn't it? More, more, more," she growled as she glared at Rosarita.

At least she's not mad at me because I want to get away from here.

"Guess what?" were the first words I heard the next morning. Mother stood at the foot of my bed waving a seersucker sundress. "I saw Grace throwing this away when I took the garbage out. Just as she was about to close the lid on their can, I saw it. Of course, she said I could have it if I wanted it. So, problem solved."

"What problem?" My mouth was so dry I felt my lips

sticking to my teeth.

"You and your packing list," she gloated. As she waved the dress again, my bleary eyes registered a wild tropical scene depicted on the flimsy fabric. Gigantic palm trees and flaming red hibiscus blossoms stretched across a gathered skirt that looked like it went on for miles.

"You can have your five pairs of shorts, the two pairs you already have and three more without buying a thing."

"That's for me?" came my groggy voice as I propped myself up on an elbow. "That's a dress, not shorts."

"I know that, you big silly," Mother teased gleefully. "There's enough fabric here for me to make two or three pairs of shorts out of it."

"Right," I coughed as I lumbered out of bed.

Construction of my camp wardrobe began immediately as Mother picked out stitch after stitch to disengage the gaudy material from its former career as a sundress. By afternoon, yards of tropical flora billowed from the dining room table as Mother laid the tissue-paper pattern for shorts atop it, pinned each piece precisely, and cut them out.

"Your shorts are going to be uglier than sin," Rosarita laughed. "But Mother's so happy she doesn't have to spend money on them that she's singing Christmas carols while she sews. I guess she forgot it's 100 degrees outside."

"Don't make me laugh," I whispered to Rosarita. "Mother will know we're laughing about her and make me stay home."

"You'd be better off staying home than wearing those shorts to camp," she warned.

I didn't care what I had to wear to start practicing for my great escape to Brazil. If I had to wear dumb shorts to Prescott to give life a try on my own, I'd do it.

I tried on my three new pairs of shorts when Mother announced they were complete. The largest of the hibiscus blossoms landed smack in the middle of my butt on one pair; on another, it rested squarely at my crotch. The third pair mercifully lacked any hibiscus, but the gigantic palm fronds all over them still made them highly unusual. But they fit perfectly. Mother used her finest skills as a seamstress to make every seam perfectly straight. The elastic around the wait didn't pull or pucker.

"These are going to work out just fine, Mother," I lied. "Thanks for making them."

"You are most welcome," Mother beamed. "But we better stop standing around admiring your new clothes and get them packed and ready to go."

"Mother, thank you for helping me with all my camp stuff."

She doesn't know she's helping me get away from here forever. I just need a few tries before the big trip to Brazil.

Mother affectionately patted down a tangle in my hair. "That's what mothers do for their little girls, no matter how silly their ideas."

By the next day, I had every item on the packing list checked off. Mother washed and ironed all my clothes, rolled up a sleeping bag she'd borrowed, and counted out the precise number of socks I would need for my two week stay. When fully assembled, my camping gear took up the entire living room floor.

"Should I go get the suitcase now so we can start packing all this?" I offered.

"What suitcase?" Mother asked sharply.

"The only one we have."

"Oh, so now it's our suitcase. Are your initials FNC? Because if they're not, the only suitcase we own is not yours. Your father is the only person who uses that luggage. That's why it's marked with his initials. You most certainly are not dragging that nice leather through the pine needles at camp."

"How am I going to get my stuff up there then? I have to have a suitcase. All this is never going to fit in a pillowcase."

"As usual, I've found a solution. Remember when Mr. Ogleby, from the bank, passed away?"

"Yeah."

"When his daughter brought in his burial clothes, she delivered them in a suitcase. She was so upset about losing her father that she refused to take the suitcase back after we took the clothes out of it. It would just go to waste if you didn't need it."

Minutes later, she dragged in a dingy brown suitcase with a long string dangling from one side where the stitching was coming undone. Fake bamboo covered the middle section of it. Inside was a taffeta lining with a scene of Hawaiian hula girls.

Rosarita bolted from the couch where she'd been reading a movie magazine. I heard the bedroom door slam shut behind her.

She's in our room laughing about the ridiculous suitcase that matches my ridiculous camp clothes. I'd tattle to Mother what she's doing, but then Mother would be mad at both of us and say I couldn't go.

Mother and I squeezed everything into the suitcase quickly and pushed it against the couch to get it out of the way before Daddy came home for dinner. With only one more day before my departure, I didn't want his tripping over my suitcase to interfere with preparations for my first trip. Rosarita stayed in her room until dinner. She kept a straight face and avoided saying anything about packing or clothing or camping through the meal.

We finished washing and drying the dinner dishes; then Mother and Daddy took the garbage out to the cans in the alley. Rosarita flashed her dimples in a wicked signal and jumped atop my tropical-themed suitcase. She wiggled her hips in a fake hula and waved her arm dramatically singing "So long, Jamie" as loudly as she could. With our parents out of sight, I too risked a good laugh at the weird camping gear assembled for me.

"Oh, crap," Rosarita shouted even louder than she had been singing.

When she stepped back onto the living room floor, an indentation the exact size of her foot remained on the side of the case. The fake bamboo unraveled around the hole, revealing the cardboard lining it.

Rosarita gritted her teeth and leaned as close to my face as she could. "Do not say a word about this."

She flipped the suitcase over so the side she just caved in was out of sight. "Act normal" she ordered as we heard the back door open and our parents return.

"I have to get an early start tomorrow. I'm getting ready

for bed," I told everyone.

I'll never make it to Brazil. I had no idea it would be this difficult to make it to another county, much less another continent.

* * *

As the Greyhound bus pulled away, leaving the moms and dads in a cloud of black exhaust fumes, many of the campers looked back anxiously. I never looked at the curb again once I lugged my weird suitcase over it. I sat next to a cute blonde girl from Scottsdale. She told me that most of the others were from Scottsdale, as well.

"Our parents like to have at least one vacation without us kids, so they send us to camp to get rid of us. But we don't care. They're going to Europe where it's old and dirty. Have you ever been there? I hate it."

"Me too," I lied. I dodged any direct references to places I'd travelled for the two hours it took the bus to lumber up the steep hills to Prescott.

Camp counselors kept us to a tight schedule of chores, hikes, horseback rides, and nature talks. For the first few days, all the campers participated. But by the second week, an attitude spread through the tents like a virus. First one girl, then three or four others began to make excuses why they couldn't participate. Some of them spent the entire day crying. I overheard two of them plotting how to get to the pay phone by the mess hall so they could call their parents to come pick them up.

"What's wrong with her? She isn't having any fun at all, and now she's trying to call home," I whispered to the girl in the cot next to mine after lights out.

"She's homesick," she whispered back. "They all are."

I couldn't believe my ears. How could anyone sob for days on end because she wanted to be at home?

The counselors tried to coax the homesick girls from their tents. Their encouraging, cajoling, and bribing only made the homesickness epidemic worse. It wasn't long before our whole ring of tents resounded with the wailing of those pleading to call their parents to come get them.

I, on the other hand, shed not one homesick tear. Before the end of our two-week stay, I was the only one who wasn't homesick. I learned to tolerate the bugs and dirt of outdoor living as long as I was free of the pink chair with its rules and regulations and secrets.

"You don't like it here, do you?" one of the Scottsdale crybabies challenged me.

"It's not so bad," I answered, trying to straddle the fence between their discontent and my happiness.

"Then you must be crazy," another of them eventually shouted through her tears. From then on, the counselors were the only ones who were nice to me. The other campers clung together, sharing their boxes of Kleenex as they suffered.

My camp experience was not at all what I expected. No one said anything about my stupid clothes, or my weird suitcase. But I became a total outsider because I didn't cry twenty-four hours a day.

Not until the Greyhound huffed back down the mountains from Prescott did I, too, fall prey to hot tears streaking my grimy face. I spotted Mother and Rosarita waiting on the curb where

I'd left them two weeks ago. My sobs were tears of frustration over my very first outing into the world alone.

By the time we rode from the Phoenix bus station to Tempe, I'd gained control of my emotions. I told my family what a great time I had out in the woods, but they didn't let my new adventures interrupt the established ritual of our daily activity. Nothing changed while I was gone.

At six o'clock, the ticking clock that signaled "60 Minutes" was beginning on TV cued Mother, Daddy, Rosarita, and I to settle in to the scratchy wool chairs in the living room exactly as we did every Sunday evening. Mike Wallace introduced the first segment. "'The Orphans of Brazil' is our top story this evening. We uncover the plight of children abandoned by their parents in this South American country. Government and citizenry alike choose to ignore these street urchins until they perish from neglect."

So Brazil isn't what I thought it was, either. Am I working so hard at getting out of here only to find that there's no place better? My disappointment rested so heavily on my shoulders I couldn't speak.

"I guess I'm still on camp time. Now that the sun's down, I can't even stay awake. Nighty night," I mumbled as I shuffled to our bedroom, climbed under the sheets, and listened through the wall to the muffled voices coming from the TV until I fell asleep.

Chapter Twelve

Car Crashes

"Jamie, come to the embalming room with me," Mother demanded.

"Can't I stay home? I'll play the piano so you can hear me. I need to practice, anyway," I said.

I don't want to sit in that cold, smelly room with my knees jammed into my chin. Just because I'm taller now doesn't mean the pink chair is bigger, too.

"No, I need you to help me with something," Mother answered.

"You want me to help with something in there. You always tell me not to touch anything in that room. What could I possibly help with?" I asked. I could feel the knot in my stomach tighten.

"That girl who died in the wreck yesterday is only a couple of years older than you are. The parents want her hair slanted across her forehead and then tucked behind her ears. They showed me a picture of her with the sides flipped up at the ends like all you girls wear it now. I don't know how to do that," she said. "The old ladies just need a few clamps in the front to make finger waves and they're all done. I don't know how to do this new-fangled stuff. Come show me how to do it so this girl will look right in her casket."

I couldn't get out of going with her to the embalming room. Worse than that, she wanted me to do stuff in there! I knew the girl whose hair Mother was doing. What if I show that I don't like seeing her dead? Daddy will make fun of me the same way he ridiculed that father who wore sunglasses to his daughter's funeral.

"I would much rather see a man behave like a man than to go Hollywood so nobody can tell he's bawling," Daddy said. "We Maguires know how to control our emotions, thank God, so we don't humiliate ourselves in public like these other jerks."

I don't know if I can count enough to keep from thinking about what that girl was like when she was alive. I can't bite my nails. I'll be doing her hair. I can't stare at the baby in the jar. I have to watch what I'm doing with the comb. I can't hold my breath the whole time I'm in there. For sure, the smell of formaldehyde is going to be all around somebody I used to know. That's a lot different from some old person I never saw before.

"Come on. I don't have all day," Mother said impatiently.

"I'm trying to find the shoes I want to wear."

"It's not a fashion show. Who do you think is going to see you? The dead people?"

Slowly, I walked through my house, out the back door, and across the alley to the embalming room. The closer I got, the stronger grew the formaldehyde smell.

"She looks really good, don't you think? It's such a nice change to have a body on this table that is still young and firm. Look at this bust line," Mother said as she tucked the white sheet over the girl's torso a little tighter. "She doesn't even need a bra. The old women's breasts are so soft that they just flop out to the sides if you don't cinch them into a bra just right. It's a real pain to do it with them lying down," Mother gabbed on. "I guess that's the advantage of dying young. You can still have a perky figure when you're in your casket."

"Her hair needs to look just right. They're going to bury her in her prom gown. I just hope they don't put a corsage on her in the casket. That never works out well. The flowers start to wilt during the funeral and it reminds everybody of how dead the person is, too."

"I don't think anyone will need a reminder that this girl is dead, with or without a corsage in her casket," I blurted out.

"That isn't nice to talk about her that way, Jamie. Now let's get to work and get her hair right."

I saw that Mother already had shampooed, rolled and dried the dead girl's hair.

"I've done everything but comb it out. You need to take it from here. You know, tease it and spray it like you girls do."

I reached for the roller furthest from the pasty white face before me. Mother handed me a brush. Within a few strokes of it, the hair went from ringlets to a satiny flow.

"I bought this especially for this case," Mother volunteered as she peeled the wrapping off a rattail comb, designed for teasing.

"Thanks," I said through clenched teeth. So far, I had not touched the scalp, but teasing would necessitate putting the tail of the comb to the head.

"She's not all beat up like most crash fatalities. How could she have died when she doesn't even look injured?" I finally managed.

Maybe if I keep talking, I won't focus on the skin so much. I can do anything but touch this dead girl.

"The bar that separates the front and back seats broke her neck. Fortunately, she didn't go through the windshield or anything. Daddy didn't have to use much wax on her at all. After you finish her hair, he'll put on her makeup and she'll look real nice."

I looked up at the prom gown hanging on the hook just inside the door.

"Do her parents know you have to cut that dress all the way down the back to get it on her? Aren't you afraid the lace on it will begin to unravel when it's cut?"

We've covered the accident. I better move on to another topic or I'll start thinking about what I'm doing.

"Of course her parents don't know we cut it. We'll tuck the back of the dress under her once she's in her casket. That way, no one will know even if the lace does start to unravel. How else would you suggest we get it on her? Have her stand up and try it on for us?"

"No. It's just so pretty. It's too bad you have to ruin it to get it on her."

"It's not ruined. She'll look beautiful if you hurry up and finish her hair."

I'm running out of things to talk about. With Mother right behind me, I don't dare start counting things. How I wish I could stand to put my fingers in my mouth now. I need to bite my nails but, after touching all these things, I might never be able to put my hands in my mouth again. What am I going to do? Everyone's going to know what a chicken I am. They'll all make fun of me. For once, I wish I could be sitting on the little pink chair. Touching a corpse is much worse than looking at it.

With the teasing completed and the strands smoothed over, I began the task of tucking the hair behind the girl's ears so I could make the ends flip up As I pulled the bangs away from the rest of the hair, the teased part underneath became entangled. I gave it a little tug to loosen it from the rest. As I did, the girl's head moved ever so slightly in the direction I pulled, but then rigor mortis jerked it rigidly back to its position on the red rubber neck rest. I dropped the hair and the comb onto the hard table.

"I can't do it, either, Mother. It's too different when someone is lying down," I said as I passed the pink chair and headed straight for the door.

"You have no patience whatsoever," Mother called after me.

One, two, three, four, five, six. One, two. One, two, three, four, five, six, seven. One, two, three four five. I'm getting out of there. I'm getting out of there. One, two, three...

The second I reached home, I counted my steps to the dining room and practiced the piano for hours.

All I'm thinking about is numbers and counting. Just keep counting, keep counting.

The next day I arrived at my first-period class, Latin, eager to concentrate on translations. As the teacher began to explain the day's assignment, I put my left hand across my paper to stabilize it while I wrote. I saw that every nail on it was bitten beyond the quick. The little scabs around my cuticles matched the ones on my right hand. But in a few seconds, I was listening attentively to the lecture.

When a few girls in the hall began talking about the accident involving someone almost our age, I walked past as though I didn't see them. I couldn't risk thinking about the stiff girl with the modern hairstyle, dressed in her newly- scissored prom gown. Today, Daddy and Max would lift her rigid body from the hard embalming table to the pillowy casket. The beautiful lace would remain in tatters long after the teenager was reduced to a skeleton.

Within a week, the funeral was over, the newspaper stories about the accident were replaced by more timely items, and the dead girl was no longer the topic of conversation among my schoolmates. With all the things swirling through my mind, I seldom remembered the horrors of my attempt at styling the hair of the dead. Still, I maintained a hectic schedule to deter Mother from relegating me to the pink chair.

Any time Mother said, "I have to do someone's hair," I immediately had an excuse to avoid it.

"I need to study. I have to practice the piano," came from my mouth involuntarily whenever the possibility of a stint in the undersized chair loomed close.

"You need to go with me this time, Jamie. I'm sure you want to say goodbye to Miss Elaine. She was always so nice to you at church."

"Miss Elaine?" I asked, trying not to sound shocked.

She's the nicest catechism teacher I ever had. She smiled and joked with us; she wasn't all serious like the nuns. Why would Mother bring her up now? I'm not in her class any more.

"Yes, the poor thing. That truck that broadsided her car killed her instantly."

"Miss Elaine died?" I inquired incredulously. "She gave me a hug just last Sunday. She's not dead."

"Don't you pay attention to anything around here? Didn't you hear Daddy leave in the middle of the night to go pick her up?"

"I heard him leave, but I didn't know it was Miss Elaine. She was on vacation. She can't be dead."

"She was in the back seat while her parents were driving to the mountains for their vacation. They drifted into oncoming traffic when her father fell asleep at the wheel. A truck hit them. Elaine took the whole impact of the crash. Her parents weren't injured at all."

"She always spoke to me at church like I was an adult. She never treated me like a kid. She'd walk clear across the room just to say she liked my dress, even if she'd seen it a million times."

She had a soft voice and pretty clothes. She winked at me during church, when she wasn't supposed to. When she hugged me, I could smell her shampoo and her perfume at the same time. People like that can't be dead. She's a real person, not a dead body.

"I know you liked her, too. You need to come with me to get her ready for her funeral."

"I don't have to help with her hair or anything, do I?" I

ventured.

"Oh, no. I'll never ask you to help again after the way you stormed out last time when everything didn't instantly go your way. You're lucky I didn't tell Daddy about that. He doesn't like it when you girls act up, you know.*"*

"When are you going?" I stalled.

"Right now. We can't dilly-dally. The highway patrol took forever to get an ambulance to the scene of the accident. They were way out in the desert when it happened. Daddy had to hurry and embalm her the minute her body arrived. Her hands were already starting to turn blue by the time she got here last night. Daddy wants me to be ready to start her hair as soon as he gets her cleaned up."

"What's the rush?"

"He's going to need a long time to work on her. You know how it is with those car crashes. The family wants an open casket, so he'll be hours with all the wax and makeup."

She doesn't need wax and makeup; she needs shampoo and perfume. You don't know what you're talking about. Miss Elaine is not dead.

Mother swung the screen door open and held it, indicating that I should leave the house and follow her to the mortuary. Without waiting to put on my shoes, I crossed the gravelly alley in my bare feet to keep up with my mother.

"Don't touch anything," Mother repeated for the millionth time as we neared the door to the embalming area.

I slipped inside and into the pink chair as quickly and silently as possible. I wrapped my arms around my long legs after I'd lowered myself to the seat of the little chair.

When I looked at the table where Miss Elaine's body lay, I let my eyes work their way up from the white table surface to the red rubber head rest and finally to the head of the body. I wasn't surprised when I didn't see hair spilling onto the table. Miss Elaine wore her hair short. Not until I looked more closely at the back of the head did I realize what I was looking at. There was no hair on the table, but there was no hair on the head, either. In fact, at the back of the head, the area closest to me, there was neither scalp nor skull. I was staring directly at the exposed brain of my teacher from church. I didn't recognize it at first because it wasn't the usual white color of the brains I had seen in anatomy books. Miss Elaine's brain was stained a yellowish red color.

"It's a shame they shaved her head to prepare her for surgery. Did anybody in that emergency room bother to see that the whole back of her head was torn off? There was no point in trying to do surgery on somebody who was already so injured by the wreck. Not only did they shave off her hair, they sprayed that iodine stuff all over her. You can see how it stained her brain and a lot of the skin around it. We can cover up most of it with a wig and Daddy can try to hide the rest with makeup. She was such a nice lady. He'll put forth an extra effort to make her look right for her funeral."

"Are you even listening to me?" Mother said when I didn't answer her.

I stared blankly at the brain of my teacher.

If I run out of here, or cry, or vomit, my family will never forgive me. I'm a Maguire. I'm not bothered by death and gory accidents. But I can't protect myself this time. I can't look away, but I can't endure what I'm feeling when I look. I'm trapped!

Slowly, a tingling sensation crept into my hands. I couldn't look down at them because my gaze was so fixed on the brain before me, but I could feel them getting heavier and heavier. I struggled to keep them clinched around my folded up legs. I felt I had a boulder, not a hand, at the end of each of my arms.

The pink chair, inadequate as it was to contain my teenaged body, began to enfold me. The fabric on the seat of my pants began to melt into the chipped pink paint of the chair. I sank downward until my skin transformed into the pulp of the wood beneath the brilliant paint. As I dropped further and further into the chair, I passed through the pink-painted surface, then the wood grain, and eventually felt my entire body become the inanimate object. The chair fully embraced my mind, as well, until I no longer existed as a separate entity. I was the chair.

Soon my mind was free of all thought. I experienced no anxiety. I had no need to chew my nails or count relentlessly. After all, now that I had become the pink chair, I'd lost my human functions.

A calm I'd never sensed before enveloped me. My breath came in long, satisfying inhalations. Even though I was the chair, I was lighter than air. In fact, I might be floating. Although I had never been the chair before, I felt I was destined to be it.

When Mother said, "There, doesn't that look better already?" my hands that were now part of the pink chair began to tingle again.

In a few seconds, the pink chair began to shrink back to its usual size. I floated from deep inside its wood to reach the seat. Then I felt my clothes touching the bright pink paint. The chair and I were separate again.

I don't want to be Jamie. I want to be the pink chair. I want to be peacefully calm all the time. Jamie is too scared and nervous and nail-biting and number-counting. I don't want to be her! I want to be the chair!

But now the chair was furniture again, and I was Jamie sitting atop it. My thoughts began to flood with the images before me. The brain of my teacher, the cold, white surface of the table, and the acrid odor of the embalming fluid hit me at once. Everything in the environment was exactly as it had been before I became the chair, except for one feeling. I wasn't familiar with it, but I wasn't afraid of it, either. I was refreshed, as though I'd had arisen from a nap. My body was energized and eager for activity. I didn't feel compelled to put my hands in my mouth or to count.

I left the embalming room without a formal goodbye to Miss Elaine. I felt no guilt about my departure from the awful scene. The kindness that was the essence of Miss Elaine was what I chose to remember, not the battered body with its internal organs spilling onto the cold table beneath it.

When I practiced the piano that day, my fingers moved with a lightness of touch that was unusual. My hands moved gently across the keys and I savored the beautiful sound I was able to force from the ugly piano. Counting or nail biting or stomach cramping never gave me the security I felt from my departure into the pink chair and away from the ugliness around me.

I've been all wrong about the pink chair. I spent all this time hating it, and yet, it's the only thing that ever protected me.

Chapter Thirteen

Nose Job

"Will you stop rubbing your nose like that?" Mother yelled. "You're ruining your face. Look at what you've done to your nose."

"It itches, Mother. I'm not doing anything to it."

"She makes me sick. She's constantly rubbing her nose around in a circle. I never saw anybody who could move the whole end of their nose around just by rubbing it. It's embarrassing. She does it in front of other people, Mother," Rosarita complained.

"I don't do anything in front of other people," I countered.

"Oh, yeah? Then how come your nose is all round on the end? You rubbed it so hard you broke it."

"You can't break your nose by rubbing it. Besides, I have to do something to stop this constant itching. It feels like bugs have crawled up my nose."

"That's just sickening. Mother, do something about her. She's just a mess."

"Jamie, really, you have absolutely ruined your nose. Why, look at Rosarita. Her nose is just as sharp at the end as your father's and mine. Then look at yours. It's rounded off at the point. You've destroyed your own face," Mother scolded.

"I don't care. I can still breathe out of my mouth. That's all you need your nose for, anyway."

"That's all you need it for. Some of us like to look normal, you know," Rosarita laughed derisively.

"Yours has always been different from the shape of our noses," Mother continued. "But recently I've noticed it's not just round on the tip. The whole thing is kind of crooked looking."

"Big deal," I said shortly as I walked out of the room.

Once my bedroom door was closed, I looked at myself in the mirror over my dresser. I knew why it was so important to my family that everyone have the same nose. Carol's nose was almost pug. Even though Daddy adopted her after her biological father died, her physical traits were a telltale sign that she was not a Maguire. Now, here I was, one of their biological own, with a nose that looked more like Carol's than like theirs.

I think Carol's nose is cute. But between having blonde hair like her and now, this funny-looking nose, I don't look like I belong to this family. It's bad enough not to have dimples like Rosarita, but now nothing in my whole face is right. I might as well be another stepchild. At least Carol has a good reason for looking different from our family; she must look like her real father. But I have no excuse for my appearance. I don't look like anybody but my half-sister. Explain that!

"Daddy, look at Jamie's nose," Rosarita started the minute we were seated at the dinner table. "Don't you think it looks funny? It's all rounded at the end. She broke it rubbing it around in circles so hard."

"Don't blame it on the nose. She's always been funny looking." Everyone enjoyed a good laugh at Daddy's humor.

"I didn't break it, Daddy. They're just saying that." I defended myself when the laughter died down.

"Show him how you rub your nose when you say you think bugs have crawled inside it," Rosarita dared me.

"This is all I do," I said, as I put my hand to the tip of my nose and began a vigorous circular motion.

"Oh, that is so disgusting. Stop it," Rosarita said.

"I'm just showing you that I couldn't have broken my own nose."

"Now that you say that, your nose does look a little different. The bone in it isn't straight. It makes you look like one of those bulldogs that snort all the time," Daddy laughed.

"So does she," Rosarita nearly shouted. "I can hear her all over the house, sniffling and snorting and scratching her nose. I hate it."

"I'm sure it will get better all by itself," Mother interjected. "Everybody grows differently."

"Yeah, Jamie's growing uglier every day," Rosarita said as the whole group burst into laughter again.

I hope they don't find out that I rub my nose at school, too. The teacher asked me if I had allergies because nobody has a cold all the time.

Try as I might, the urge to rub my nose overwhelmed me. I started carrying a Kleenex in my hand constantly, trying to hide the rubbing behind the tissue.

This tissue hides my hands, too. I just fold it over my

fingernails when anyone gets close enough to see them. Then no one knows my nails are bitten to the quick.

"You use too much Kleenex. I get so sick of seeing them all over the house where you drop them," Rosarita complained.

"I need them. My nose is always stuffed up," I said.

"Mother, you should take her to a doctor. I can't stand listening to her sneezing and blowing and scratching every single day," Rosarita threatened.

"Don't, Rosarita," I mumbled out the side of my mouth. "You know how Mother makes me go to the doctor over every little thing already. Don't you remember the last time with those bruises on my legs?"

I spent much more time looking at my nose in the mirror than I admitted. I began to notice that one side of my profile looked entirely different from the other. When I turned one way, my nose was straight. But, from the other side, it dipped down in the middle and turned up at the end.

Nobody has two different noses from two different angles. I'm going to get in a lot of trouble when Daddy finds out that I really did break it. How do you fix a broken nose, anyway? I can't have a cast on it like kids do when they break an arm.

As Friday approached, not even Rosarita's harping about my disgusting habits distracted everyone from the anticipation of the next boxing match on TV. Every week, Max and Grace joined Mother, Daddy, Rosarita, and me for the "Friday Night Fights" on the console television set in our living room. Rosarita and I longed to be out with the other teens but, having few friends, we seldom had an opportunity to escape from the adults. Mother and Grace were usually whispering about something totally unrelated to boxing, but Max and Daddy were as close to the screen as they could get, shouting at the winner to knock out the opponent or groaning when the loser took one right in the face.

"Oh, Jesus, that's going to leave a mark," Max laughed as a boxer's neck snapped back from the force of a blow.

"Hit him back, you damned chicken," Daddy urged.

"Get him. He's going down."

"He'll never make it through another round."

"This is great. He's bleeding all over the ring and they still won't stop the fight."

"He's down for the count. Ring the bell and get it over with."

"Wasn't that a great fight, girls?" Daddy asked after the referee stopped the fight due to one boxer's bludgeoning.

"Yes, Daddy," we answered in unison.

"I don't know why you like to see other people getting beat up," Grace said.

"They get paid for it." Max began the usual argument. He stopped short when the camera zoomed in on the losing boxer's face.

"Jesus Christ, will you look at that?" he shouted. "That poor guy's nose has been beaten so bad he has two different profiles. Look at that. He has a straight nose from one angle, but it looks turned up at the end when you see him from the other side. How does he even breathe out of that thing?" He and Daddy roared with laughter.

"I'm going to bed, Mother. I'm tired of watching this," I said hurriedly.

That boxer's nose looks just like mine. I saw how it got that way. He sure didn't get it to look like that by rubbing it too hard when it itched.

I finally fell asleep after hours of lying in bed, listening to the others through my bedroom wall as they talked and laughed about the boxing match.

By breakfast on Saturday morning, the fighter and his nose were no longer the topic of discussion.

I think everyone has forgotten all about the fight. I'm going to remember not to rub my nose so much and maybe everyone will forget about my nose, too.

"Jamie, I think we're going to have to consult a specialist about your nose," Mother told me as she cleared the breakfast dishes from the table.

"It's okay, Mother," I countered. "A lot of kids get colds that last a long time."

"You know we have tuberculosis in our family. Your grandfather died from it," she said.

"But didn't that happen when you were just a baby?" I asked.

"It doesn't matter when it happened, Jamie. Our family has had some very serious medical problems and we have to take care of them quickly before they can cause another tragedy," Mother warned.

"Do you get a runny, itchy nose from tuberculosis?" I dared.

"Haven't you heard those tubercular's cough? Don't you think all that congestion in their lungs began with a runny nose?

I'm not going to lose anyone else to that disease."

"You have to catch it from somebody, though, Mother. You don't inherit tuberculosis. I'm pretty sure I'm fine," I argued.

Within a week, Mother had an appointment for me with an ear, nose, and throat specialist in Phoenix. As we approached a building with ornate carvings near its doorway, Mother announced, "There are some very fine physicians in this building. I hope you understand what a privilege it is to see one of them."

Mother's happy that we can go to a place where kids are so sick their mothers get a lot of sympathy. I just hope she doesn't try to convince them that I have tuberculosis.

"It's going to be quite an ordeal to get your stuffy nose cleared up. We may have to come here every week for shots or something. They'll have to run a lot of tests on you to find out if you have tuberculosis or something else. You're going to have some answering to do about how you smashed your nose all up by rubbing it so hard."

Mother beamed as the doctor opened the door of the examining room.

"It's such an honor to see a specialist in this beautiful building, Doctor," she fawned. "Those general practitioners in Tempe just don't have the brilliance to cure a young lady like Jamie here." The doctor looked right past Mother and straight into my face.

"What happened to her nose?" he demanded before he even had time to shut the door.

My face began to burn as the humiliation of admitting my nose-rubbing habit brought all the blood in my body to my cheeks.

"Why don't you tell him what you did," Mother said. "You are not going to believe what this child has done to her own nose."

"I rub it real hard," I muttered with my head cast down. "It itches so bad, I rub it around and around in circles. I only do it because it feels like bugs are crawling around in it."

As I made my confession, the doctor placed a strap around his head that supported a high-intensity light attached and leaned as close as he could to the table where I was sitting.

"Look up," he commanded flatly.

I tilted my head back.

The doctor moved his head just right to aim the searchlight up my nostrils—first one, then the other. The light was so big and so close that I felt its heat on my face.

"Inhale for me," he ordered.

I sucked in a long breath through my mouth.

"Breathe through your nose, not your mouth," he requested.

"I can't get any air through my nose," I answered timidly. "It's okay. I don't mind breathing through my mouth. I just part my lips a little bit and it's just as good as breathing with my nose."

"We're not really here about that, anyway," Mother broke in. "You see, I have a long history of illness in my family. My sister died from leukemia and my father had tuberculos…"

"That's of no consequence here," the doctor interrupted.

"A family riddled with disease doesn't matter?" Mother rallied, indignantly.

The doctor slowly rolled his stool away from the examining

table. Pulling his glasses far enough down his nose to see over them, he looked Mother squarely in the eye.

"No disease, and certainly no child rubbing it, could create a nose that looks like this," he stated.

He paused for Mother to reply. She stared at him in silence.

"This is a referral to an allergist," he said, as he handed a business card to Mother. "Get her in as quickly as possible. The allergist will tell you when she is ready to come back to me to prepare for her surgery."

Suddenly, Mother perked up. "Surgery?" she asked, with an expression I recognized as delight.

"Correct," the doctor answered as he opened the door to leave. "This child is a nasal cripple," he finished as he shut the door behind him.

Mother and I left the office without a word.

As we rode down in the elevator of the elaborate building, I could tell Mother was experiencing no conflict of any sort. She had the peaceful expression of someone confident of having achieved a goal.

She'll forgive the doctor for cutting her off about her diseases if she gets to have hospitals, operations, and bandages. She's going to tell people that the doctor said I'm crippled. She'll let everyone see how hard it is for her to have a sick kid.

"We'll call this allergist the minute we get home," she told me. I could hear the eagerness in her voice as she began planning another medical adventure.

If the doctor was so certain I didn't make my nose this way, then why does it look like this? I'm not a boxer.

I had little time to wonder about the source of my nasal problems. Mother, in a flurry of anticipation, was setting the stage for my surgery. Preparations began immediately.

"We have to start getting everything ready for you to go into the hospital," she told me the next morning as she threw the blanket covering me to the end of the bed. "Get up, there's a sale on nightgowns and stuff at Penney's. You can't go to the hospital without new gowns. You'll need a robe and slippers, too. I'm not having those nuns and nurses turn up their noses at me because you have grubby looking pajamas. All dressed up in their white uniforms and habits, I'm sure they talk about patients and their families behind their backs if they're not dressed right."

"How do we know what they think is right? Don't you have to wear hospital gowns, anyway? Who will know what my nightgowns look like if they're folded away in a suitcase the whole time I'm there?" I asked. "Come on, Mother, I want to sleep just a little bit more."

"No, we have to do this. I'm not having you embarrass the family by wearing your old pajamas in there. Most of those people that work at St. Joseph's know your father. We don't want to lose business because people think we aren't careful about appearances. Would you send somebody to a mortuary that couldn't even make their living relatives look right? Those nuns recommend mortuaries to people when their loved ones die in that hospital. We're not taking any chances that they'll get the wrong impression about how we take care of people."

I got out of bed and prepared for a day of shopping. Mother and I left immediately in our quest to avoid family shame at the hands of hospital personnel.

Hours later, we returned home from the store with bags full of nightgowns, robes, house slippers, and underwear. We saved a few dollars by skipping the racks that held bras and slips.

"You won't be wearing those at the hospital. But you can't have any torn elastic or faded lace on the underpants. The nurses will see those for sure," Mother warned me.

"You bet they will," I said. "I'm not getting caught in one of those hospital gowns with the ties all the way down the back. I'm keeping my underwear on at all times. I've seen people with their butts hanging out the rear end of their gowns. I'm not having that happen to me," I said.

"Look at all the stuff Mother bought me for the hospital, Rosarita," I said when my sister came in.

"Have you picked out a new nose from the catalog of schnozzes yet?" Rosarita asked.

"They don't have a catalog to choose from," I retorted.

"When you get your hair done, you get to choose your new style from magazines about hairdos. I bet they have magazines showing all the latest styles in noses. After all, there are different sizes and shapes and colors. Maybe that's what you should do. You should get a colored nose right in the middle of that pasty white face of yours. Can't you just picture it? Big, wide nostrils and dark brown skin? Maybe they'd throw in a pair of big, black lips to match it," Rosarita laughed.

"That's not funny. I'm going to look like you and Mother and Daddy after they fix my nose. It's going to be long and sharply pointed like yours. Then maybe people won't ask if I'm adopted," I replied.

"It's going to take more than a nose job to make you look like us," Daddy added as he entered the room. "This guy is a surgeon, not a magician," he joked. He and Rosarita laughed.

"I got all new nightgowns, and robes and slippers, too," I said. "Hey, Mother, do you think I could get some new books to take along? I'm going to need something to keep me occupied after my operation. I don't want to get bored just lying in bed all day with nothing to do."

"You don't seem to have any trouble lying in bed all day when I want you to go shopping," Mother answered. "But, yes, you can have some new books if you think they'll keep you happy."

"I hope it doesn't hurt much. Sure, I'll be asleep during the whole operation, but, I'm kind of scared about when I wake up."

"Me, too! Haven't you ever seen those Frankenstein movies? I hope they don't have to resort to using spare parts from other people to finish the job," Daddy laughed.

"That's just what I said, Daddy. Don't you think Jamie would look good with a nose from a Negro? It would make her face so much more colorful," Rosarita chimed in.

"Seriously, I think they use mallets to break bones in those operating rooms. A guy I knew in the Army had to have his arm reset and he told me they broke it with a mallet that looked like a sledgehammer," Daddy shared. "Don't worry about being afraid of anything until you see the mallet headed for your face, Jamie," he said, and laughed again.

"Very funny, you guys," I retorted.

Several weeks later, when all the tests and waiting periods were over and the allergist said I could have the surgery, Mother and I walked the long series of stairs into the front entrance to the hospital.

"Isn't this beautiful?" Mother gasped, as we walked across the polished marble floors to reach the admissions desk.

"Yeah," I said shortly.

"Well, let's get you into your room," Mother said as though she were giving me a stay at a luxury hotel.

"Okay," was all I could answer back.

"Oh, your room is on the fifth floor. I bet the view from there is beautiful. I can't wait to see it," Mother enthused as a nurse ushered us into the elevator.

"Let's get you out of those old shorts and into your pretty new nightgown," Mother encouraged as soon as the nurse left my room.

"Okay," I mumbled.

"I wonder if the doctor is going to come by today," Mother chatted cheerily. "Sometimes they check on the patients before the surgery. Any time I have surgery, I always like it when it seems like they care enough to visit with me ahead of time."

"Okay," I answered again.

"What is wrong with you?" Mother demanded. "This is the fun part. You better start appreciating things now before they do stuff that hurts, young lady."

"Sorry."

Mother settled herself into the plastic chair next to the bed. She moved her big gathered skirt around until it was placed perfectly over her knees.

"I wish that doctor would get here," she said after a few minutes. "I would really like to talk to him, but I have other things to do today, too," she said impatiently.

"It's okay, Mother, you can go. I'm fine."

"You just want me to leave so you can start reading all those stupid books you insisted on bringing."

"You said you had things to do."

"Here's your roommate," Mother said eagerly as the door opened and a girl in a wheelchair rolled in. A nurse pushed the chair, and her mother walked soberly behind them.

"Maybe she's sick," I said about the brunette teen who was climbing into the hospital bed next to mine. "Don't bother her now," I cautioned.

"I'm not going to bug her. I just want you to be friendly with someone for a change."

Then Mother leaned close to my ear and whispered, "She's wearing a shirt with the name of a Scottsdale school printed on it. She's probably snotty, but just be nice to her. She already thinks she's better than us. Don't make matters worse by ignoring her."

"This isn't summer camp, Mother. We're not going to be friends. We share a hospital room."

"If you're going to snap at me sarcastically like your father does, I'm going to leave. Then you'll see how much fun it is to be here all by yourself."

Leaning in close again, Mother whispered into my ear, "I bet that girl's mother is going to be here all day and night. At least I have the good sense to get out of here."

She walked toward the wide door. Turning only to wave a short goodbye, she disappeared.

I listened to the voices behind the drapes separating my bed from my new roommate's. She and her mother were discussing how she was having an operation to put arches in her feet.

I broke out my new copy of *Gone with the Wind* and soon forgot all about what was going on around me. I was in the Deep South, waiting for the Yankees to invade the plantation. But my time in the Civil War was interrupted by a priest who came to ask if I wanted holy communion before my surgery in the morning.

"No, I don't think I'll have enough time," I told him. "They say my operation is first thing in the morning."

"They'll wait for me if I tell them to," the priest replied.

"I'd really just rather get it over with, if you don't mind," I answered.

"I don't mind, but the Lord will. Won't your parents be disappointed if they can't take communion with you when something so important is about to happen?" he pressed.

"They don't really get involved in things very much," I said.

"Oh, they'll be involved when it comes to something like this. How did the accident happen that broke your nose?" he asked.

"It wasn't an accident. My parents are mad because they said I did it to myself by rubbing my nose too hard when it itched. But then the doctor said nobody could do this to their own nose, no matter how hard they rubbed."

"So, what broke it?"

"Nobody knows."

"Nobody knows, and that's the end of it?" Suddenly, he reached for my hand atop the blanket and said softly, "Jamie, dear child, young girls' noses don't just break all by themselves. God knows how this happened to your face. Those who did this to you will be held accountable in the next life."

He continued to hold my hand while he said a silent prayer over me and blessed me. He didn't question me any further about communion the next morning or about joining my parents before the surgery.

When the nurse came in to administer my sleeping medications, I was nearly nodding off already. I read my book until the print on the pages was too blurry for me to see.

In the middle of the night, I awoke to a nurse standing at the end of my bed.

"Are you all ready for tomorrow?" the nurse asked. "If you're frightened about anything, you can ask me what's going to happen."

"No, I'm fine. I don't really get scared about gory stuff. I've spent a lot of time around people who are a lot worse off than I'm going to be," I told her.

"Okay," the nurse replied, but I could see that she looked confused.

"I live in a mortuary. Nothing about blood and stuff bothers me."

"Sleep tight," the nurse said.

At the crack of dawn, nurses, orderlies, nuns, and interns converged on my room en masse. Even though I was the patient, nobody spoke to me.

Mother and Daddy said they would see me before I went into surgery, but they were not at the hospital when the gurney rolled from my room to wide double doors under a sign that read "Surgery."

I hope someone notices that I'm not asleep yet. The nurses are getting everything ready to start the operation and I'm wide awake. I wonder if I should say something in case they think I am asleep.

I recognized the doctor when he came in.

"Nurse, remove my wrist watch, will you? It's not shock resistant. I don't want to break it when we begin the fracture," the doctor said.

Fracture! There's going to be a fracture and I'm still awake!

The nurse pulled the elasticized band of the doctor's watch over his gloved hand, being careful that the jewelry and the latex didn't touch.

With his watch secured, he ordered, "Mallet."

Daddy was right. They do use mallets to break people's bones. He's going to smash me in the face with a mallet while I'm wide awake. I can't wait any longer. I have to speak up.

Mustering all my courage, I said quietly to the nurse, "Hi. Did you know I was awake."

"Of course you're awake," the doctor interrupted. "You'll choke on the blood if you're asleep. Just remember to keep swallowing. If you get too much blood in your stomach, we'll go after it later."

They aren't going to put me to sleep. I'm going to be

awake when they break my nose. And, just exactly what does he mean about "going after" stuff in my stomach?

"This won't put you to sleep. It'll just numb your nose so you can't feel the procedure," the doctor stated flatly. "This is going to hurt," he continued as he aimed a syringe with the longest needle I'd ever seen. My eyes crossed as I followed it coming closer and closer to my face until it hit its target, the skin separating my nostrils. The pain was so intense, I gasped as he inserted the needle to administer the local anesthetic.

My composure evaporated in a second. I could feel hot tears running from my eyes into the bonnet covering my hair.

If Mother and Daddy find out I cried in public, they're really going to be mad at me. Crying in a hospital is almost as bad as crying at a mortuary. Think about the pink chair. Think about the pink chair. Think about the pink chair.

I didn't feel myself sinking into the cold, hard table beneath me. I couldn't feel myself disappearing into the floor beneath it. No matter how hard I concentrated, I couldn't tap into my best defense when I needed it most.

It's so different here. People are talking and rattling instruments right next to my ears. I can't slow my breathing down. If I can't be the pink chair, I'm just going to keep on crying, and that's making everything worse.

For four hours, I watched and listened and thought I was going to drown in my own blood.

"Keep swallowing. Keep swallowing," the doctor commanded. "Don't cough, just swallow. We can get it later."

After several strikes of the mallet, I watched as the doctor stood back to assess his work.

"This is much too long," he pronounced. "The tip is much too sharp."

I went cross-eyed watching a little saw with a long handle get closer and closer to my face. Then I heard the grinding back and forth, back and forth as it narrowed the bone in my nose. Then, I watched the doctor use an oversized pair of tweezers to pull a bloody piece of tissue from my nostril.

"That should take care of that sharp point," the doctor told the nurse.

When I moved my arms to begin feeling my face, they jerked back down onto the hard table.

My hands are strapped down. I can't move my arms. They can do whatever they want to me and I can't even push them away.

When I coughed to clear my throat of the hot liquid pouring down it, red splattered the doctor, the nurse and the equipment surrounding them.

"Stop coughing. Stop that," the doctor yelled. "Keep swallowing. We'll get the blood later."

As he held my chin in his hand to examine his work before continuing to shape my nose, the doctor turned my head away from him. It was then that I spotted it. I blinked as hard as I could to clear my eyes of the tears streaming from them. Then I stared deliberately at the sight just across the room.

I can't believe I missed it all this time. But what is the baby doing in here? Did somebody else put their baby in a jar of formaldehyde? And, if they did, why is it here?

I stopped struggling to get my hands free from the straps holding them to the table. Even though it tasted terrible, I started swallowing the blood running down my throat like the doctor ordered me to do. Even the tears stopped running down my cheeks into my hairline.

I stared at the glassful of liquid across the room as hard as I could. Is there a baby in there? I think it's floating around in there just like the one in the embalming room!

I strained my eyes as hard as I could to try to catch a glimpse of it as it drifted around in the liquid. I could see it. The light bounced off the side of the glass container in a straight line. The liquid it contained floated perfectly still. The baby it supported came in and out of my view. My recollection of the pink chair became crystal clear in my mind. I felt myself sinking into it, becoming it. The pores of my skin united with the grain of the wood beneath the pink paint. My breath came in long, slow patterns that slowed my heart rate as well. My fists began to unclench beneath the straps holding them to the table. In the midst of the chaos of the operating room, I had disappeared. I wasn't dead, but I wasn't alive, either. I simply wasn't.

I didn't reappear until I was out of the operating room, down the hall, and entering the hospital room I left hours ago.

"What did you do to my daughter, you son of a bitch," I heard. I opened my eyes to see Mother and Daddy beside my hospital bed. I wasn't on the table anymore. My hands were free. The hot liquid wasn't running down my throat, choking me. The baby in the glass jar was out of view now.

My father was moving menacingly close to the doctor's

face. His fists were clinched as though he were going to punch him. Mother was crying, holding Daddy's arm to keep him from launching a blow.

What's happening? Why is Daddy mad at the doctor? Mother loves doctors. Why is she crying? Daddy doesn't usually care what people do to me.

The doctor looked at me, then back at my parents. "She bled profusely," he said flatly. "She'll be fine as soon as the bruising and swelling subsides."

Weeks later, the bruising gradually ebbed, the swelling receded, and I felt fine, except for the bandages that still covered the middle of my face.

"I can't wait to see how your nose looks under those bandages," Mother said.

"We'll know after today. Of course, anything would be an improvement," was Daddy's chuckled rejoinder.

"Rosarita, are you going to the doctor with us? They're taking the bandages off. I bet my nose is going to look just like yours," I said. "Even Daddy is going with us. Come on."

"I'm not riding all that way in the hot car just to find out you look as bad as you always did. You didn't even choose a new nose from the catalog like I told you to. I've seen your old face one too many times already. I'll wait here in the cool house to see it again."

My parents and I made the long, hot trip to Phoenix in the family sedan without Rosarita. I hoped we would use the Cadillac limousine with air conditioning, but no one suggested it.

On this visit to the doctor, Mother didn't stop to admire the koi pond in the courtyard or marvel at the intricate architecture of the clinic building. Daddy was all business, too.

"Jamie," the nurse called out sweetly when it was time for me to see the doctor.

"We'll come along, too," Daddy stated. He was already out of his waiting room chair and walking toward her before she could respond. "Mother, you come, too," Daddy ordered.

All three of us packed into the tiny examination room where the doctor would remove my bandages. I was eager to see how much I now resembled my family.

"Doctor," Daddy said with a nod when the white-coated man entered.

The doctor ignored Mother and Daddy and went straight to the table where I was perched on the edge.

"How are you feeling? Have you had any more bleeding?" he asked me.

"No, I'm not bleeding anymore. I feel pretty good except for these bandages. They're getting itchy."

"Oh God, we don't want that to happen. You'll start rubbing it around like before and mash it right back to the way it was," Daddy interjected.

Again, the doctor completely ignored him.

"Let's get these off," he said directly to me. He drew a long-handled pair of scissors with rounded tips from his pocket.

"Are you sure you want to stay in here when I remove the splints on the inside? It won't be pleasant," the doctor asked, finally recognizing my parents.

"Oh, we can take it," Daddy remarked. "We're in the

funeral business, you know," he continued conversationally.

The doctor didn't reply; instead, he shone a light up my nostrils.

"Tip your head back for me," he ordered.

He inserted the longest tweezers I had ever seen into my nose. From one nostril and then the next, he slowly dragged the splints from my face.

I couldn't help but grimace when the stench hit me. Blood trapped for weeks by the splints reeked like rotten meat.The doctor saw me squint in revulsion. He almost broke into a smile when Mother turned white.

"It looks good," was his assessment as he moved from side to side to gain various angles of my newly-revealed nose.

"Do you want to see it?" he asked me.

"We do, too," Daddy interrupted from his seat behind the doctor.

Again ignoring him, the doctor handed me a mirror and said, "Take a look."

When I looked into the mirror, the sharp-nosed girl I expected to see was not in the reflection. Instead, it was the same old Jamie, except her nose was now straight.

Although my profile was the same from both sides once the bandages were removed, I still looked nothing like anyone else in my family, except Carol.

I went through all of that misery and my nose is not pointed or long like everyone else's.

The doctor didn't wait for comment from me or my parents. He ripped the searchlight from his head and took the few steps to the door.

"I'll see her again in another month," he said to the nurse in the hallway. Then he warned me, "Don't bump that nose. It's still not completely healed."

"Okay," I replied quietly. My parents and I rode back to Tempe through the desert heat without uttering a sound.

"Told you so," Rosarita laughed when I walked into the living room where she was watching television. "It looks just like it did before. You should have picked out a new one."

There was no danger that I would bump my new nose. I seldom left my bedroom in the weeks after the bandages came off. I played the piano a little and read books for hours, but I didn't feel like being around other people now. I didn't have the energy to talk to them.

"You'd better perk up, Chatterbox, and quit sulking around the house like something's wrong," Daddy warned. "You know, you could show a little gratitude. Your mother was very upset to see you all bruised and bloody like that. And let's not forget that your sisters received a watch for their fourteenth birthday gift. It cost me a hell of a lot more than that to straighten out your nose. That was some expensive gift. Next time I'll get you a watch and save myself some money. "

"I'm sorry, Daddy. I'm glad you gave me the operation instead of a watch. I was just hoping my nose would look like yours. It looks like Carol's. I'm just surprised, that's all," I said.

"That's all we need around here—another pug nose. I should get my money back from that bastard doctor. I don't know what he did to you in that operating room, but you looked like you'd gone through the windshield of a car when we caught up with you in the hospital. Believe me, I've seen plenty of car crash victims and you were a dead ringer for one of them." After a short pause, he continued, "At least I'm glad it didn't kill you. Those windshield cases are a bitch to get ready for an open casket. I'm the only guy in town who can use a little wax and makeup and keep them from looking like a freak of nature at their own funerals," he went on, "but it takes a hell of a lot of effort. I'm not up for one of those cases right now. I'm tired." He flopped down into his overstuffed chair to prove his point.

Everyone enjoyed a hearty laugh, and the discussion of my surgical outcome ended permanently.

Chapter Fourteen

Home Economics

I cowered, sweating, in the doorway of a classroom filled with sewing machines. Beyond them, I spotted another room divided into eight kitchens.

"Don't be shy. Come in and find a seat behind any machine," called the most perfectly groomed woman I had ever seen. Every hair on her head was teased and sprayed into a flawless bubble. The makeup on her eyes, cheeks, and lips precisely matched the colors in her madras plaid shift. She floated to the door with a gait that was a testament to hours of practice with books on her head. Neither the two-inch spike heels nor the sharply pointed toes of her pumps encumbered her graceful glide across the room. I recognized the alligator logo on the sweater draped across her shoulders as she neared us.

The only people I've seen look this great were dead. People don't walk around with their hair, makeup, and clothing perfectly matched unless they're about to be buried.

"Cool!" "She's pretty." "I'm gonna like this class," came the voices of the popular girls behind me.

These girls think they look just like her. They see their rat's nest hairdos, raccoon eyes, and glittery braces as equal to her perfection.

"Crap!" "Don't tell me she's our teacher." "This is waste of time," came the voices of the creepy girls beside me.

Creepy girls know they'll never look as good as her. They see their greasy hair, pimply skin, and chapped lips as insurmountable obstacles to social acceptance.

"Get out of the way. Go in. Are you going to just stand here?" I heard as the traffic jam I created at the door became larger.

School is the one place I excel. Now we have to do this kind of stuff, I'll never make it. I need books and tests, not sewing machines and ovens.

I grabbed the first chair I stumbled across and piled my notebooks next to the machine before me. I stared at the line drawings of dresses on the walls and the plastic bins lining the shelves. To my horror, one of the bins already had my name written on it.

"These totes store all your sewing materials, girls," Miss Perfect pointed out. "I know, they look like plastic bins, but we decorate them up real cute and then they look more like fashionable totes, don't you think?"

She makes up names for things she doesn't like. I wonder if she has a cute name for kids like us. She knows we can't be "decorated up real cute," so I bet she doesn't.

Before her stood a long table piled with paint, glitter, yarn, stickers, markers, plastic flowers, construction paper, pipe cleaners, and popsicle sticks.

"You can use any of these materials to customize your

tote so you'll always recognize it as yours," she said. "This is our first adventure in creating beauty from the simplest of things. That's what homemakers do. Now that you are taking home economics, you can learn all the secrets of turning a house into a home. So let's make these plain old bins into totes we can be proud of." She waved her arm across the colorful array before her.

The popular girls squealed with delight, plunging headlong into the materials. Within seconds, one of them created a girl with popsicle sticks for a body, a plastic flower for a head, and glitter on a triangle of construction paper for a dress. Another one bent pipe cleaners into her initials and drew in little hearts for the periods after each letter.

"Keep going, girls, you're doing a fantastic job," Miss Perfect cheered. She circled the table, watching us transform our bins into totes.

Mine still looked like a bin, and I had no notion of how to make it look any better.

"Reach in, Sugar, don't let these loud girls push you aside," Miss Perfect egged me on. "You all are so grabby," she giggled as she winked at the popular girls.

"Another part of being a good homemaker is time management, ladies, so keep your eye on the clock. You need to finish before the bell rings."

I looked desperately at my bin. The class period was almost over and I hadn't added anything to it.

"Clean up time, girls," Miss Perfect chimed. "A clean home is a beautiful home," she carried on.

I grabbed the bottle of white glue, squished out a huge blob of it onto my bin and dumped the entire contents of the red glitter bottle on top of it. Anything that didn't stick, I swept onto the floor.

"Everyone put your totes away," the teacher shouted above the blasting of the bell.

I jammed mine onto the shelf with the others.

"These are adorable. Look how cute they are all lined up like this," Miss Perfect began. "Why, Miss Maguire, I believe you used every bit of my red glitter."

The red shimmers that didn't stick to the glue were not on the floor, as I intended, but down the front of my gathered skirt, and even atop my white Keds. There were so many of them they fell as I walked, leaving a shiny red trail from my seat to the classroom door.

"Sorry," I mumbled while I shook my skirt. The specks fell from my cotton dress, but stuck tight to the canvas of my sneakers.

"Look at this, you guys. Jamie has red glitter shoes," one popular girl called out. "Click your heels and see if you go back to Kansas."

"She's just being creative, now. Don't make fun," Miss Perfect corrected.

I can't tell if she's defending me or mocking me. I couldn't see if she winked at the popular girls again. I think I'm part of their inside joke.

While I fled for the safety of my English class, the usual din of the hallway lowered a bit. I saw the popular girls from my home ec class walking arm in arm. Everyone laughed as they skipped by me. As they passed, I heard them singing, as loudly as they could, "Follow the Yellow Brick Road." Everyone caught on to the joke and sang along. The hallway was alive with their taunting.

Most of these kids don't even know why they're singing. They just want to copy whatever the popular girls are doing so they can be popular, too.

I ran to my next class as fast as my red glittered shoes would carry me.

When I got home from school, I raced past Mother as fast as I could and shut my bedroom door behind me.

"What's wrong with you?" Mother demanded as I flew past her.

I grabbed Rosarita's nail brush and scrubbed furiously at my red-speckled sneakers. The top layer came off quickly, but some of the glitter was so small that the brush embedded it into the canvas.

If anyone finds out about home ec, I'll have to live through the taunting all over again. I have to destroy the evidence or my family's going to make fun of me, too.

Rosarita's nail brush had no upright bristles any more. They curled out to either side from the pressure I'd placed on them. Specks of shiny red told the tale of how they became so freakishly bent.

As I rummaged through our closet trying to find a good hiding place for my ruined Keds, I spotted Rosarita's bottle of white shoe polish on the shelf next to her pumps. I grabbed it with relief, tore the cap off, and shook it violently to get the liquid to saturate the spongy applicator. I spread shoe polish as thick as I could over the canvas, rubber edging, and even the laces of my sneakers. The white liquid completely obscured the remaining glitter. The only trace of color left on my shoes was the dingy soles on the bottom.

I stepped back to admire my handiwork. I had created a masterpiece that would disguise the day's events in class.

"Can you at least show some common courtesy now?" Mother asked when I emerged from the bedroom, once again breathing normally. "I thought you were going to mow me down before."

"I was just anxious to get started on my homework. This year my classes are harder than before. I'll have to study more to keep my grades up," I lied.

"In the higher grades, they just expect that you know a few things related to real life. You can't keep your nose buried in your beloved books all the time and expect to do well in classes like home ec. Didn't you enjoy learning something useful for a change?"

"Yeah, it was fine."

"Don't bubble over with enthusiasm. If I asked you about English, I bet you'd ramble on for days about literature or essays."

"Sorry."

"Don't be sorry. Tell me what you did in home ec. I loved that class when I was young. I could take it all over again just for fun."

"We made totes out of plastic bins."

"You got to decorate your own sewing box. That's darling. I can still remember how I glued yarn to spell out my name in cursive when I first learned to sew. Everybody loved it. Other girls tried to copy it, but the teacher saw I did it first and made them take theirs off. I was the teacher's pet. She favored me even more when she saw what a good seamstress I was."

We ate dinner as usual with the black and white Zenith turned toward the kitchen so we could watch and eat at the same time.

"How was school, girls?" Daddy asked.

"Boring as usual," Rosarita griped.

Daddy smiled. "I should have known you'd say that."

"My English teacher is kind of cute," Rosarita volunteered. "All the rest of them just ramble on about stuff I don't care about."

"What about home ec? I bet that was interesting," Mother tried.

"It was better than the rest of them, but I still didn't like it. They want us to learn how to run a nursery school. I don't want to make little kids as miserable as we are. Why don't they just let them run and play like they want instead of cooping them up, trying to make them say abc's and listen to dumb rhymes," Rosarita answered.

Daddy shook his head and chuckled. "That's my girl. You wish you were outside instead of being cooped up, too. We've got quite the young scholar here, Mother."

I don't mind if they forget I went to school today, too. The less I have to say about my classes, the better.

I nearly forgot about the stress of the first day of my new school year until I got dressed the following morning. Minutes before we had to pile in the car, I dared to rummage to the back of the closet to retrieve my sneakers. They looked great! Now that the polish was dried, they looked brand new. I couldn't see red glitter anywhere.

I jammed my foot into the left one and grabbed for the laces. As I did, I heard a crackling noise. The laces were stiff with shoe polish.

As I wrestled the resistant laces into a bow, a patch of white speckles appeared on the bedroom floor beneath me. When I took my first step, the brittle coating on top of my shoe broke into a million pieces. With each step I took, more and more polish fell off. By the time I made it to the front door and into the car, I'd left a trail of white that tracked my path exactly.

Mother's going to find this when she gets back. Everyone's going to know what I did!

The popular girls were gathered by the lockers where they could watch everyone come into the school. One of them called out, "Hi, Jamie. See you in home ec."

This cued the others to recall yesterday's fiasco. High-pitched laughter and snippets of the tale of the red glitter reached me, but I pressed ahead. I watched my shoes as I scrambled past them. With each step, more of the white polish came off and more of the red glitter reappeared.

I tried to tuck my feet into the book shelf underneath my desk in first period math.

"Cool shoes," I heard someone say. Across the aisle of

210

desks sat a boy wearing a leather-fringed vest. His notebook was covered in a tie-dyed rainbow pattern.

"Me?" I asked as quietly as I could.

"Yeah, cool shoes," he repeated. He thrust his Converse hightops into the aisle and I gasped to see them covered in Magic Marker peace signs.

Neither of us spoke another word to each other, but the knot in my stomach began to ease as the teacher worked out problems on the blackboard.

When the bell rang for my next class, home ec, I decided not to try to cover my goofed up shoes.

The popular girls don't like me, anyway. I don't care what they say about my shoes.

Miss Perfect greeted us at the door, winding a tape measure through her fingers.

At least this isn't some new creativity I can screw up. I know how to measure stuff.

"Line up quickly, girls. We need to get your measurements so you can choose your patterns," she announced.

The popular girls ran to be first in line. Miss Perfect asked for a volunteer to write the numbers as she called them out. The most popular of the popular girls crowded her way to the tablet on the teacher's desk.

"I'm ready when you are," she giggled.

"You're always ready, aren't you?" Miss Perfect chuckled as they winked at each other affectionately.

The first girl approached the desk with confidence. I couldn't hear what Miss Perfect said to her, but she suddenly pulled herself into an exaggerated posture that thrust her chest out further than the rest of her body. Miss Perfect stepped closer to her and wrapped the tape measure beneath the girl's outstretched arms.

"Thirty," Miss Perfect called out to the girl with the tablet. *She's measuring how big our boobs are and yelling it out to everybody in class! That popular girl is writing it down.*

I gawked in horror as Miss Perfect moved the tape to the waist and finally to the hips. She told the tablet girl every measurement as she moved down the torso. She moved quickly, but not quickly enough that the popular girls didn't have time to comment on each girl's figure.

"Sexy," one of them laughed as a girl about the size of an average first-grader stood red-faced before Miss Perfect.

"Is that tape long enough?" another shouted out when a Mexican girl with breasts bigger than Miss Perfect's stepped up. All the popular girls laughed until the teacher shot them a disapproving look.

"Forty five!" the girl with the tablet repeated loudly when Miss Perfect told her the measurement. The popular girls put their hands over their mouths or turned their faces to the wall, trying to contain their laughter.

"Let's all be ladylike," Miss Perfect warned. By now, the Mexican girl's skin had turned from caramel brown to ashen gray. She didn't make eye contact with anyone as she returned, slump shouldered, to her desk.

No one, skinny or buxom, dared comfort the Mexican girl. The popular girls were the judges of who was cool and who was not. The other girls and I watched helplessly as girls of every size, shape, and color received their evaluation.

"And, Jamie," Miss Perfect gushed as I shuffled toward her when everyone else was measured.

I tried to focus on the wall behind her to avoid looking straight into her face when she was close enough to wrap the tape around me. I knew the number she would call out would be smaller than everyone else in the class. I put my arms out straight as she told me. I looked down and saw a long tail of tape dangling loosely down my body as Miss Perfect held the rest of it taut to measure my bustline. The knot in my stomach was so tight I could scarcely breathe.

I hate this class more than anything I've ever endured. At least in the pink chair no one else can watch me and laugh.

"Did you say twenty eight?" the tablet girl yelled out to Miss Perfect.

Miss Perfect nodded silently.

"I thought you might have said thirty eight because she's so tall, but then I looked at how skinny she is and I got all confused. I just wanted to write down the right number," the tablet girl giggled on. The other popular girls were starting to titter.

"She's tall, but she's no bigger than a minute," Miss Perfect said. "You know, models are tall and skinny. Jamie's going to be an attractive woman some day."

"Not today," one of the popular girls mumbled under her breath, causing the others to laugh out loud.

Miss Perfect tried to save me, but nothing can stop the popular girls. The boy with the peace sign shoes and my home ec teacher want to rescue me, but they can't. If things get too bad, I know how to rescue myself, though. I can use my pink chair trick and not even see these people.

Sewing could have been interesting if I didn't know how critical Mother would be. I managed to stretch my material across the long cutting tables and pin my tissue paper pattern onto it before Mother demanded a retelling of each halting step I took.

"Did you stretch the fabric diagonally and tug on it before you placed your pattern pieces on it?"

"No, but I was real careful how I cut it."

"You already cut your material? Oh good Lord, I bet you didn't have it on the fabric correctly."

"The teacher said it was okay to cut."

"The teacher doesn't know how flighty you are when it comes to practical things. I bet you slapped the pattern on and cut it out just so you could finish and get back to your books."

"I'll be more careful from now on."

Mother phoned Carol to commiserate about all the sewing errors she presumed I'd made. I could hear her through my bedroom door.

"She cut the material without letting me see it first. Can't you just imagine what it's going to look like?" Mother paused long enough for Carol to answer.

"What do you mean? Girls can take their sewing home for their mothers to check. Rosarita did it all the time. How do you think she got such good grades in home ec? I re-sewed everything she brought home. It was so poorly done."

Again, Mother paused while Carol spoke.

"I think she better quit spending so much time worrying about the school rules and figure out how to get that fabric home to me, or it will be a complete mess."

I learned how to trace my pattern onto the fabric, sew in darts to make room for boobs I didn't have, and blind stitch the hem of my blouse without incident. But I hated every minute I spent in the sewing lab.

It's only a matter of time until I screw this up so bad Mother and the popular girls will see how dumb I am at anything except books.

"Line up, ladies," Miss Perfect called out as she swept back a floor-to-ceiling curtain at the end of the sewing machines. "Today, we're going to try on our new blouses, and tomorrow we start practicing how we'll model them for our mothers at the tea next week."

Behind the curtain was a row of full length mirrors. Ten girls at a time drew the curtain behind them, tried on the blouses they made, and walked out for everyone else to see. The popular girls made a beeline for the curtained area. Twelve of them crammed into a space meant for ten. They screamed and giggled as they ripped off their expensive clothes to reveal lacy, pastel-colored bras with cups larger than I had ever seen.

"I hope my boobs can fit into this," I heard one of them yell. An answer rang out from behind the curtain. "If they don't, you can just model your bra. It's big enough to be a bikini top."

"Let's allow everyone to have some time in front of the mirror, girls. You've been in there long enough," Miss Perfect remonstrated.

One of the popular girls peeked out from behind the curtain. She glared at the group where I stood.

"We have to hurry so the creeps can get in here," she whined to her friends. "I don't think they should be allowed in the fashion show. Nobody wants to look at them, anyway. One of them can't even walk around without looking at the floor the whole time. Maybe she's checking what color is coming off her shoes, red or white."

"We're hurrying," they giggled, pushing the curtain aside while many were still dressing. They strolled out still buttoning their clothes over their ample chests and adult-size bras.

I stepped behind the curtain with the other creeps. We turned our backs to each other so no one had to bear the humiliation of revealing our training bras. We relinquished our street clothes and struggled into our sewing projects in silence. The odor of fear wafted through the room as sweaty armpits huddled inside poorly constructed blouses.

"Now, girls, we walk slowly, with our chests held high, as we approach the platform," Miss Perfect shouted over her shoulder as she demonstrated how we should model our clothes. She stepped up the two steps on the wooden platform in the middle of the room. "Watch carefully, ladies, and do exactly as I do," she instructed as she placed her feet perfectly and executed a pivot so all sides of her clothing were visible.

"You see? That's not so bad," she encouraged.

The popular girls couldn't wait to duplicate our teacher's moves. I glanced up long enough to see the creeps beside me. I was certain the last creep in line was going to throw up any minute, so I moved closer to the back. We began the march to the platform with the enthusiasm of those stepping up to the gallows.

"Heads high, chests out, smiles toward the audience," Miss Perfect coached as the popular girls charged out to the limelight as we creeps straggled along behind them. "It's almost time for the bell to ring. Everybody change back to school clothes. We're all girls in here. Don't wait to get behind the curtain; just change at your desk. The other teachers will be mad at me if I make you tardy for your next class."

Clothes flew through the air. The popular girls ran between the sewing machines trying to snap the elastic on each other's bra straps. The creeps and I tried to get our blouses off and another one on without exposing our flat chests. When the bell rang, we bolted to the hallway, desperate to get out. I didn't care that I'd buttoned mine so that one side of my shirttail was much longer than the other. I could hide in the bathroom and fix that later. At least I was out of the horrors of the home ec room.

"When do we get to see your masterpiece?" Rosarita goaded that evening. "Are you going to model for everyone?"

"Shut up, Rosarita. You know they're making us show our moms what we made. It's not a fashion show with models and everything," I mumbled.

"You are practicing how to walk and turn, aren't you, Jamie?" Mother joined in. "You have a hard time looking up when you walk. I hope your blouse is sewn correctly. Most people in town know I make your clothes; they'll be expecting a good job from you, too."

"I don't want to talk about it, you guys," I muttered under my breath as I headed for my room.

Mother questioned me about the fashion show every day. "Are you practicing your walk? Are you going to wear lipstick? Is your blouse too plain without some accessorizing?"

"I'm sure it's too plain. I picked the easiest pattern so it would be easy to sew," I answered.

"You're going to need something to jazz it up a little."

"Okay."

"How about these pearls?" Mother held up a string of slightly yellowed fakes. "I've been saving them in case your father ever took me to a place where we could get dressed up, but we all know that's never going to happen."

"You don't have to give them to me, Mother. I'm sure Daddy will take you some place nice eventually."

"He hasn't in the last twenty years; I can't imagine him starting now."

"Aren't you going to feel bad if you give up your pearls and then Daddy wants you to get dressed up?"

"No, just go ahead and take them. He's not really married to me. He's married to the mortuary. I don't know why I ever bought them in the first place."

"Okay, I'll just borrow them for the fashion show and then give them back to you. I don't ever go anywhere dressy, either."

Rosarita laughed until Mother shot her a look that sobered her up.

"I was just thinking about where Jamie would go with her pearls," Rosarita defended herself.

"Well, we don't need anyone making Jamie feel bad about her sewing. I know she struggled with it," Mother said.

The day of the fashion show, my stomach was so knotted I could scarcely stand up straight.

Miss Perfect is going to be so mad at me if I don't do everything just right. Step, step, turn, pause, step, step.

Through math class and even English, all I could think was the sequence of movements and the posture and the facial expression I was to maintain while modeling my blouse. When the bell rang for third period, home ec, my hands started to tingle.

My nails can't get any shorter. If I count, I'll look down. But I can think about the pink chair. I could be the chair again and not have to experience the nightmare ahead of me.

I heard the popular girls squealing with delight before I reached the curtained room. I didn't spot Mother among the ladies in the folding chairs, but I knew she was there. I changed my blouse with as much modesty as I could and pulled Mother's pearls from my purse. Slowly, I worked my way past the popular girls and the little band of creeps gathered in the corner until I reached a spot where I could see myself in the mirror. I leaned in toward the mirror and threaded the hook through the clasp.

"Everyone line up," Miss Perfect commanded. The creeps could not have looked any unhappier had they been lining up to face a firing squad. The popular girls wore enough makeup and perfume to asphyxiate the entire group.

"Oh, one last thing." Miss Perfect interrupted my inner dialogue. "The last girl in the modeling line must say, 'Now please join us for cookies and punch' to the moms."

I wasn't so smart after all. I let everybody go ahead of me in the line and now I have to invite the moms too. Rehearsal raged in my mind. Step, step, turn, step, step, now please join us for cookies and punch. Step, step, turn, step, step, now please join us for cookies and punch.

The popular girls thrust their giant boobs straight out and grinned broadly as they mounted the platform and turned slowly for everyone to admire their blouses. I stood rigidly, repeating the mantra of instructions. A soft sound interrupted my practicing. Something bounced off the tile floor beneath our feet. After the first slight ping came several more in quick succession. Yellowy pearl beads rolled from the dressing room out to the floor and the platform. I gasped and quickly grasped the neck of my blouse. All I had left was a clasp with a broken string hanging down each side.

The popular girls waited on the other side of the platform for the creeps and me to do our modeling. The first creep stepped out from the dressing room to make her way to the platform. I replayed the sequence of stepping and turning in my mind in an effort to get both of us through the experience. As she began her second step, her foot landed on one of the pearls. She slid, arms flailing wildly, until she did a split. Her ample thigh slapped onto the floor with the sound of Jell-o plopping out of a mold. Pearls rolled crazily in every direction from her landing spot. Not even the meanest of the popular girls cracked a smile. The silence in the room was deafening.

"Oopsy," chirped Miss Perfect as she pushed the rest of the creeps toward the platform. Everyone stared at the floor, trying to avoid the beads. The creeps nearly ran across the platform and collapsed into the waiting arms of their group on the other side of the room. The show ended in a matter of seconds.

I approached the platform at the same brisk pace as the last girls, studying the floor intensely before each step. I heaved a sigh of relief heard throughout the room. But, then I saw Miss Perfect gesturing maniacally. I was the last model in line. I had to invite the moms for tea.

Having abandoned my mental recitation of the steps and the turns in light of the pearl fiasco, I couldn't remember what I was supposed to say. My face was so red it burned as students, mothers, and teacher alike stared at me expectantly.

"Now please join us for cook and punchies," I blurted out shakily. I wasn't sure I'd made a mistake until the crowd erupted into laughter.

Even the creep who did the splits minutes before joined in the mockery; I guess I got paid back for what I did to her. Mother inhaled a cookie in one bite, grabbed her purse from under the folding chair, and bolted for the door before I could even talk to her.

By dinnertime that night, Rosarita and Daddy would have an entire comedy routine worked up about pearls and punchies. I gritted my teeth and approached the lion's den at the kitchen table.

"What's new, girls?" Daddy began his usual conversation.

Here it comes. He's going to get Rosarita to tell the story instead of him.

"Nothing," Rosarita and Mother answered robotically.

"What about you, Chatterbox?" he directed at me.

I*s this a trap?   Can I possibly get away with silence? Surely Mother told everyone about my mess ups.*

My mouth was so dry, I couldn't speak.   I shook my head silently.

"What's new with you, Daddy?" Rosarita mercifully continued the same conversation we had every evening.

Daddy launched into his monologue on affairs of the day. Not one person at the table mentioned the fashion show, the tea, or the pearls.

I am getting away with this.   Mother didn't tell.

We finished our meal, cleared the table, washed and dried the dishes, and hauled the garbage out to the cans in the alley with no deviation from our daily pattern.

After we gave Daddy his good night kiss, Mother caught my eye as I walked past her toward my room.   She didn't say anything, but she smiled at me with a conspiratorial glint in her expression.

I'd humiliated myself so much at school that she spared me the derision I faced at home.   Tears of relief gushed from my eyes as I scrambled into bed, turned my face into the pillow, and sobbed myself to sleep.

Chapter Fifteen

Secret Meetings

"How would you girls like a job?" Daddy asked.

"Okay," Rosarita and I answered in unison.

"We're going to be having a little meeting here. You know how I'm an officer on the school board? Instead of meeting at the school, the board is meeting at our house this time. You girls can serve cookies."

"Okay, Daddy," we repeated.

"Now, this meeting. It's going to be like a lot of other things around here. You can't repeat anything you hear. You can't even say that you saw the people at the meeting."

We don't care about anybody who comes here. Why do they have to have the meeting here and not at the mortuary? We can't even play our radios if they meet here.

"You girls just wait in your room, and Mother will tell you when it's time to come out. She's making coffee for everyone," Daddy said.

"When is everybody coming?" Rosarita ventured.

"Right now," Daddy stated. I noticed his voice had the edge it got when somebody called for an ambulance.

"Is everything all right, Daddy?" Rosarita pressed.

"Everything is going to be fine. There's nothing for any of you to worry about," he said, again in terse phrases usually reserved for hysterical callers begging him to rush the ambulance to an accident site.

Mother began her assigned task of making coffee; Rosarita and I retreated to our bedroom to wait for Mother's cue to come out.

It's weird being quiet when nobody's dead. Something is really wrong for Daddy to be acting like this about people who are alive.

Daddy stood guard at the front door so that those attending didn't even have to ring the doorbell. I heard him greet each of the attendees with the barely audible grunt he reserved for those he didn't really want to speak to.

"What's going on?" Rosarita asked me in a whisper. "Why are people coming over here all of a sudden, and Daddy doesn't seem happy when he lets them in?"

"I don't know what's happening, but it's not good. I can't recognize the voices of the people who are here. They're all men, though."

My bed was pressed against the wall it shared with the living room. It was the perfect vantage point for eavesdropping. I pressed my ear to the wall to increase the volume.

"It's about school. It's the high school board of education in there," I reported to Rosarita, who sat on the other bed.

"We should have known it would be something boring like that. Daddy thinks he shouldn't tell us about all the stuff they talk about in their school board meetings. Who cares?" Rosarita said.

"He's really afraid we're going to tell about this one," I responded.

"Why aren't they meeting at the school, anyway? There's a whole room there just for their meetings. I've seen it. It's right next to the principal's office," Rosarita complained.

"Be quiet. I want to hear what this is about," I whispered when I heard one of them say the meeting would begin.

Daddy had let in four board members, the principal, and the superintendent of the high school district. I knew that, with Daddy as the fifth member, the entire board was assembled in our living room.

Everyone spoke so softly, I could only pick up the interjections at first.

"Jesus Christ," one voice said softly.

"God damn it," another spat.

"Son of a bitch," came through the living room wall into our bedroom.

"I don't know what you're straining to hear. It's the school board in there. It's going to be something boring," Rosarita predicted.

"Wait, wait, stop talking," I urged. "They're talking louder now."

"It's about Mr. Garland," I relayed to my sister. "They're really mad at him. One guy sounds like he's going to cry," I reported.

After a pause for listening, I said, "He did something queer." I stopped whispering to listen again. "He ran an ad in the paper for a yard man. Did you see anything in the paper like that?"

"No. I don't even like the newspaper. It's boring, too," Rosarita grumbled.

"They say he did something queer to a man who answered his newspaper ad for a yard man. They won't say exactly what he did," I went on.

"Wait a minute." Rosarita suddenly sat up in her bed with a gleam in her eye. "Did they say Mr. Garland *did* something queer or he *is* a queer?"

I pressed my ear against the wall as close as I could.

"The guy that's about to cry just said it. He's said Mr. Garland *is* a queer."

Rosarita gasped.

"Act busy," I ordered as I heard Daddy approaching our bedroom door.

"We need to take a little break in here, girls. Why don't you go to the kitchen and Mother will tell you what to serve everyone," Daddy said when he poked his head in the door.

Minutes later, Rosarita began a parade from the kitchen carrying a tray of our best cups and saucers. Behind her came Mother with a thin trail of steam wafting from the spout of our percolator. I came last with a plate full of Mother's homemade oatmeal cookies. Rosarita flashed her dimpled smile at each of the men as she offered them a cup. Mother demurely kept her eyes on the coffee as she circled the room. I thrust the plate of cookies toward each of the men without uttering a word. I had no winning smile to deliver. Not one of the men reached for a cookie. With the cups filled and the cookies offered and rejected, we marched, single file, back to the kitchen.

"I'm not surprised they didn't want any cookies, Mother," I commented when we returned there. "Most of those men look like they're going to get sick. Rosarita and I will eat them, though. They're really good."

"You can each take one back to your room," Mother allowed. "I think the board members are a little too upset to eat right now." She offered no opinion as to why the men were anguished.

I resumed my fact-finding mission with my ear pressed to the thin wall.

"They're saying he'll get beat up if anyone else finds out he's a queer. They should make him move to protect him, one guy is saying. But how is he going to teach his classes if he doesn't live here anymore?" I asked.

"Because, moron, he's not going to teach anymore. They don't let queers teach school. I told you that before," Rosarita replied.

"But Mr. Garland's a really good teacher. They should ask the kids; they'd tell him he's a good teacher. He grades fair and he's nice. Why won't they let him be a teacher any more just because he's queer?"

"I don't know. But they won't," Rosarita stated flatly.

"You can't even live here anymore if you're queer?" I asked incredulously.

"Not unless you want to get beat up every day like that tap dancer," Rosarita said. "Believe me, it's that bad. Don't you remember when somebody beat up our tap dancing teacher? That's because he was a queer," Rosarita continued.

"He was? I never knew that," I said.

"Oh, yeah, he wasn't queer. He just taught tap dancing all day and got beat up in a men's room at night." Rosarita shot back sarcastically.

"I thought he was just a good dancer. I felt bad when somebody gave him those black eyes," I said.

"Queers do not get treated well around here. If Mr. Garland is one, they're probably planning how to beat him up right now," Rosarita predicted.

"The school board doesn't beat up people. He's a good teacher. They probably aren't going to do anything to him. I don't see what the big deal is. The yard man doesn't go to our school," I reasoned. "It doesn't matter what Mr. Garland did to him. He's nice to all of us."

"Oh yeah? Then why is the school board meeting here instead of school, where everybody can see them? They're going to do something really mean to him, you just wait and see," Rosarita warned.

How can something so awful happen so quickly? Mr. Garland is a good teacher. What difference does it make if he's queer?

"Let me listen," I whispered, holding my finger to my lips to hush Rosarita.

After a pause, I said, "They're going to do it in twenty-four hours. They're saying they're going to give him twenty-four hours."

"Are they going to beat him up in twenty-four hours?" Rosarita asked eagerly.

"I can't tell. Let me listen some more," I said.

"They're leaving," I reported when I heard the front door open. "It's over. They decided to make him lose his job and move out of town in one day. Now they're all just going home."

My sister and I stared at each other for several minutes. With everyone gone, Rosarita reached for the radio to tune in the rock and roll station she liked best.

"It's getting late. I'm going to bed," I said.

"It's not even nine o'clock," Rosarita argued.

"I know, but I'm tired," I lied.

I needed time to think without Rosarita constantly questioning me. Pretending to be asleep was the only way I could have some solitude.

Mr. Garland would have been better off to have killed the yard man. If he'd murdered somebody, he'd at least get a trial and be able to defend himself. He won't even get that. The school board found him guilty in a secret meeting and will send him into exile immediately. He won't even get a chance for parole in a few years.

I knew that Mr. Garland would never be allowed to return to Tempe High or any other school. His life was ruined. He was a teacher; that was his job. But somebody took it away from him without warning for actions I didn't fully understand. Just what was it about being queer that made people beat you up, or drive you out of town and your chosen profession?

What does a person have to do to avoid being plucked from their very existence? Miss Elaine was nice to kids, attended church regularly, tried to help others, but she was snatched out of this life by a truck. What else could she have done to have her life spared? Mr. Garland isn't dead, but maybe his fate is worse. Miss Elaine lives with the angels. Mr. Garland will have to keep moving until he finds a place where it's okay to be queer. Just where in the world is that?

Thoughts of hundreds of people I had seen lying on the tables in the embalming room filled my mind. In an avalanche of uncontrolled memories, I recalled the litany of tragedies I'd observed. Sure, the old people had lived out their natural life spans, but there were plenty who had not. The girl who was buried in her prom gown was just as nice as any of the other girls. What did Duane do to deserve living his life with only one arm? Surely the baby floating around in the formaldehyde couldn't have harmed anyone. Why did these people have to die or be maimed? When was it going to happen to me?

As my thoughts raced behind my closed eyes, I felt a tingling sensation in my hands. It was the same feeling I experienced when I became the pink chair.

Lying flat on my stomach with my head turned toward the wall where I'd eavesdropped only hours before, I directed my thoughts to one phrase. "Be the pink chair."

It began to work. My tingling hands became so heavy I could feel their weight denting the padding of my mattress. My breaths became deeper and deeper each time I inhaled. The oxygen coursing through my system made me feel much better. My tensed muscles began to uncoil, first unclenching my jaw and slowly working down my body until even my toes were flush with warmth. Rather than sinking into the chair, this time

I felt the starched and ironed sheets Mother fastidiously folded around my mattress begin to give way to a nourishing caress. My pajama top became a part of the sheets as I drifted further down. I passed through the ticking stripes of the mattress covering and disappeared into the cottony softness of its stuffing. I, as Jamie, no longer existed; I had become the bed the same way I had become the pink chair. Deep inside the shelter of the mattress, I fell into a sleep that lasted the rest of the night.

When I awoke early the next morning, I felt unusually rested and alert. I began my day without the anxiety that frequently crippled me.

I can be something else when I choose. If being Jamie is too painful, I know how to be an inanimate object. I can control this escape with my own mind. Oh, thank you, pink chair!

When I saw the substitute teacher in Mr. Garland's classroom the next day, I didn't tell any of my classmates about the meeting of the night before. The real estate agent who put the "For Sale" sign in Mr. Garland's front yard told everyone the same story the teachers at school were spreading—that Mr. Garland had gotten a better offer at a school in the East and had accepted it and left suddenly.

Many of my classmates were angry at Mr. Garland for not even saying goodbye to them when he found a better job.

"Maybe he'll come back and visit us this summer. I really miss him," one student said. "Do you think so, Jamie?"

I silently shrugged my shoulders.

Chapter Sixteen

Horseback Rides

Menstrual cramps made the pink chair worse than before. The embalming room was so cold that I huddled in pain, longing to get out. During the school year I rarely got trapped there, but summer, with my new maturity preventing trips to Tempe Beach for a week every month, increased my vulnerability to my assigned spot at Tthe Place.

"Mother," I shouted as I held the receiver out to her. "It's Carol. She wants me to come visit her. Please, oh please, oh please, say yes."

Carol and her husband had moved to a small town in the mountains where people went to escape the heat of Tempe summers. Covered in ponderosa pines, the area was a stark contrast to the barren desert only a few miles away. If I was allowed to visit my sister in Pine, I wouldn't have to spend every day at the pool or risk ending up in the pink chair until I could go back to Tempe Beach.

Besides that, I loved being around Carol. Ever since she'd married and moved away, I felt the sting of her absence in a million different ways.

Born during our mother's ill-fated first marriage, Carol

was named for the magical time of her birth, just days before Christmas. She didn't carry the name of someone dead like Rosarita and me. Carol, unlike the Maguires, valued life more than death, it seemed to me. She carried about her an eagerness to experience the world, not to avoid it, like others in my home.

"Carol, what is all this commotion about?" Mother said into the phone. I could tell by the irritated tone of her voice that the answer would not be favorable.

"You know how your father feels about little girls not being in their own beds at night," Mother told Carol.

I stood nervously by as I heard Carol's muffled answer through the phone.

"Come on, please," I silently mouthed to Mother.

"Well, I'll ask Daddy, but I'm sure he'll say no," Mother conceded.

Daddy wouldn't be home from work for hours, and I knew better than to interrupt him at the mortuary. I bounced around the house in anticipation, sometimes resorting to nail-biting to stand the anxiety.

When Daddy opened the back door to come to the dinner table that night, I could scarcely contain myself.

"Carol wants Jamie to come stay with them for awhile," Mother said sourly.

"Oh, Christ, not this thing about spending the night at someone else's house again. I have told you girls I don't want you to be anywhere at night except in your own bed in your own home," he stated.

"I know, Daddy, but this isn't like those slumber parties

you won't allow us to go to. This is my sister, and she's already a grown-up. I'm not going to be with a bunch of kids," I reasoned.

"Doesn't Carol have anything else to do to keep herself occupied? She just couldn't wait to get married and move away, and now she wants the rest of us to come trailing along after her," he grumbled.

"I'll be really good, Daddy. I won't cause her any trouble, I promise," I pleaded.

"Let me eat my dinner in peace, will you?" Daddy asked. "We'll talk about it when I'm finished with my meal."

He doesn't have a good enough reason to say I can't go. He's stalling for time to think of something.

"Have you decided yet?" I asked the second he took the last bite on his plate.

"I don't understand why you want to go live in a hick town when I've provided a perfectly nice place for you here." He paused, glaring at the refrigerator as he made up his mind, then said, "Go ahead, if that's what you want to do."

"Thank you, Daddy," I replied as solemnly as I could manage. I didn't risk jumping for joy like I wanted to, or Daddy would say I had insulted his home and change his mind.

A week later, a pickup truck pulled up in front of the mortuary. I couldn't wait to pile into the back of it as though I was part of the construction materials Carol's husband Henry was hauling back to Pine.

Henry needs this stuff to build cabins. I need it to build an escape from here.

"Put this scarf around your head," Carol warned before

we left. "I don't want Mother saying you got an ear infection because of the wind in the bed of the truck."

I wrapped the scarf around my head and tied it snugly under my chin.

Through the trailer parks on the outskirts of Tempe, past the miles of sand and cactus of the desert, and, finally into the pines we drove. I didn't mind that I couldn't hear anything but the rush of wind past my ears as I rode amid the lumber and tools. Henry stopped at a drive-in restaurant and bought me the biggest cup of soda I had ever seen.

"Use both hands or you'll drop it," Carol warned. "It has to last you all the way to Pine. We don't want to waste time by stopping again."

"That's fine with me."

It was dark by the time we reached the tiny town. With no street lights or other houses nearby, I would have had no notion where I was except for the smell of the pine trees. I inhaled deeply and let the cool air fill my lungs before I grabbed for my pillowcase stuffed with clothes and began groping my way through the darkness to Carol's front porch.

"Hurry and get ready for bed," Carol said when we were inside. "We have a big day tomorrow."

I was so excited I could hardly relax, but the heat and wind from the ride made me sleepy in spite of myself. In minutes, I was asleep on the folding cot in Carol's living room.

Away from the constant presence of our parents, Carol and I enjoyed every pleasure the region had to offer. We rode horses, picked fresh vegetables, took hikes through the pines, and attended dances in the church hall.

"Do you do all this stuff when I'm not here?" I asked one day.

"Sometimes, but it's not as much fun without you here," Carol answered.

Why does she like me to be here? Mother and Daddy think I talk too much and make too much noise around the mortuary. Carol makes it seem like she really likes having me around.

But the week I spent with Carol passed with lightning speed. Before I knew it, it was time for me to go back home and risk ending up in the pink chair again.

"Let's call Mother and see if you can spend another week," Carol suggested.

"No, Mother won't let me," I immediately responded.

"Well, let's just try," Carol persisted.

"We can try it, but you have to call," I said.

"Go pour us a soda. I'm going to call. We haven't had enough time to do everything I wanted in just one week," Carol replied.

I went to the kitchen to put ice and soda into the two glasses on the counter. By the time I walked back to the living room, Carol was just putting the receiver back into the cradle. She was beaming.

"How do you like that?" she laughed. "They were just starting someone's funeral so they didn't have time to talk. I asked if you could stay another week and Mother just whispered, 'All right, all right, we're busy.' Am I a master of timing or what?"

"I can't believe it. I can really stay longer?" I asked. I

was astounded first by anyone's desire to have me around, and second by Mother's easily allowing it.

"Let's celebrate," Carol said. "The Forest Service got two new horses in. Let's go see if we can borrow them and go for a long ride."

"You bet," I yelled. I was already halfway out the door.

"You girls have to be careful," the forest ranger told us as he saddled the horses. "This is government property. I shouldn't let you borrow them, but no one will find out if I do. Nobody comes up here, anyway."

He helped each of us as we grunted and groaned, trying to hoist ourselves into the saddles.

"Do you think we're good enough riders to do this?" I asked Carol.

"Sure we are," Carol answered. "If we can get you out of that mortuary for two whole weeks, riding these horses is going to be nothing."

Both of us laughed and loosened the reins for the horses to go through the gates in front of the ranger station.

"We'll be back soon," Carol yelled over her shoulder.

Side by side, the two horses walked placidly down the country road. I could smell the scent of the pines and enjoy the aroma of wildflowers along the roadside. The cool air drifted around me refreshingly, unlike the still heat of Tempe.

"Isn't this nice?" I asked as I came astride Carol's horse.

"It is," Carol agreed. "Let's see if we can make them go a little faster, though."

"Okay, but remember, we don't know much about

horseback riding. We better be careful."

"You sound just like Mother. What do you think is going to happen? We're not going to fall off. We're fine." Carol nudged her horse with her heels. It began to trot, and she pulled ahead of my horse. Carol was bouncing up and down with such force that she looked like a rag doll. Her hair, swept up into a pony tail, landed with a plop on her neck with each lunge forward. I could see daylight between Carol's butt and the saddle, she was bouncing so far off it each time hooves met the ground.

I was laughing so hard, I couldn't speak, much less keep up.

"Whoa, whoa," Carol yelled as she pulled back on the reins.

"What are you doing?"

"That just about shook my teeth out," Carol said between bursts of laughter.

"You should have seen how you looked from behind," I remarked. "I think that trotting stuff is definitely a little too advanced for us. We'd better stick to walking."

The two horses walked slowly, side by side, as Carol and I giggled and laughed at our lack of horsemanship. We passed the construction site where Henry was building a summer cabin for someone. Then we clip-clopped beyond the old school house and out into the new residential areas on the edge of town.

Without warning, my horse broke into a trot.

"Oh my gosh, what is the matter with this thing?" I shouted as I pulled on the reins with all my might.

Instead of reverting to the slow walk, the horse trotted even faster.

"Whoa, whoa, stop, slow down," I shouted. The horse

continued to move faster and faster. I was bouncing around so much in the saddle that I grabbed for the saddle horn to hold on. The horse continued to pick up speed.

Suddenly, the horse made a *U*-turn and began heading in the opposite direction, moving even faster now.

I moved from being slightly annoyed at the bouncing of the trot to sheer terror as my horse became nearly airborne. Travelling at a full gallop, I felt as though I was flying for seconds at a time, only to be jarred with a thud when the hooves met the pavement again. I raced by the houses we'd passed only minutes before. The cool breeze I'd experienced before was now a hurricane-force wind raking over my skin as I streaked down the road.

I knew I needed help, but Carol was nowhere in sight. I had only one hand to use to pull back on the reins. I needed the other to maintain my death grip on the saddle horn so I wouldn't fall off. I knew the situation was beyond my control now. All I could do was cry for help.

"Help! Help!" I attempted to shout. Each time I got out the first part of the word, the horse landed again, jarring the breath from me. "Heh" as I lifted from the saddle, "pa", as the air flew past my lips on the crash landing. "Heh-pa, heh-pa," rang out over and over again as I set a land speed record through the countryside.

Soon it became even more difficult to speak. As I passed back through the pines, whose beautiful scent I'd appreciated only minutes before, I couldn't coordinate flying off the saddle, landing back down on it, pulling back on the reins with one hand, holding onto to the saddle horn for dear life with the other, and screaming for help simultaneously. Clearly, I had more to do than I could possibly manage. Avoiding the low branches of the needled trees I was hurtling through was the final blow.

"Heh-pa" (slap in the face, slap in the face, as tree branches hit me). "Heh-pa," (slap in the face as pine needles raked over my skin).

I managed a reprieve from the pine boughs in the face only to be doused with cold water as the horse crossed the creek with lightning speed. Just as I was about to give up on getting any assistance, I heard the sound of hoof beats on the bridge above the creek my horse and I were splashing through. When I reached the far side of the water, my horse also heard the sound of the hoof beats above us. In one gigantic leap, the horse and I joined the traffic on the road.

I looked to my side to see who it was who was riding to my rescue. With horror, I saw that the rider astride the horse on the bridge was Carol.

Carol's horse was travelling at the same speed as mine. It had been doing so for so long that Carol's ponytail had fallen down and her hair was flying everywhere. The cute bangs that usually fringed her forehead were now standing upright at her hairline like a very long crew cut.

"Make your horse stop," she yelled as we rode side by side.

I was moving so fast, I couldn't force enough air out of my lungs to fight the wind going in. I looked back at Carol with a desperate expression. We galloped through the town, past the school house, and into the yard of the ranger station in record time.

"Boy, you sure didn't take a very long ride," the ranger said as he came out of the office.

I couldn't verbalize anything because I was so out of breath, but Carol managed, "My foot is stuck."

I looked at Carol's foot to see what she was talking about. It had slipped completely through the stirrup. Her legs were shaking so much she couldn't pull her ankle back through it.

"If I would have fallen, I could have been dragged to death," she said.

"I can't get my hand off this saddle horn," I said as I peeled my fingers, one by one, from the horn I had been squeezing furiously.

"Hey, it looks like this horse got the bit in his teeth," the ranger said as he began to lead the horses back to the barn.

"They ran away with us," Carol finally managed to get out.

"Oh, these horses couldn't run more than a few yards. They're work horses, not race horses," the ranger laughed.

"Then why is Jamie's face all scratched up from running into pine trees?" Carol asked.

"Because she doesn't know how to duck." The ranger laughed again.

With the relief of knowing we were safe, we began to relax and, with considerable help from the ranger, get down off the horses.

"What's Mother going to say when she sees your face all scratched like that?" Carol asked.

"As though you don't know," I replied. "We're both going

to be in big trouble if she finds out about this."

As we drove back to Carol's house, we giggled slightly, then laughed out loud. By the time we reached the house, we were so hysterical we looked as though we were crying.

"Your butt was hitting that saddle so hard, your whole body bounced on every step," Carol laughed.

"At least my hair didn't look like a crew cut. Your bangs were standing straight on end," I answered as I wiped a tear from my eye. "My side hurts from laughing."

"What do you expect when I'm traveling ninety miles an hour with no windshield to protect me?" Then, falling into the leather recliner, Carol laughed and said, "I just want to have a seat on something that's not moving beneath me."

"Same here," I managed as I stretched full-length on the sofa.

"We deserve a little break after that ride. Then we can put the roast in the oven for dinner."

Several hours later, Henry startled us when he opened the screen door to the house. We were so exhausted from careening through the forest at breakneck speed, and relieved that we'd survived it, that we'd slept the rest of the afternoon.

The next morning, with our scratches and bruises and aching muscles, we sat down to devise a plot so Mother wouldn't find out we had been in danger.

"How long do you think it will take for those scratches to clear up?" Carol asked.

"I don't know. Can't you figure out a way to put makeup on them to cover them up?"

"That will just make them more obvious. Mother is going

to find out. She'll run straight to Daddy and both of us will be in trouble. We have to think of a way out of this."

"I think both of you are getting a little old to be afraid of your parents. What are they going to do if they're unhappy with you? Spank you?" Henry laughed.

"You haven't lived with Mother. You don't understand," I said.

"She might not come out of her bedroom for days. Then Daddy will blame us for upsetting her," Carol added.

"If you're that scared, why don't you just stay here until your scratches heal?" Henry asked.

Wide-eyed, I asked, "Do you think I could?"

"Why not?"

We didn't have an answer.

"Let's tell Mother that you want to go to the rodeo up here next week," Carol suggested

"She's isn't going to let me be away from home that long," I argued.

"She will if we say it's for a special occasion."

Mother never saw my face scraped up or Carol's ankles bruised purple. She didn't know how much my hand hurt from squeezing the saddle horn so tightly, nor did she get to sympathize with the pain of her daughters' pulled muscles after their tumultuous ride. But I could tell she knew something was out of the ordinary from the moment I called with my story of going to the rodeo.

"You don't like rodeos," she told me. "You've never even been to one. Now, all of a sudden, you can't come home after weeks of being away because of some dumb cowboy circus."

"I don't care as long as you don't miss any school." Daddy answered. "The Perry Como Show is on TV. Let's talk about it when that's over."

I went to the Rodeo in Payson, a slightly larger town than Pine and only a few miles down the mountain, and my scratches and bruises healed in the next week. My sophomore year at Tempe High would begin in days. I had to go home.

When Henry's pickup pulled into the driveway of the mortuary, Mother was out the front door in a second.

"It's about time you came home. Didn't you get sick of her? She's been at your house for weeks," Mother began before I could grab my pillow case out of the back of the truck. "Come in," she continued. "I've made dinner for everyone."

"Oh no, Mother, we need to start back. We don't like to drive those mountain roads after dark," Carol began, making excuses.

We're trapped. We haven't been home five minutes and Mother is starting the interrogation.

"You want to stay and eat, don't you?" Mother asked Henry.

"Okay, Gertrude," he answered obediently.

The second the last bite of Mother's elaborate dinner was consumed, Henry and Daddy disappeared into the living room. I could feel the tension in the air already. I knew the men in our family didn't want to be part of the explosion to come.

"So, what did you girls do all those weeks in Pine?" Mother began conversationally.

"I don't know. Carol, what did we do?" I faltered.

"Oh, you know, we just took it easy," Carol began.

"Well, the television doesn't work up in those tall pines. How did you pass the time?" she pressed.

"Jamie went to a dance," Carol ventured.

"Jamie doesn't know how to dance. Who would she dance with, anyway? She doesn't know any boys in Pine."

When we were silent for several seconds, Mother dropped the bombshell we both knew was coming.

"So, tell me about this rodeo that was so important you couldn't even come back to your own home," she said.

The trap is being set and we're walking right into it. There's no way out now.

The three of us skirted the issue for hours, with Carol and I refusing to give Mother any reason for punishing either of us.

When Carol and Henry left well after dark, I felt a sense of true pride that Carol and I presented a united front and withheld the information Mother so desperately wanted.

"You'd better tell your sister thank you for keeping you in Pine for the whole summer, Jamie," Mother prompted as everyone stood by the pickup to say goodbye.

"Thanks, Carol. I had a really good time," I said.

"Don't start that crap," Mother said as Carol's eyes filled with tears. "You know your father can't stand a bunch of crybaby women."

I held back my own tears until I was safely in bed for the night. At least I had the satisfaction of knowing that Mother had not broken me into revealing my horseback experience.

Almost a week passed before Mother brought up

Carol again.

"What did you girls talk about all day if you didn't have anything to do up there?" she started.

"Oh, just girl stuff, you know."

"Carol isn't a girl. She's a married woman. What did she talk about?"

"Not much. I better go practice my piano. I've been away from it for a long time."

"The piano can wait. Something is going on with you girls. Why do you always plot against me? What did I ever do to make you so hateful toward me?" Mother said, chin beginning to quiver.

Here it comes. She's going to throw a fit until I tell her everything.

"I think you girls were saying bad things about me. That's why you won't tell me what you did up there. With no TV or anything else to do, I bet you spent the whole day gossiping about things you don't like about me, didn't you?"

"No, Mother. Carol loves you. We wouldn't say bad things about you."

"I know I've made mistakes, but no one is perfect. Why do you girls sneak around to talk about me behind my back?"

"Mother, we didn't. I promise."

"Then why won't you tell me the truth about what you did up there? And I also want to know why you stayed so long. I know you're covering something up."

"We didn't do anything to cover up for, Mother. We just messed around."

"I don't know what you mean by messing around, but I know you girls have stabbed me in the back. You stayed up there so long so everyone would think Carol was better to live with than I am."

"Carol isn't better than you, Mother. We were just having fun."

Mother lapsed into open sobbing. "I don't care what you girls say about me. I'm not giving you the opportunity to gossip and lie about me all day in some dinky little town again. Don't bother asking if you can go to Pine again. I know what you did the last time, and I won't allow it to happen again," she finished, slamming the bedroom door behind her. I heard her flop across the double bed and begin the wailing that would eventually bring our family to its knees.

Though we never openly discussed why, Carol and I knew there would be no more lengthy visits to Carol's house. Unable to break our code of silence, Mother resorted to her guilt and shame routine and won the battle anyway. I found little satisfaction in knowing that Mother couldn't punish me for risking a horseback ride; I was already being punished for something I didn't even do.

It's not enough to get away from the pink chair. No matter how long I stall, it's always there, waiting for my return.

Chapter Seventeen

Dead Soldiers

Mother decided I could never go back to Carol's. It didn't matter that the reason was unclear to me; I wasn't returning to Pine and I had to accept it.

When the new school year began, I risked confronting Mother and Daddy about attending the slumber parties and overnight visits the other girls my age were experiencing.

"If Daddy won't let me spend the night with other girls, can they come here and stay with me sometime?" I ventured when I was feeling most courageous. "I'll only ask the quiet ones. I know who all the rowdy girls are, and I would leave them out, okay?" I suggested.

"You know how your father feels about girls being in their own beds at night," Mother answered.

"But, these aren't Daddy's girls. Their fathers don't care if they spend the night at a friend's house," I argued.

"Hey, you guys, do you think your parents would let you spend the night at my house if I could talk my parents into letting us?" I asked a group at school.

"Oh, that would be so cool. Could we play in the caskets? I would love to jump out at somebody who thought I was dead because I was in a casket," one of them chimed in.

"We can't do that," I said grimly.

"Can we get inside the hearse and pretend we're driving it?" another asked.

"My parents wouldn't allow that," I replied disappointedly.

"Let's wait until real late and then get in the ambulance and turn on the siren and scare everyone," somebody else suggested.

I felt the knot in my stomach begin to tighten.

"We'd have to stay in my house and be really quiet, especially if the phone rang. Somebody might die and my father would have to talk to their family on the phone. We can't make any noise at all while that is going on," I cautioned.

"We could toilet paper someone's house," a girl said.

"My parents wouldn't let us out of the house after dark," I told them.

Nobody wants to sit silently in our house all night. They just want to come to my house because they think it's creepy to be around dead people. They don't want to be with me, they just want to have scary stories to tell everybody else.

"I don't think my parents would let me do it anyway," I said dejectedly. "I was just wondering if you guys would come. It's not a good idea after all," I concluded as the group began to back away and talk among themselves. I went back to doing my geometry homework alone while the other girls wrote notes to each other in class.

"I could have told you not to ask them," Rosarita told me after school. "Mother and Daddy don't like other people being around here during the day. Why would they let you have girls stay all night?" she asked.

"You get to go out with boys, though. I thought if they let you have dates at night, they would let me have girls over," I defended myself.

"They only let me have dates because I go other places with the boys. They wouldn't let me have anybody spend the night here, either. You're so dumb. Why don't you just get a boyfriend? Then you can go places with him," Rosarita told me. "You'd better hurry up, too. A lot of the cute guys are already in Vietnam."

"Yeah, right. I'm going to get a boyfriend. I don't even know any boys," I retorted.

"There are boys in your classes at school. Just flirt with them a little bit and they'll ask you out. Then you can get out of here sometimes, too. You know you're never going back to Carol's; you can forget about that for your hideout. Mother thinks you did something in Pine that you won't tell her about. She's mad at you and Carol for keeping secrets."

"It's all right. I don't really mind staying here all the time. I only get bored on weekends sometimes."

"Keep your big mouth shut about it or Mother will make you go to the mortuary with her," Rosarita warned.

"I know, I know. What do you think, I want to sit in the pink chair all day?" I asked.

Rosarita laughed, "You look like such a goof sitting in that dinky little chair with your ten-foot-long legs sticking out in front of it."

"You wouldn't think it was so funny if you were the one

crunched down on that thing for hours. Your legs start to cramp after a while."

"That's why I have boyfriends. They keep me away from all that," Rosarita continued. "A lot of the boys who graduated last year are already in the Army. I think they look really cute in their new uniforms. You could go out with one of them. They'd be interested in you if you would do something about your appearance."

"Like what?" Get a mask to cover my face?" I inquired sarcastically.

"No, just wear some neater clothes and walk with your head up. You stare at the ground like you think your feet are going to fly out from under you. How can any boys see you smiling at them if you keep your head down all the time?"

"Boys don't care if I'm smiling at them or not. I don't have dimples like you do. Nobody wants to see some dumb girl grinning at them for no reason."

"It's up to you. But remember, you walk all the way home from school alone while I get rides from boys in neat cars. That's because I keep my head up and I smile. You're going to be walking home in the heat the rest of your life if you don't lift your head up. Or are you counting the lines in the cement like you used to? What a jerk," Rosarita laughed as she walked away.

Rosarita's right. I am going to be alone forever, walking in the heat, looking down at the sidewalk. It's none of her business if I count or not, though.

I took my time making my way home after school. If I

rushed, there would be more time to risk the pink chair. I strolled through the 100 degree temperatures of the desert atmosphere for more than a mile five days a week. Some days I passed the piano store, others I crossed the street and shot a furtive glance into Parry's Pool Hall, a place Mother forbade me ever to look.

"There are child molesters in that pool hall. Don't you think they can see girls walking past and follow them home? The next day they'll be waiting by their houses to molest them," she warned me.

What is the connection between playing pool and molesting girls? I never see any of those men do anything but drink beer and play pool.

I always lingered for a few moments when I got to the window of the flower shop I had so loved as a child. Billie made beautiful displays of seasonal flowers and carefully positioned them in the picture window in front of the shop. The smell of carnations floated out to the sidewalk as people opened and closed the doors. Even though I didn't go in after Duane's accident, I still relished the beauty of the shop itself.

Immediately beyond the flower shop stood the mortuary. The little patch of grass in front of it was always perfectly manicured. The metal letters spelling "Maguire Mortuary," backlit with a light green neon light, shone night and day on the façade. The maroon-and-gold stained-glass panels in front of the chapel reflected their colors onto the gray sidewalk.

The soldiers who appeared ever more frequently around the family business were strangers. They didn't look much older than me, but they neither looked nor behaved as though they were young. They stood motionless in front of the mortuary, gazing endlessly at the patch of grass in front of the building. Their eyes held no expression.

"Going to the airport again," Daddy announced as he fidgeted into position on the velvet-upholstered seat of the hearse.

"Not another military funeral," Mother said.

Daddy didn't answer as he eased the long, white vehicle from its parking spot in the garage near the back door.

"We're getting a lot of shipments from out of town now, huh?" I asked my mother.

"They're those poor boys coming home from Vietnam," Mother answered. I heard the catch in my mother's voice as her emotion overwhelmed her.

"Is that why soldiers are always hanging around outside the front door to the mortuary?" I asked.

"They're not hanging around," Mother replied as she instantly snapped out of her sentimentality for those lost in battle. "They're military escorts. They stay with the body until it's properly buried. Don't ever say anything to them when you see them. They're not supposed to be talking to people. They're on guard, protecting their comrades in arms."

I bet their comrades wish they would have been this protected before they ended up dead. What are they being protected from now, being killed a second time?

"Some of those soldiers are Rosarita's age. They should have stayed in college so they wouldn't get drafted and have to go over there," I replied.

"So now you're going to agree with those dirty hippie kids from the university? President Johnson knows what's best for our country. If he says they have to fight, they do. Don't you ever let your father know you don't agree with the war. He's the commander of the American Legion for the whole state of Arizona. I don't know what he would do if he thought one of his own children didn't agree with war."

"Rosarita doesn't like it, either. She thinks the boys look cute in their uniforms, but now too many of them are getting shipped out. It would be kind of funny if she didn't have any boys around to take her on dates. Besides, Daddy's always saying how yucky it was when he was in the Army. I bet he doesn't think we should send more men to this war, either."

"Now you're saying that your own father is on the side of those hippie radicals who don't even get haircuts? You don't talk like that in this house, young lady. You keep it up and I'm going to tell your father just exactly what you said. Then we'll see what you say about soldiers," Mother threatened as she stomped from the room before I could answer.

I don't want to be a hippie; I just don't want people to die. If the President could see what bodies look like after they're dead, I bet he wouldn't make anybody risk getting killed in the war, either.

I was shocked that I had factual data to support my disagreement with my parents. Could it be that I knew something my parents didn't? Some of the newspapers and TV shows told how many Americans died each day. Their numbers for soldier mortality were much higher than the number reported by the military. Even Walter Cronkite thought we should get out of Vietnam. I didn't say "I told you so" when Cronkite admitted his opposition to the war right in the middle of his newscast. Once again, my ability to hide my feelings saved me from the disdain of my family.

During debates in my social studies classes, the side arguing against the war always won. I was a fierce competitor when it was my turn to speak. I'd compiled a stack of note cards with every fact I could gather about the war. Surely no one could read them and still want to fight.

But my parents agreed with the war, so I had to agree with it, too. I'd agreed with all their past opinions. I didn't socialize with people of dark skin, I didn't spend the night with other girls, I got good grades in school…but this topic stopped me in my tracks. People my age were dying for a cause I felt was wrong. I didn't voice my opinion at dinner, nor wear flowers in my hair, nor attend peace demonstrations at the university, but I was a full blown dove.

I found myself reviewing other opinions my parents demanded I share. The notion of independence began to creep into my thoughts, slowly. Maybe they're not right about everything. If my feelings about a subject are different from theirs, it doesn't automatically mean I'm wrong. I observe actions every day that confirm my beliefs.

Funerals for the fallen soldiers were marked by crying and hugging and carrying on by the families left behind. But I didn't have a lot of sympathy for them. After all, they let their sons and brothers get involved in the foolishness of war in the first place.

But the dead soldiers' girlfriends were not so easy for me to dismiss. I saw them in the hallways at school. They made a big show of receiving letters with a red and blue border around the envelope. Everyone recognized the stationery. The girls would act real scared before they opened the letters, like they were afraid the boys had written them just before they got shot or something. I found the entire scene pretentious and attention-seeking.

But when their boyfriends really did die in battle, they were stunned by the reality of their new lonely lives. I watched as they stumbled from the chapel to the family limousine, in such a trance thatt others had to usher them around like they were old ladies.

Now they're just like me. All alone. The only difference between us is that they once enjoyed the luxury of being someone's girlfriend. I've always been alone.

Some of the meaner, more possessive mothers of the dead soldiers, who didn't like the girlfriends, wouldn't even let them ride in the family limo. I heard some of the families specifically ask that the girlfriends not be given any special privileges at the funeral. It was as though the mothers wanted to be the only females getting any sympathy, I thought. The mothers saw to it that the girlfriends were deprived of any intimacy they shared with the boy they thought they would marry someday.

They were the most important person in the world to at least one boy, and now they don't belong to anyone. I can't imagine how painful that must be for them. They aren't used to loneliness like I am.

Most of the funerals began at two o'clock in the afternoon, so they concluded just as I walked past the mortuary on my way home from school each day. The chapel would empty first of the young mourners and their families, people I recognized from around town.

I stood silently watching as the flag-covered caskets were carried from the mortuary and placed in the back of the hearse. The six teenagers who had become soldiers and then pallbearers within a matter of months, stepped up to the casket handles and grasped them tightly in their white-gloved hands. They walked the space from chapel door to hearse with exact precision. I saw them glide the casket onto the metal fittings and back away in unison as one of them closed the door.

Something about the way they maneuvered the casket struck me as odd the first few times I saw it. But the same thing happened almost every time the soldiers brought the casket from chapel to hearse. Not one of the pall bearers struggled to maintain his balance or shifted his position to support the weight of the casket.

These young soldiers had no difficulty at all carrying the bodies to the car. At the funerals of civilians, most pallbearers broke into a labored sweat as they nearly buckled under the weight of body and casket. When their hands were so wet from perspiration they could no longer keep a firm grip on the casket handles, Daddy would solemnly step in front of them, giving them a chance to dry their palms down the sides of their suit pants before trying again to maneuver the burden of the casket into the hearse with the formality required.

As I stood watching the uniformed pallbearers walk past me, each step in unison, with no effort required, the solution to the mysterious strength of the uniformed pallbearers dawned on me.

Days later, I said to Mother, "There's nothing in the caskets that come back from the war, are there? Those families and girlfriends are sobbing over empty boxes. I know it."

"Oh, Jamie, you've always had such an imagination. Why would the military bury an empty casket?"

"Haven't you seen the pallbearers bring them out to the hearse? They're strolling along, carrying the caskets with one hand, and they don't even break a sweat. Those caskets are empty. I know it. You might as well admit it."

"You sound just like those dirty hippies. Burying empty caskets, my foot. You accuse the government of your own country of the most horrible things. What do you think they did with the bodies if they're burying empty caskets? You make no sense at all and frankly, I don't like your insinuation that your father, a decorated veteran himself, is involved in some military scheme to hide the bodies of soldiers. What do you think he's doing with them? Holding them for ransom?"

"No, Mother, I don't think Daddy is doing anything wrong. I can just tell that those caskets are too light to have anything in them. It just made me wonder where the bodies went if they're not in the caskets they send home."

"There will be no further discussion of this preposterous idea of yours, young lady. Why, if the men at the American Legion Post knew that the daughter of their commander thought the Army was hiding something about its dead soldiers, they would be very disappointed in your father. Is that what you want? Do you want Daddy to have to answer to his fellow veterans about why his child has sided with the filthy hippies?"

"No, Mother. I don't want to disgrace Daddy in front of the American Legion."

I pushed the gruesome thoughts about the dead soldiers to the back of my mind until I came to the mortuary to ask Daddy for his signature on a permission slip for my school field trip.

"Will you sign this, Daddy?" I began as I walked into the chapel. I knew he was preparing for a funeral by the way the pink torchiere lamps were placed at either end of the casket.

I glanced inside the open coffin to see a military uniform folded inside it. All the ribbons and medals were placed as precisely as if someone would be wearing it soon. Yet it was folded into a perfect rectangle.

"How come you're putting it in there?" I asked Daddy as he gingerly laid it atop a satiny pillow.

"It's his uniform," Daddy answered solemnly in the tone he reserved only when referring to the dead.

"Where's his body? Aren't you finished with it yet?" I asked.

"It's right here," Daddy said softly. He lifted the edge of the perfectly folded uniform to reveal a sandwich-sized plastic bag. Inside it, I saw about two cups of ashes and dirt.

Without waiting for my question, Daddy said, "Helicopter crash."

My hands began to tingle and I sat down instantly on

the wicker chair nearest me. Daddy continued his reverent placement of the uniform and closed the casket for the last time.

I was right all along. Daddy picks up empty caskets at the airport. People my age have been reduced to a bagful of ashes. Their families are mourning over remains that might not even be their kids. How could the Army keep track of whose ashes were whose following a fiery crash from the sky in a foreign country? Their girlfriends are in love with someone who doesn't even exist anymore. If they wanted to give one last hug before burial, they would be holding onto a folded uniform, not a person they loved. Oh my God, I hate this war.

The next morning, as I prepared for school, I saw the permission slip with Daddy's signature on it. I followed my usual morning routine of bathing and dressing, gathering books and eating breakfast. Everything was just as it always was except for one thing; I had no memory of anything that had happened between the time I saw the ashes and when I woke the next morning.

I must have walked across the alley to come home. Nothing in my room suggested I had done anything out of the ordinary in my preparations for bed, but I could recall nothing from the night before except seeing the bag of ashes. Like a needle stuck on a record, my mind played over and over and over again, "I'm right about the war and my parents are not."

Chapter Eighteen

New House

"Well, girls," Daddy began. I recognized his tone of voice. Something bad had happened. "They finally did it to us, the bastards," he went on as though we already knew what he was going to say. "We're being driven out of our own home."

Rosarita looked panicked. "What are we going to do? Where are we going to live?"

"Oh, what's to become of us, Rhett? The Yankees are taking over the plantation," I said in a fake Southern accent.

Mother shot me an expression of rage.

"The city wants to make room for new development," Daddy continued. "They say our house is on land that could be used for new businesses. If we won't accept the price they're willing to give us, they'll condemn the property and take it anyway. We have to move. There's no way around it."

"I cannot believe I'm being driven from my own home," Daddy grumbled. "I paid cold, hard cash for it. I didn't rely on a bank to provide my housing. And now I'm the one the city throws out so they can make way for new development. I wonder how those bastards at city hall would like it if I threw them out of their homes?"

"It's the sixties," Daddy said in a high-pitched voice, mimicking the mayor. "Everything is changing. We have to make way for modern improvements. Don't you remember how exciting it was right after the war when all the new housing developments went in? This is the same thing, except it's the business district this time. You want what's best for the town, don't you?"

Daddy shook his head in disbelief as he mocked the mayor's words. Rosarita dabbed tears from her eyes as she saw Daddy glance her way.

Thank God, we're moving away from the mortuary. I can tell people where I live without having them laugh. We won't have to sneak around quietly so we don't interrupt somebody's funeral. We can have neighbors who are alive. Hooray!

"I've slaved over this house for twenty years, and now the city can just claim it as its own?" Mother asked incredulously. "Are they going to include the price of the tulip bulbs I just planted? Are they going to pay me back for the whole row of sour orange trees that are six feet tall now? I wonder what value they gave to the drapes I stayed up all night to sew myself," Mother shouted.

"There's no point in getting upset, Mother," Daddy replied. "We have to move. We might as well make the best of it."

"Make the best of it?" Rosarita questioned. "I already have the best of it. I don't want the hassle of moving now. After I finish beauty school, I'll be living in my own place next year. Can't I stay here while the rest of you move? I don't want to haul my stuff all over town twice in a year."

"I'll find you something worth your trouble, Rosarita. Now don't fret. You'll get your mother all upset."

"So we get to pick out a new house?" I asked. "Do we get to go with you to find one?"

"I'm not sure that's something you girls want to get involved in," Daddy replied. "I think it's going to be awful hard on you to know you can't keep this house."

I'll tell you what's been hard on me; it's been living here my whole life. I can't wait to get out of here. I can kiss this place goodbye in a heartbeat.

"Mother, do you want to be involved in selecting another house or will that be too much for you? If you want, I can just find something as much like this house as possible and buy it."

No! We don't want another one like this one. I want my own bedroom. I want a living room big enough to contain a record player and a desk. Imagine the possibilities. We might even get furniture that doesn't make our legs break out in a rash every time we sit on it.

"We have to find one that's for sale by owner. We can't afford those pricey real estate agents," Mother asserted.

"I could read the ads in the real estate section of the newspaper for you," I offered.

"You can all do what you want, but I'm having no part in leaving this house. This is where I've always lived, and I plan to continue doing so," Rosarita stated.

"We're going to have to stick together on this one, Rosarita," Daddy said as he put his arm around her shoulder.

Since when do we stick together about anything? Until

now, it's been every man for himself.

When we were in our bedroom alone, I asked, "Rosarita, you really don't want to move to a new house?"

"Of course I don't. You know what it's like getting a picnic basket ready to take to a park. Can you imagine what Mother will be like packing up a whole house? Not even a mansion would be worth the trouble of moving into it."

"Come on, Rosarita. You know how Mother exaggerates things. I'm sure she'll be excited to move once she sees a pretty new house."

"No, she won't. She told me about how awful it is to live with neighbors so close they can spy on you to see if you're as rich as they are. Then they gossip about you to all the others neighbors."

The next day, Mother launched her offensive in the battle not to move. "When we go to look at new houses, don't say you like any of them. If we hold out long enough, the city will change its mind and we can stay right here," she assured us.

"I don't want to do that, Mother. I think we should participate in finding a new home," I countered. "What if they decide to tear our house down and we still don't have a new one to move into?"

"Tear it down?" Mother screeched. "They're going to tear down our house? I will stand here and let the roof cave in on my head before I'll allow someone to tear down my house?"

She started to cry. I knew the exact number of steps it would take her to get from the living room to the bedroom where she could throw herself across the bed and refuse to come out for days.

Wham! The house shook to its foundation with the force of the tirade. I looked calmly at my sister. She turned and headed for our bedroom. My father looked tired.

My plan to escape life ruled by the dead accelerated feverishly as the opportunity to relocate loomed. I awaited the arrival of the *Tempe Daily News* every day. Skipping all the front page news and the feature stories inside, I flipped straight to the real estate ads. If anyone came in while I was reading, I turned to another page. I knew that even reading the ads would be seen as an act of family treason. But I had my own opinions now, separate from anyone else's. I kept my mouth shut and acted on my own thoughts, not theirs.

For weeks, I ran out to the front porch to retrieve the paper, only to be disappointed by ads for houses my family would never agree to. Most of them were listed with real estate agencies. That put them out of the running right off. Others were too expensive, too large, or too contemporary.

Uncharacteristic of my earlier stressful times in life, though, I didn't bite my fingernails. When I thought about what I was doing, I felt some mild anticipation, but I wasn't nervous or fearful like I used to be. I knew I was going to leave here even sooner than I'd planned.

Walking home from school, I spotted a sign in the front yard of a house along my route. "For sale by owner" it read. I could tell from its small size that it wouldn't be very expensive. I put my books down on the sidewalk in front of it and wrote down the phone number listed at the bottom of the placard.

I'll have to wait until everyone is in just the right mood before I mention this house. If I act as if I like it, nobody will agree with me. I'll just bring it up casually when the time is right. I stuffed the piece of paper with the phone number into my purse and continued the long, hot walk home. I knew today was not going to be the day to bring it up the minute I opened the door.

"Do you know what happened to me today?" Mother demanded the minute she saw me.

"No, what?" I asked with dread.

"Some real estate agent called here asking if we were in the market for a new house. That can only mean one thing," she said menacingly.

"What's that?" I asked.

"Someone in this household is sharing our personal business with other people. You girls know that you are never to repeat anything you hear in this house. One of you has betrayed our family trust. I know you have because neither your father nor I have spoken word one to anyone outside these walls. Rosarita still thinks she's going to stay here even if the rest of us move. She certainly isn't telling her friends that she's moving. I want to know just what you think you're doing, talking about your family all over town," Mother demanded.

I felt my stomach tighten for a second, but regained my sense of calm quickly.

"Mother, there was an article in the newspaper about the city buying this property for redevelopment. It was on the front page last week. I didn't talk to anyone about our personal business. Everybody read about it themselves. Didn't you see the story?" I asked.

"Oh, so now you think you're smarter than I am because you can't keep your nose out of that stupid newspaper? Don't you think I see you dashing out to the porch to grab it every afternoon? Now you think you can throw it in my face because you saw something that I didn't? Well, let me tell you, everyone in this family knows your attitude about the move. It seems to me you could quit sneaking around telling people we want to buy a new house and show a little loyalty to your own family."

I didn't feel sick. I didn't bite my nails. I didn't even start counting everything. I was hurt by my mother's words, but I focused my thoughts on facts, not feelings.

"I'm sorry you think I did that, Mother," I said quietly. I turned and went into my bedroom.

Mother doesn't have anyone to fight with if I don't answer back angrily. I just avoided screaming, crying, and days of Mother locked in her bedroom, refusing to come out. I can't believe I can do this.

For several days, I reflected with satisfaction on my ability to thwart Mother's tantrum. I'd experienced events much worse than my mother's outbursts and knew by now that I had an arsenal of weapons to combat the anxiety that had riddled my earlier years. I was feeling almost self-assured.

My recent self-confidence dwindled in a second, though, when Mother burst through my bedroom door screaming, "Who is he? Who is he?" Daddy was only a few steps behind Mother.

"Who is who?" I asked in a tremulous voice. My stomach

was in a huge knot.

"Your dealer," Mother shouted.

"I'll kill the son of a bitch," Daddy said through gritted teeth.

"Dealer?" was all I could get out of my mouth.

"You left your purse on the kitchen table," Mother said. "I wasn't snooping. You are the one who left it standing wide open for me to see into."

"You went through my purse?" I asked, bewildered.

"Yes, I did. And I'm mighty glad I did it, too."

Daddy nodded in agreement.

"What do you have to say for yourself?" Mother demanded.

"About my purse? You're right. I left it on the table. I'm sorry. I'll put it away in my room next time."

"Oh, don't be coy with me, young lady. The cat is already out of the bag about you," Mother snarled.

"Just what the hell were you thinking?" Daddy growled.

I was terrified. Neither of my parents made any sense, but I was obviously in deep trouble.

"Show her, Mother. She's never going to admit it on her own," Daddy challenged.

As Mother sobbed and Daddy maintained a cold glare, she pulled from the pocket of her housedress the incriminating evidence she had gathered from my purse.

A packet of individually wrapped red tablets were in one hand. In the other was the scrap of paper with the phone number I had written and stored in my purse. I still hadn't found a time when everyone was in the right mood to bring up the idea of buying the house with the "for sale by owner" sign and the phone number in Mother's hand.

"Where did you get these? Did you get them from the dirty hippie whose phone number you were hiding?" Mother raved.

"That's not a hippie's phone number," I replied.

"This is not the time to get into semantics, young lady. I don't care what you call them. Those people are well-known for dealing drugs," Daddy accused.

"You think I bought drugs from hippies?" I asked.

"So you're going to play this out, are you?" Mother said. "Well, Daddy, if she won't admit it to us, should we just go ahead and call the police? My daughter is going to reform school. What did I ever do to deserve this?" she rattled on.

"I'm not going to reform school. I didn't do anything wrong," I pleaded.

"Let's just slow down a little here," Daddy said. "Do we need to call the doctor to get your stomach pumped first? How long has it been since you took one of these?"

"I chewed one this morning," I reported.

"Oh, Jesus, you chewed it? You know, I'm a graduate of embalming college. I know a few things about the human body. If you chew these things, they get into your bloodstream even faster. God only knows if you've already done damage to your brain."

"I'm pretty sure I haven't damaged my brain. But, if you think I have, call Dr. Dandridge and ask him," I said.

"Dandridge the dentist? So, it's that long-haired kid of his who is peddling this crap?"

"No, Daddy. Jeff Dandridge isn't dealing drugs. Dr. Dandridge gave me those pills himself."

"We're not stupid. No dentist hands out pills to high school girls. If he thought you needed medication, he would write a prescription for it, not hand it out himself in little plastic packets," Mother asserted.

I could feel my hands beginning to tingle. I hadn't called up the image of the pink chair myself; it came to me automatically. But this time I didn't allow myself to sink into the chair and escape my parents' wrath.

I have concrete evidence and an adult to verify my story. I can prove I'm telling the truth. All they can do is figure out they accused their own kid of doing something horrible. I'm not the one who needs a means to escape this time.

In a completely calm, level voice, I said, "Dr. Dandridge cleaned my teeth and gave me my annual check-up last week. Do you remember when I went to my dentist appointment?"

When neither of my parents answered, I continued.

"He gave me these tablets to help me do a better job brushing my teeth. He said if I used them, I could reduce my chances of getting cavities. You chew them up, and any places on your teeth that are not thoroughly clean turn red. He told me to keep brushing until the red marks went away. That way I would know all the bacteria was out of my mouth."

My parents stared back at me without a word.

"If you don't believe me, call him. You must have come across my next appointment card in my purse, too. That has his number on it. Call him. Do it right now," I demanded.

Who is saying these things to my parents? I think it's me, but it's a me I never knew existed. The Jamie I've known my whole life is scared to death to talk back to her parents, but this new Jamie is doing a terrific job!

"So you're saying these aren't some kind of illegal drug you've been taking?" Daddy asked finally.

"No, Daddy. They're not. Dr. Dandridge said it was real important that I protect my teeth. He says I have a smile like the girls in the Ipana toothpaste ads. He said I shouldn't do anything to harm something so pretty."

Mother wiped the tears from her eyes. By this point in most confrontations, she had already stormed off to her bedroom to sulk.

"That story may or may not be true," Daddy conceded. "But the issue of the hidden phone number remains unanswered."

"There's no issue. I didn't hide it. I just put it in my purse to save for a time when I thought you guys might want to use it."

"See that?" Mother interrupted. "She's higher than a kite right now. She loves her psychedelic trips so much she thinks we want to join her."

Then the New Jamie said something I thought I would never hear. She openly addressed Mother's exaggerations for exactly what they were.

"Mother," New Jamie said, "we've already established that I don't take illegal drugs. I am not high now. I have never been high. I don't ever want to be high in the future. Do you understand that?"

I watched in wonder as New Jamie, a girl who looked

exactly like me but whose boldness was astounding, waited for my parents to answer.

"That phone number is not for a hippie drug dealer, it's for someone who's selling their house," she stated boldly.

"This is the number for somebody who wants to sell a house?" Daddy asked meekly.

I nodded silently. New Jamie was still present, but didn't answer. Instead, she returned my parents' stares eye to eye.

"I'm going to call this number right in front of you, Miss Know-it-all," Mother went on. "Then we'll see how cocky you are when you talk back to us."

I was telling the truth when I answered. "I didn't talk back to you." I didn't include that my alter ego was doing most of the talking now.

"We don't need to discuss who said what," Daddy said quietly. Mother glared at him for his lack of support.

"I wish you would dial that number," New Jamie said. "The person at the other end of the line is someone who is selling a pretty house close to my school. I'm sure he would like to talk to you about buying it from him. I don't think he would put a sign in his front yard unless he wanted people to inquire."

"Hmm, well, I guess you never know," Daddy said. I could see his face was turning a little red. I was pretty sure it wasn't from anger this time.

"You're just going to believe her and act like nothing has happened, aren't you?" Mother turned on Daddy.

"Well, Mother, it seems like she has a mighty good alibi."

"It's not an alibi, it's the truth," New Jamie said.

"Oh, sure, make this all my fault. I'm the one who keeps tabs on the welfare of this whole family. Then you swoop in like the big hero at the last minute and all is forgiven. This is just about the last straw," Mother yelled as she began her trip to the bedroom door. Daddy and I braced ourselves for the slam that we both knew would follow in a second.

Wham! The whole house shook from the impact of the door against the frame.

"I guess that didn't work out very well," Daddy said.

This is the closest I'll ever get to an apology from him. We both know I deserve one, but receiving it would send Mother into a tantrum that could last for days. No matter how much I deserve an apology, they'll never say they're sorry.

My hands were beginning to tingle again. I could feel that the old anxiety-ridden Jamie was soon to be alone again in her battle for survival. I had to rely on my own courage now.

With Mother behind closed doors for who knew how long, Daddy and I ended our confrontation. Each of us went a different direction to avoid the awkwardness of the moment.

Mother's mood became incrementally more civil as the next few days passed. She eventually stopped wailing inside the locked bedroom. Then she came out to the kitchen, but wouldn't speak to anyone. By the third day, she was watching TV with everyone else and giving short verbal responses to others while still pouting. By the fourth day, she and the family had negotiated a silent pact to behave as though nothing had ever happened.

"I heard about a house the owner is selling down by Jamie's school," Daddy mentioned casually, as though he had never heard of it before.

"Is it as nice as our house? I don't even want to look at it if it isn't better than where we're living now," Mother started.

"Now, Mother," Daddy placated, "you know we may not be able to find a house as nice as this one. But, with your handiwork, I think you could turn a shack into a lovely home. I can remember what this house looked like when we first moved in. There were no flower beds, no beautiful lawn. Let's not forget how ugly these windows were before you made curtains for each and every one of them all by yourself. They look a lot better than the ones Grace bought at the store for their house. I'm sure you can work your magic on anything we buy."

"Oh, thank you, Daddy," Mother said demurely. "I guess I can make a place look better, but it takes a lot of work."

"You bet it does. But look what all that effort can produce."

"How about we take a look at this place and see what you think you could do with it?" Daddy ventured cautiously.

"Okay, I'll look. But I'm not saying I'll agree to buy it if I don't like it."

"Of course not. There's no harm in looking, right?"

Daddy called and arranged our visit with the owner. Rosarita maintained her sullen resistance to moving. Mother still nurtured her skepticism that any home would meet her standards of perfection. Daddy was reduced to the role of a jittery chauffeur. I couldn't wait for the chance to see if this house, far away from the mortuary, would be our new home.

"Step right in," Mr. Hoffman, the owner, said dramatically as he opened the door wide for all of us to enter. "I'm so delighted you're interested in the house. You know, we've met before," he said to Daddy. "You buried my mother almost five years ago."

"Of course," Daddy said. I could tell by his expression that he had no recollection of the man's dead mother. "You sure have a lovely home here," he added, changing the subject.

"We're quite proud of it," Mr. Hoffman went on. "We've lived here for twelve years. We wouldn't be moving now except for my wife's arthritis. We're going to Sun City, where the houses are designed for those who have a little trouble getting around."

He ushered us through each room of the house, indicating the many reasons his house was superior to any other for sale.

"Everything here is original. We haven't changed a thing. Some of the neighbors around here have remodeled so often—trying to keep up with the Joneses, you know—that the houses have lost all their original character. We liked ours the way it was when we bought it, and we've kept it that way."

I could see he was a man of his word. The twelve-year-old carpeting was so worn that bare spots showed through in the heavy traffic areas. Several of the ceramic tiles in the bathroom were cracked. The appliances in the kitchen were clearly well-used.

I don't care what's wrong with this house; I can't see a casket for miles. It's perfect. If we lived here, no one would know, just by driving by the house, that we're in the funeral business. I could have friends come to see me and not be embarrassed. If I ever had a boyfriend, he could pick me up at a real house, not a mortuary.

"Thanks for letting us see your home," Daddy was saying all too soon. "We'll let you know if we have further questions."

"What did you think?" Mother asked as soon as we were in the car.

"It doesn't make any difference to me. I'm not moving, no matter what," Rosarita sulked.

"I told you it would be awful living in a regular neighborhood," Mother said. "We're just going to have to accept that fact."

"The yard was real pretty already, Mother. You wouldn't have to do much to make it as nice as ours," I interjected.

"But I'm positive you could improve on it," Daddy said hurriedly. "Nobody has a green thumb like your mother," he said over his shoulder to us in the backseat.

Daddy continued his campaign to win Mother's approval to purchase the new house. When, several days later, she finally acquiesced, I was floored when the roles my parents played in the scenario completely reversed. Once Mother decided she wanted the house, Daddy became a nervous pessimist. He spoke constantly of the financial strain the new house would put on the family. He warned us daily of the sacrifices each of us would have to make to be able to afford it.

"Every month I'll owe the bank a hundred dollars, or they can take this house away from us," he warned. "I have never owed anything to anybody in my life before this," he complained.

"I'm so sorry you have to go through this, Daddy," Rosarita said as she softly patted his shoulder. "I wish you would be like me and just stay here no matter what. That's what I'm going to do."

"I always say that if you can't pay for something in cash, you can't afford it. But with the city buying us out, I have to be like everyone else and get myself into debt. You girls know that I'll have to work even harder and be away from home even more because of this new house."

I feared the entire transaction had faltered. Daddy stopped his constant calculations of income and expenses, Mother quit measuring the curtains on our current windows to see if they would fit the windows at the new house, and Rosarita was reabsorbed into her pursuit of beauty and boys.

Then I overheard Daddy talking to the loan officer at the bank. In a flash, everything changed.

"Are you girls ready to start packing?" Daddy called out when he hung up.

"This is going to be so much work. I don't know how I'll ever get us ready. You'll hide out at the mortuary until I get everything done. The girls will be no help, either. They'll claim they have things to do for school. Just like everything else, the full burden of this move will fall on my shoulders," Mother complained.

"There's no need to worry about that, Mother," Daddy announced. "I have the moving arrangements all worked out." He began telling Mother the details, but I was too excited to hang around and listen.

Chapter Nineteen

Moving Day

Curled into the fetal position, I wriggled a fraction of an inch to the far edge of my mattress so the curve of my back touched my bedroom wall. I yanked the bedspread until it covered my entire body except for the pink lace hairnet that held my brush rollers in place through the night. As my fingers grazed my cheek, I felt my usual mask of Clearasil dried and cracked on my face. My eyes were closed, not clinched, shut. My breathing was slow and measured. I lay as perfectly still as I did every other Saturday morning. With the backdrop set, all I had to do was act out my part as soon as sounds of the household coming to life signaled the beginning of the ruse I'd planned.

I'm getting out of here. I'll never have to wake up in a mortuary again. I'm going to live in a normal house.

I felt no need to take one last look at the view out my bedroom window. I couldn't be happier that soon I would have neighbors that were alive. I felt no nostalgia for the patch of grass that separated my room from the garage of hearses and ambulances before it angled toward the embalming room. Today was my first chance, even earlier than I dreamed, to say goodbye to gruesome sights, so long to putrid stench, and adios to grief on a grand scale. Still, I had to execute my plan for liberation flawlessly or I could ruin the entire scheme.

Shuffle, shuffle, shuffle, I heard Mother's dilapidated bedroom slippers cross the shiny linoleum floor of the kitchen, collect static electricity across the wool carpet of the living room, and slow to squeeze between the record player in the hallway and our bedroom door.

"Jamie, it's time to get up," Mother yelled as the door made a popping sound when the vacuum created by the fan of the swamp cooler gave way to her shoulder.

Nothing in the new house is warped from the moisture of evaporative cooling. Modern air conditioning makes everything dry and easy to open. Without Daddy's signature paint job over anything movable, I'll be able to open doors with the turn of a knob.

"I'll have none of this lounging around until noon today," Mother rambled on. "We all have to help in this moving business, whether we want to or not."

"All right," I said, making sure my voice was low and grumbly, as though I'd just woke up.

"Don't tell me that okay stuff and then go back to sleep. I'm warning you. You have to get up and get going."

"I'm up, I'm up," I said. I turned my legs so they stuck out from under the bedspread, but kept my head on the pillow.

"I mean get all the way out of bed. Sticking your feet out doesn't count. Do you have any idea how much work it is to move an entire household?"

I slowly pulled the bedspread from the rest of my body and

lowered my dangling feet.

"There, I'm up," I announced.

"That's a little more like it. You know you're not the only one who dreads this day."

Don't walk too fast or they'll suspect you're anxious to go. Keep your head down so they won't catch a glimpse of the eagerness on your face. Just nod in agreement with anything anyone says or they'll detect the glee in your voice.

"I don't know why I have to help moving," Rosarita whined. "I want to stay here, but nobody will let me."

Mother and Daddy comforted her with hugs and assurances that they too felt doomed by a future without the familiarity of the old house and mortuary. I remained steadfast in my plan, though. I didn't risk blurting out anything to mess up my plan for this day.

"I have worked my fingers to the bone getting all this stuff packed and ready," Mother moaned. "But at the new house, our old furniture is never going to look right. And, of course, we can't afford to buy anything new because your father has gone into tremendous debt to buy the house. We'll never be able to have nice things again because any money he makes will going into the house," Mother told us.

I looked out at the overstuffed sofa and the tropical print chairs temporarily parked on the front porch waiting to be loaded into the moving van. Mother was right. The new house needed the clean lines of Danish modern furniture that everyone else had now, not the big gaudy sizes and upholstery of the thirties and forties that we owned.

Keep quiet. No outdated furniture can keep me from getting out of here. I don't care if I ever make another purchase as long as I live. Mother's looking for any excuse to cancel the move.

"And don't talk about this to anyone else, Jamie," Mother warned. "We don't want people thinking we can't afford to live in the new house. You know the neighbors will be watching to see how we live, deciding if we're good enough to be in their neighborhood. One mention of money is all it will take for them to decide we don't belong. And then what are we going to do? Move back into the old house? It'll be torn down and we'll have nowhere to live."

If we don't have enough money to buy food, I will starve. If we have no money for clothes, I will wear rags. If we can't have a car, I will walk.

"I know how hard you have worked to get us ready to move," I said, turning toward Mother.

I can't risk Mother getting mad because we're not grateful to her. The risk is too great today. I can leave no detail of my plan to chance. The whole family has to remain calm or all will be lost. I have one foot out the door already.

Carefully monitoring the grin that could betray my elation that this day was, at last, at hand, I asked calmly and slowly, "So when do we go to the new house?"

"I don't want to leave this house. I want to stay right here and see if anyone can bully me out of doing exactly as I please," Rosarita repeated for the millionth time, tears rolling down her dimpled cheeks.

"None of us want this, but we have to face it. This is just

the way things go in this world. Just when you think you're set for life, somebody comes along and jerks the rug out from under you," Daddy said. Mother nodded in solemn agreement.

Why would anyone want to stay here when they can live in a normal neighborhood? From now on, everybody around my house is going to be alive.

After today, my shortcut to walk home will be jaywalking on a residential street, not slipping through a garage lined with caskets.

When we fill out our registration information at the beginning of the school year, I can write "Palmdale Drive," not "Fourth Street." Numbered streets were the business district. Every year, some dumb teacher would blurt out, "But where is your home address?" when I turned in my forms. Giving the explanation about the mortuary invariably led to the same questions every year.

"Have you ever been in a casket?" some boy would shout.

"Have you ever seen a dead body?" a girl asked as she shivered with fake fear.

"Do you get to use the siren on the ambulance if you want to?"

"Is your house haunted?"

With my new address, all of these inane pryings would be avoided.

I took a long, last gaze at the only home I'd ever known.

I should feel nostalgic, at least. Maybe if I remember just the general atmosphere, not specific details, I can experience the regret my family feels.

Despite its location in the middle of the Arizona desert, our old house seemed cold and damp, both inside and out. The swamp cooler attached to the side of the house incessantly dripped into a puddle where wasps built their nests. The flood irrigation that lingered for days, nurturing millions of mosquito eggs to maturation, made the entire fishy-smelling environment soggy. The orange trees that formed a six-foot hedge between our house and the body shop next door bore fruit too sour to eat. The limbs were covered in thorns so sharp they cut through the skin of anyone who touched them.

If I concentrate on what it's like inside, I'll remember something I can recall fondly.

The stained cement and linoleum floors that Mother waxed until they reflected like glass deflected so much of the moisture in the air that the house felt constantly clammy. I remembered Daddy dashing across the slick floor to answer The Big Phone. When he slipped onto a throw rug, he rode it like a toboggan all the way into the hall. Our furniture, inherited from dead people, was upholstered in heavy wool. I suffered rashes on my legs from sitting on its prickly fibers. Even the sounds in the house were sharp. Every time anyone opened one door, the vacuum created by the evaporative cooling made another door slam shut.

No one would miss the cold, wet, slippery, scratchy, noisy house we're leaving behind. I'm not sentimental about this house; I just want to escape it as soon as possible.

The sound of Daddy's voice interrupted my reverie. He told us we couldn't afford professional movers because we bought the new house. But, he added, he'd already figured out how to get our outdated furniture to the new home.

Who cares? Let's just get out of here. I'll carry the furniture myself if it will speed this up.

At last, my waiting was ended.

"Here they are. Everyone get ready to help lifting this furniture," Daddy announced as I heard the sound of a truck approaching.

My family and the owners of the truck trudged back and forth, transferring twenty years of accumulated belongings from the house to the vehicle. Even when the Arizona sun beat down so hard we had to stop for water and rest, we pressed on until the truck was full and the old house was empty.

"We'll follow you in the car," Daddy yelled to the truck driver.

That was my signal to gather the few things I could carry by hand and scramble into the back seat of the family sedan. I wanted to dance and leap and skip to the carport, but I was too smart to fall for that temptation. Instead, I walked placidly to the curb in front of the house I so disliked. Slowly, I opened the car door and climbed into the backseat without a hint of glee.

I rode silently as the caravan of truck and sedan passed through the business district on Mill Avenue and into a quiet, residential street south of Broadway Road. My plan for relocation and self-reinvention had worked perfectly; I now lived in a house like everyone else's.

As we drove up, Daddy maneuvered the car ahead of the truck so he could pull it into the carport. The truck was then able to occupy the entire driveway, making unloading easier.

When I looked out the car window to catch a glimpse at my lovely new surroundings, I caught sight of "Brooks Casket Company" painted in enormous blue letters on the side of the truck containing our furniture.

"They brought their furniture here in a casket truck," I overheard a neighbor saying.

"I wonder if they have caskets in their house," another one commented.

"I don't want my kids going over there if they do," her friend answered.

"You don't think they drive dead people around in that truck, do you?" a third chimed in.

The sign on the truck dashed my hopes for a new identity at my new address before I could get out of the car.

My perfect plan wasn't so perfect after all. I went to all that trouble to act just right and I'm still inseparably linked to the mortuary. No matter where I go, dead people are going to follow me forever.

My fingers didn't automatically jerk to my mouth to start the endless gnawing that would make them bleed. I walked from the car to the house without counting even one step. My hands didn't tingle in preparation for drifting into the pink chair. New Jamie moved into the new house in spite of the judgmental neighbors.

I'll be fine. It may take time, but I know where I'm headed. I can get there from here.

Epilogue
College

"Purple haze, all around," Jimi Hendrix screamed from the pink plastic clock radio next to my dormitory cot. I slammed my hand on the snooze button and gained fifteen more minutes of wrestling the itchy blanket to the precise spot where it covered my toes but left my chin unscathed by its scratchy fibers.

"You're the one dumb enough to sign up for a 7:40 a.m. class. Don't wake me up, too," my roommate grumbled from across the room.

"I know, I know," I muttered under my breath as I shoved my feet into the fuzzy slippers that protected them from the cold tile floor. I glanced in the mirror on our closet door as I dragged myself into the bathroom that connected our room with the bedroom next door to us.

I climbed into the minuscule bath tub and cranked the faucet for hot water as far as it would go. Tepid water trickled from the showerhead as I lathered a glob of Breck shampoo onto my hair. Mother said it left my hair too greasy, but I used it every day now. The scent was luscious.

My jeans slipped on just the way I liked them, skin tight over the thighs with floppy bell bottoms at my ankles. I grabbed a tee shirt wrinkled into a little ball and stretched it out as much as I could before I put it on. Nobody in our dorm ironed clothes and none of us stayed in the steamy laundry room to get our clothes out of the dryer the minute it stopped, either. So we all wore wrinkled clothes.

I glanced at my watch, hoisted my enormous *History of Western Civilization* text atop my notebook, and ran for the elevator. Five other girls stood impatiently waiting for its arrival. I dodged into the stairwell and scrambled down four flights before the elevator girls could beat me to the last of the jelly doughnuts in the cafeteria.

I was so late for class that I didn't wait for the traffic light to turn green before I dashed across University Drive. Two drivers honked at me to get out of their way, but I ignored them. I ran down the mall, reached the Social Science building, and plopped into my assigned seat in the lecture hall within seconds of the bald professor beginning the lecture that would drone on for an hour.

I am a first class hell-raiser, I congratulated myself as I uncapped my pen to begin taking notes. I used green ink for my class notes, not the blue or black that teachers demanded in high school. Nor was I compelled to use a three-ring binder with a colorful divider separating each subject; I used a different spiral notebook for each class on my schedule. I thrilled to the sound of the tiny holes in the paper giving way, leaving their once-forbidden confetti in their tracks, each time I tore a page from them. I used only the notebooks stamped with the seal of Arizona State University smack in the middle of the front cover.

I left no room for doubt that I was a college student, not in high school anymore. With my counter-culture school supplies, my wrinkled clothes, and my disrespect for traffic rules, I was a different person from the Jamie who wore starched dresses to high school and counted the number of steps from class to class.

I was so lucky Mother and Daddy believed my tale of needing a dorm room so I could study more than I'd be able to at home. My new neighbors in the all-girl housing almost blew it for me before I could even move in. As Daddy brought the last of my moving boxes into the lobby, he saw the girls kissing their boyfriends goodbye and engaging in a variety of behaviors he disapproved of.

"This isn't a dormitory," he said loudly enough for the young lovers to hear. "It's a glorified whorehouse."

Please don't say I can't stay. I'm not kissing anybody, the others are. Don't punish me now, when I'm so close to being the furthest I've ever lived from the mortuary.

The no-refund policy on the dorm rental fee swayed him to allow me to stay in my new immoral home. At night, the girls were so loud as they shouted to each other in the hallway that I couldn't study without my deepest concentration. But I was prepared. I focused on my books the same way I used to focus on the baby in the jar. I heard no more of their boisterous voices.

The division of popular versus creepy girls faded away completely when sorority members needed to rescue their GPAs. I was so delighted to interact with them that it made no difference to me that I gave them free tutoring. Some of them were so far behind in class that I couldn't help them pass the tests. I began writing their papers for them to average into their dismal test scores. They brought me candy and soda from the vending machines as I typed away on my portable Smith-Corona. Most of them handed over generous amounts of hard cash as their grades improved.

"How can you afford to buy all these dresses that are too short for you?" Mother challenged when I came home for Christmas break. "I wouldn't make anything for you that displays your legs well above your knees. You better not say you traded your well-made clothes that I sewed for these shabby things that don't even fit you properly."

"I save the spending money you give me and then I buy them for myself. I would never trade the clothes you custom made just for me."

I felt no need to share with my parents the cottage industry I developed writing for the rich sorority girls. If ever there were a person well-prepared for keeping a secret, it was I. Keeping my mouth shut about someone else claiming my writing as her own was much easier than keeping silent about dead bodies.

While many of my dorm mates piled on the freshman fifteen pounds, I remained tall, skinny, and flat-chested. No one noticed my figure, though, with my new wardrobe catching the eye of both boys and girls when I strolled through the lobby of Palo Verde West. No one laughed or pointed or made jokes about me. I was just another, albeit extremely well-dressed, coed. I had so many people to say hi, or give a wave, or flash a smile to, I no longer had room in my thoughts for counting.

Daddy was so busy commuting back and forth from the

new house to the mortuary that he hardly noticed I didn't live with him anymore. I rarely talked to my parents or sisters except occasionally by phone. The conversations usually centered around their fears about my attitude toward the war in Vietnam. Daddy called to tell me the latest police gossip about the punishment that awaited war protesters. Rosarita warned me of how humiliated she would be if I participated in any hippie activities against the war. Mother said I was getting "a little too cocky" in my remarks about the government. She hinted that she would influence Daddy not to pay my tuition for the next semester if I didn't stop arguing that the war was wrong.

My family's greatest concern about my new identity was that I would become an activist against the war. I had no desire to do that. I was already at peace. Not with Vietnam, but with myself.

Acknowledgments

I credit my husband, Kurt Mahoney, with this book ever being written. His belief in me and this story have been unwavering throughout its production. My daughters, Maryann Early and Cheryl Klein, provided as much technical as emotional support. They encouraged their husbands, J.D. Early and Marc Klein, to exhibit their same blind faith in this book. I cannot thank them enough for this. I must doubly thank my sister, Marilyn Patterson, for validating our childhood and supporting its re-telling.

My dearest friends and long-suffering readers cannot be overlooked in this story coming to print. Brenda Pickard May, Vicki Pickard Brown, Tom Brown, Sally Brooks, Marilyn Peters Anderson, Sandy Miller, Chris Ellingson and Marcia VanScoy volunteered their time and expertise to the early versions of this story. I am so very grateful for their help.

Nick Ligidakis and the staff at Inkwell, particularly Ron Birchnough, provided a hand to hold during the publishing process. Their work is deeply appreciated.

Secrets from the Pink Chair is Patty Mahoney's debut novel. She spent her childhood in Tempe, AZ where she lived at her family's mortuary. She earned her undergraduate degree in Print Journalism from the Walter Cronkite School of Arizona State University. In graduate school, also at Arizona State, she completed three Masters degrees, one in education, another in school counseling and a third in mental health counseling.

Patty began her career teaching English and journalism at McKemy Middle School. For many years she worked at McClintock High School, first as an English and journalism teacher, and, later, as a counselor. She served as adjunct faculty at Arizona State, where she taught journalism and at Mesa Community College where she taught psychology. She went on to become a nationally certified counselor, working primarily with emotionally disturbed children.

Patty retired from these positions several years ago. She resides at her condo in Scottsdale and her home in Sedona with her husband, Kurt, a retired psychologist.